NECTANEBO

Traveller from an Antique Land

Herbie Brennan

Dedication:
For Audrey, who made it possible, and Jacks for all the rest.
With special thanks to the forty-nine backers who pledged their hard-earned money to lay the ghost.

© Herbie Brennan 2019

Print ISBN: 978-1-54398-375-3
eBook ISBN: 978-1-54398-376-0

TABLE OF CONTENTS

NECTANEBO

Traveller from an Antique Land

Herbie Brennan

A novel by
New York Times Best-Selling Author
Herbie Brennan

INTRODUCTION
The Story of a Haunting

M y name is Herbie Brennan, and I'm a writer. You can find my details on the Internet. Back in the 1980s, I was involved in the whole fantasy role-play (FRP) movement, enjoying Dungeons and Dragons, writing solo adventure gamebooks and creating a couple of boxed FRP games. As a work in progress, one of my scenarios involved a dark wizard. I cast about for a name and eventually made one up, loosely inspired by the term "necromancy." I decided to call him Nectanebo.

In my mind's eye, I saw Nectanebo as an ancient Egyptian, perhaps even a pharaoh, with a fearful reputation for the practice of magic. I had a very clear idea of what he looked like—similar to Akhenaten in many respects—and the complexities of his character. I saw him as someone deeply involved in politics, a power-hungry plotter and schemer.

Before I got to writing the scenario, I thought I'd do a bit of library research to refresh myself about ancient Egypt so I could include a few authentic details that would make the character more believable.

And that's where it started to get creepy. The first thing I discovered was that there was, or had been, a real-life Nectanebo. Indeed, there were two of them, uncle and nephew, but the one that matched my wizard was Nectanebo II. He was Egypt's last native pharaoh and had a fearsome reputation as a sorcerer. He was power hungry and seized the throne by force.

It's easy to argue what might have happened here. I'd long had an interest in ancient Egypt and read a good many books on the subject. Maybe I'd read about Nectanebo at some stage, forgotten all about him, then dredged him out of my subconscious when I started to write my scenario.

Could be, but it didn't feel like that. It felt like Nectanebo's ghost had crawled into my head and wouldn't leave. Nectanebo wanted his story written: not just the little role-play scenario I'd planned, but a proper full-length book that would bring his name before the modern world.

He nagged and nagged at me to write it. For weeks, then months, I couldn't think of anything else. Eventually I gave in, put aside my other work and started on a biography of Nectanebo.

But I ran into trouble right away. Very little was known about the historical Nectanebo at that time. My research turned up the barest outlines of his life, running only to a few paragraphs. Try as I might, I couldn't find anything else. Yet Nectanebo still insisted I tell his story. Under the circumstances, the only way I could do that was in the form of a novel. So I started to write one called *The Chronicles of Nectanebo*. It went like a charm. It was as if the old pharaoh were dictating it to me.

My literary agent at the time was Murray Pollinger. After a few refusals, he found me a publisher. We signed a contract, and the publisher promptly went bust. Murray took the manuscript out again, and before long it had been declined by every major publishing house in Britain. I decided the story wasn't commercial enough and rewrote it completely with a modern twist. Murray went out with it again, but without success. So I rewrote it again.

And again.

And again.

I'd had forty or fifty books published by this time, and that sort of rewriting was something I just didn't do. But Nectanebo kept pushing me. We offered the manuscript in America, and still nobody wanted it. Murray eventually retired, and my new agent, Sophie Hicks, took on the job. Several publishers made nice comments about the writing and plot. One said it would make a great movie. But none was prepared to publish it.

Around the turn of the millennium, I managed to break free of Nectanebo while I wrote my Faerie Wars novels (which made the *New*

York Times Best Seller list), but a few months ago, he was back with a vengeance, still demanding, still insisting. I've been interested in psychical research all my life, and I know a haunting when I see one. I decided the only way I was going to get this pharaoh off my back was to publish his story myself.

So I mounted a Kickstarter campaign to raise the funds to do just that.

By then I had the novel rewritten for the sixth time in the form of a science fiction thriller set in the modern day, but with Nectanebo's fictional (channelled?) biography threaded through it.

You know how the story is supposed to end, of course. The Kickstarter money flooded in, I published the book and it's the very volume you are now holding in your hands. Well, nearly, but not quite. With two days left before the Kickstarter deadline expired, only a quarter of the target funding had been pledged. Since Kickstarter operates an all-or-nothing system, that meant my hopes would be dead in forty-eight hours.

But the following day, everything changed. I was off-line for much of the morning, but when I went back on around lunchtime, there was an email from Kickstarter with the news that the target had been reached. For maybe five minutes, I actually thought it might be a scam. But when I checked, it turned out to be true.

So how did it happen?

It seemed that the extra money—several thousand euros—had been funded from the estate of a very dear friend of mine who had died some years earlier. Her executors decided she would have wanted me to complete the Nectanebo project and made the pledge on her behalf. So the spirit of my friend was instrumental in ensuring I could lay the pharaoh's ghost to rest.

What follows is the novel that had to be written. I hope you enjoy it.

May they be as nothing, those who attack my Name, my Effigies, the Images of my Double, my Foundation. They will be deprived of their Name, of their Ka, of their Ba, of their Ku . . .

Egyptian Tomb Curse.

Book One: Death

ONE

Helen Weiz's consulting room contained an examination table, monitoring equipment, a large desk, two armchairs, a light table and a sound system that played Mozart—"Music proven to reduce blood pressure" she'd once told Luke Webb.

"How's the headache?" Helen asked. She was an overweight, middle-aged brunette with brown eyes glittering in a heavily lined face and a voice like a saw cutting plywood.

"Gone this morning," Luke said. He took a seat in one of the armchairs without being asked.

"Was it my prescription, or do you think it just went of its own accord?"

"I think it may have gone of its own accord," Luke said. "I'm afraid the stuff you gave me only stopped it for the rest of the day. I slept well enough, but the headache came back next morning."

"And then?"

"And then it hung around low-key for a couple of days, bad again last night, but this morning it was gone." He looked at her soberly. "Have the results come in?"

"They're clear."

"All of them?"

"I'm waiting for a couple, but they'll be clear too."

"How do you know?"

"I know these things. I'm a doctor. How's your grandfather?"

"No change," Luke said. "I'm going to visit him this afternoon."

Weiz picked up a folder from her desk and carried it round to sit in the other easy chair. "I hope he makes it. I love that man."

"Do you think he will? Make it this time?"

3

She shook her head. "No. What's really wrong with him is old age. He may hang on for a few more weeks, but his body's worn out. You, on the other hand, are going to live forever."

"Despite the headaches?"

"I didn't say you were going to enjoy it. What did you think you'd got—a brain tumour?"

"The thought crossed my mind."

"Tell it to keep going. You don't have a tumour. The scans are all through, and you don't have anything growing in your head. You don't have an aneurysm or an embolism or an infection or an invasion of little green men from the planet Zog. And that's just your head. When it comes to your body, you're healthy as a horse and twice as pretty. My husband should have your body."

Luke smiled, which was probably what she wanted. "So what's causing the headaches?"

"Migraine," Weiz said. She spread her hands. "I know, I know. You're going to tell me the pain level is off the scale. You're going to tell me you can't think, you can't eat, you can't make love to your girlfriend. You're going to tell me the pressure feels like your skull's about to burst."

"I think maybe I am," Luke said.

"That's migraine. It's other things as well, but in your case it's migraine. Your reaction to the medication just confirmed it. That tablet was the wonder drug of the decade when it came out. Absolutely, positively guaranteed to cure migraine. Of course it didn't. It stops the symptoms for a day after you take it; then there's a bounce-back and the migraine runs its course. Exactly what happened to you. God in heaven, I wonder about the drug companies these days. It frightens me. It really does." She stopped and added mischievously, "Hope it wasn't one of yours."

"I wouldn't know," Luke told her. He glanced past her through the window. A pigeon was strutting self-importantly along the sill. "Where do we go from here?"

"Well, there's good news and bad. The good news is it won't kill you, no matter how bad it gets. Unless you count suicide, of course. The bad news is we don't really know how to cure it."

Luke stared at her blankly. "So I have to put up with it?"

"Not quite: there are treatments," said Weiz.

"I've been feeling a little weird as well," Luke put in. He was no longer in pain, but he needed to be sure she wasn't missing anything. He still didn't buy her migraine diagnosis.

"Dissociated, can't take noise, feel you're walking on cotton wool? Except this morning when you woke up it looked like somebody had washed the world?"

"That's right."

"It's migraine. If I'm wrong, you can have your next of kin sue me. Nine times out of ten it's stress." She looked at him soberly. "Are you one of those clowns who gets upset when their doctor mentions the word 'psychosomatic'?"

"Yes," Luke said.

Helen Weiz sighed. "Doesn't mean imaginary. Doesn't mean you're not suffering. Just means the root cause of the problem isn't physical. You're worried about Stanislav, aren't you?"

"Among other things," Luke nodded. Of course he was worried about Stanislav. He didn't want the old boy to die. The man was more like a father to him than a grandfather. But if he did die—and he couldn't last much longer—there was the whole nightmare of the Foundation. The network of corporations, clinics and facilities was almost too big for one person to understand, let alone control. More to the point, Luke didn't want the job.

For once Weiz dropped her banter. "I can imagine. Who inherits?"

"My mother." It was no secret. The financial media had begun to speculate five years ago when Stanislav was hospitalised with a prostate infection that was misdiagnosed as cancer. To shut them up, the old boy had released details of his will. His wife was dead, so the provisions were simple enough. His grandson was provided for by a massive trust. His daughter got the business.

"She doesn't want it, Luke."

That was the trouble. Luke nodded. "I know."

"Are you going to take it off her hands?"

Luke said, "Let's just stick to my migraine, Helen. What are you going to do—give me tranquilisers?"

"At your age? I'm going to give you a bottle of vitamin B12 and some advice. The advice is this: you're a spoilt brat rich kid, but you're also kinda nice. You take life far too seriously, you work far too hard and you're far too quick to take responsibility. You listening?"

Luke smiled thinly. "I'm listening."

"The vitamins you take every day, one tab in the morning after breakfast—you don't skip breakfast, do you?"

"No," Luke lied.

"Good. Your pee will turn green, but that's harmless so don't add it to your worries. This is not a cure. The vitamins are to help your body cope with stress. The cure is to reduce the stress. You're not going to change your lifestyle—I know that; men never do—but you can revise it. By which I mean start leaving a little time for yourself. Take in a movie, walk in the park, eat a hot dog, go cheer your favourite team. Whatever helps you let go for an hour. Start this afternoon."

"And this is going to stop my migraines?" Luke asked hopefully.

"Can't hurt," said Helen Weiz.

The Chronicles of Nectanebo: One

I became pharaoh in Egypt after this manner:

The priest Khonsu, in the years before he was my mentor, dreamed a great dream. In this dream, a cobra of vast dimensions reared up beside a broad river that flowed through desert wastelands. As Khonsu watched, the cobra was attacked by a hawk that was, however, immediately killed by the venom of the snake and swallowed whole.

The dream did not end there but, rather, seemed to begin again. Once more the hawk swooped. Once more the cobra struck. Once more the hawk died and was eaten.

And again the dream recurred, but now something changed. Across the desert sands strode an ibis that stood before the towering serpent and bobbed its head so that the cobra, watching it, fell into trance. Thus, when the hawk swooped again, it did not become prey to the cobra but, rather, struck deeply into the body of the serpent and killed it.

But, then, while the hawk was feeding on the giant corpse, a curious metamorphosis occurred, and the bird became a snake, identical to that which it had so recently killed.

It is in the nature of dreams that they melt beneath the heat of day, but this dream endured. When Khonsu awoke, he was haunted by it like a ghost. It seemed to him of significance beyond superficial appearance. He determined to discuss the dream with a sage named Amsu, called after the god Amsu of Coptos, Lord of Kebu.

Amsu interpreted Khonsu's dream in the following manner:

The great serpent rearing up out of the desert was the pharaoh himself. The cobra is the king of snakes and consequently associated with the king of Egypt, even to the extent that the royal headdress traditionally incorporates the motif of a cobra erect and poised to strike.

That the serpent reared beside a river was seen as further confirmation, for the river was the Nile, which made fertile the Egyptian desert and was mother to the Egyptian nation. Where else would the pharaoh rule but by the Nile?

The meaning of the hawk was less clear. Amsu interpreted the action of the bird as a rash attack on the pharaoh by some pretender to the throne which, nonetheless, succeeded against all odds. But who the hawk represented, the old priest could not say.

The fact that the hawk became a cobra in its turn simply meant that the usurper took the throne and ruled in Egypt.

On the matter of the ibis, Amsu's interpretation was even more interesting. The ibis is, of course, a holy bird, skilled in magic. As such, it might be taken to represent the god Thoth, patron of magic (who, of course, has an ibis head) or one of his servants. Amsu leaned towards the latter interpretation and further suggested the ibis was Khonsu himself.

The dream, said Amsu, was a vision of possibilities. It indicated that any attack on the pharaoh must fail unless supported by one such as Khonsu. But should Khonsu lend his priestly power to the cause of the usurper, the pharaoh would fall and the usurper would, in turn, become king.

For Khonsu, this was a bewildering and uncomfortable revelation: bewildering because he had no political ambitions, uncomfortable because he was actually quite fond of the reigning pharaoh. (Achoris of Mendes was still on the throne then, a ruler popular since he had increased the wealth of the nation and kept it free from external attack.) He was loath to adjudge Amsu in error and presented the old man with expensive gifts as a token of his esteem. But privately he wondered if this venerable sage might not be mistaken, his mind at last growing fogged by the weight of years.

On the day Khonsu spoke of his dream to Amsu, I was three years old.

Khonsu did not forget the dream, but neither did he take any action which might have given substance to Amsu's interpretation. Achoris lived out his days as pharaoh without threat of revolution. His son Nepherites, however, was dead just four months after acceding to the throne. It was my uncle, Nectanebo of Sebennytos, who killed him, and the central symbol of his family arms was a hawk.

This development set Khonsu thinking deeply. There was much in Nectanebo's usurpation that matched the symbolism of the dream, but one important factor was missing—Khonsu himself or, indeed, any priest-magician who might have been represented by the ibis. Khonsu had taken no part in the plot against Nepherites and did not even know my uncle personally before he became Pharaoh.

By this time, Khonsu and I had already met, and he was growing interested in my potential as a priestly initiate. He has always sworn he did not then relate me to the bird of prey in his dream, although the hawk emblem featured as prominently in my family arms as in those of my uncle. But all that changed when Nectanebo, my uncle, died and Tachos stepped into his father's shoes.

Tachos was a fool with dreams of glory. One of his earliest adventures was an attack on Palestine with Spartan and Athenian aid. It was a sortie Egypt could ill afford. Friction developed among the allies, and, more importantly, money ran low. The war dragged on inconclusively. In an attempt to secure quick funds, Tachos imposed swingeing taxes and seized Temple property. Khonsu was only one of many priests who were outraged.

Until this time, Khonsu never talked to me of politics: our conversations were strictly confined to religious matters, philosophy, the arts and the occult. But this should not be construed as suggesting I had no interest in the subject. I was my uncle's nephew, an intensely ambitious young man, arrogant enough to despise my cousin and determined enough to be laying my own plans for the seizure of the throne. These were, however, ill-formed, naive and not entirely serious.

Khonsu changed all that. He was an intensely practical man despite his mystical leanings, and a man of considerable, if concealed, temporal power. He used this power to the utmost, once he had made up his mind Tachos must be deposed. Before even approaching me, he had laid a firm foundation for our coup. I was supported by the majority of Temple priests, by all the important noble houses and by nearly half the key generals in Tachos's own army. Perhaps more importantly—and certainly more amazingly—Khonsu had reached a tacit agreement with both Greece and Sparta that I would be accepted if I succeeded. The gods alone knew how he kept all this scheming secret, or perhaps I was simply the last to know. In any event, none betrayed me. The only real danger came from an old and dear friend.

I loved Darius. I can say this now, having passed through the portals of death, without fear of disbelief. He was the friend of my childhood, the companion of my youth. We played together, explored together, laughed and cried together, grew together. In manhood we hunted together, trained in military skills together. He was as a brother to me, dearer than my own flesh.

When Khonsu first explained his plans for my ascension to the throne, I was surprised, unnerved and excited by turns. At this time, I had not yet reached my thirtieth year, so the world and all its wonders were still fresh to me. The throne was a bauble I desired, rather than a responsibility I would shoulder. The deposition of Tachos was a glorious game; a sober, dangerous and important game, to be sure, but a game nonetheless.

Khonsu had an eye for detail—most priests have—and schooled me for almost half a year on the precise moves we would be required to make to ensure the overthrow of Tachos. He cautioned careful, thorough preparation. I would have moved far sooner had it not been for his restraining hand.

It was impossible to keep a matter of this import secret from Darius, nor did I wish to, for I assumed he would be my staunchest supporter, as he had always been my closest friend.

But Darius had a wife, and his wife was Gegum.

TWO

Two large men fell in step beside Luke as he walked into the street. Ahead, another large man, in uniform this time, opened the back door of a Mercedes with windows as black as its bodywork. Luke stared at it for a moment before climbing in. He sometimes felt like separate people: the private Luke who'd inherited his grandfather's curiosity and liked nothing better than to investigate the workings of the universe, and the public Luke who needed staff, including bodyguards, to fulfill his obligations to a foundation his grandfather could no longer control and in which his mother showed increasingly less interest.

One of the large men got into the front with the driver. The other slid into the seat beside Luke, his eyes wary. The young woman already in the car was wearing a severely cut business suit that did nothing to hide a model figure. She glanced at him and raised an eyebrow.

"I'll live, Sandra," Luke said shortly. He leaned back in the leather seats and closed his eyes. "What have we got?"

Sandra glanced at the clipboard on her lap. "For now there's the opening at the Wyemar Gallery . . . meeting with Van Flandern, loosely scheduled for three thirty . . . drinks reception with the Labats at five—"

"Yes, yes," Luke interrupted wearily. "Can I fit in a call to the hospital?"

"You're supposed to be visiting him this evening."

Luke nodded. "I know. I want to bring it forward."

Sandra studied the clipboard. "I don't see how we can." She frowned. "The Labats live quite close to the hospital. I suppose if we kept Van Flandern strictly to half an hour and got lucky with the travelling time, you could have twenty minutes with Mr. Regis before you went on to the reception. Van Flandern won't like it, but—"

"Twenty minutes isn't long enough," Luke said. Nothing seemed long enough these days. Stanislav once told him that time started to contract as you got older and the things you most wanted to do somehow never got done. But it wasn't supposed to happen when you were thirty.

Sandra shrugged. "Okay, suppose we cut back on the time you spend at Wyemar—it's only a flag show for the Foundation, after all. Then we can—"

"Fuck it," Luke said quietly. He was thinking of Helen Weiz's advice. She was right, of course. He didn't leave enough time for himself. He didn't even leave enough time to do the things he really needed to do, like sit with his grandfather, who, though nobody came right out with it, was dying. He still wasn't sure his headaches were just migraines, but Helen was on the button when she told him he was stressed.

"Fuck what?" Sandra asked.

Luke leaned forward and knocked on the glass partition that separated the front of the car from the back. When it slid open, he snapped, "Pull over." As the car drew up to the kerb, he said to Sandra, "Call Wyemar, Van Flandern and the Labats and give them my apologies. You can reschedule Van Flandern, but not for less than two weeks. I'm taking the rest of the day off. When you've made the calls, you can do the same." He reached across the big man beside him to open the car door. "So can you and Abe, Frankie."

"Excuse me, Mr. Webb," Frankie said frowning, "but this may not be such a hot idea."

"Let me out, Frankie," Luke said quietly. The big man slid out of the car and held the door open for him. As he stepped outside, the air suddenly tasted clean and fresh despite the traffic fumes. He patted Frankie's face with genuine affection. "I'll be fine." He smiled. Suddenly he felt like a kid let out of school.

"Where will you be, Mr. Webb?" Frankie asked. He had the expression of a man who didn't quite believe what he was hearing.

"Probably eating hot dogs," Luke said.

Sandra stuck her head out of the car. She had a mobile phone in her hand. "What excuse will I give?"

"Tell them I have a headache," Luke said, then walked off down the street.

THREE

The building looked more like an abandoned fish-processing factory than a television studio. There were only a few small windows, high up, relieving the sweep of a grubby brick façade. No one had thought to put out a sign. If there was a main entrance, it was far from obvious. Not so much as a broadcast aerial on the roof announced this place for what it was. Even the street outside seemed mean and empty, the sort of district people instinctively avoided. They were still avoiding it now, by all appearances. Apart from Taymur's Ford, the only other vehicle within a hundred yards was a laundry van pulled halfway on the kerb.

There was no security worth mentioning. Taymur walked to an unmarked side door, stared directly into the lens of the closed-circuit camera and pressed the bell. One look at his well-cut suit and neatly knotted tie, and the receptionist buzzed him in. She didn't even ask who he wanted to see.

Taymur found himself facing a flight of concrete steps that would not have been out of place in an underground car park. Here again, there was no indication where he should go. He looked around for an elevator, found none and began, unhurriedly, to climb. There were no security cameras on the stairwell.

He reached a narrow landing with an unmarked door, but it proved to be locked, so he continued his climb. He was a slimly built man in his early forties with large, luminous brown eyes and the sort of skin that suggested hours spent on an expensive yacht. His shoes were hand-made Italian. His shirt, like the suit and tie, was silk. Even without the briefcase, he would have looked like a prosperous businessman, or maybe a lawyer.

On the second floor, the stairwell opened out into a reception hall, and suddenly there was carpet under foot. Taymur glanced around. It seemed obvious the building was a converted warehouse and the work had been carried out with an eye to function rather than style. He liked that. Too many New York offices were designed to impress, not as efficient work units. Here you had a floor with three small desks, a couple of doors presumably leading to other floors, a space-saving metal staircase spiralling somewhere, and that was it. No potted plants, no abstract art on the walls. He saw a notice board with thumbtacked schedules. The carpet was industrial standard.

As Taymur stepped forward, a casually dressed girl in her twenties looked up from one of the desks and grinned at him expectantly. Beyond her, a plump man in his shirtsleeves rose and walked out briskly through a door, muttering to himself. The third desk was unmanned. Taymur turned his attention to the girl. She had a monitor screen in front of her and a half-eaten sandwich on a paper napkin beside it. Beside that was a heap of files. It looked as if her job involved more than just reception, which might explain the lax security.

Taymur smiled at her. "Paperwork," he said amiably, as if it explained something. He hefted his briefcase to the edge of her desk, and she hurried to clear a space for it. "Thank you," Taymur said. He flicked the catch and opened the lid so it blocked her view of what was inside. "Please allow me a moment."

"No hurry," the girl said pleasantly. Her eyes were interested, a little amused. She was still smiling.

Taymur took the 9 mm silenced Beretta from his briefcase. *God's will*, he thought, and shot her through the forehead.

FOUR

Luke avoided the hot dogs, which he loathed anyway, and found himself in a gallery less familiar, but apparently no less expensive, than the Wyemar. It was full of tortured sculptures in stone, wood and twisted wire.

"Hardly your taste, Mr. Webb," a soft voice murmured as he stared at one of the more extreme examples.

Luke turned to find a slim, fair-haired man at his shoulder. He was wearing a velvet suit with a floppy cravat, and Luke disliked him at once. "Have we met?" he asked coolly.

"Dear me, no—I've never moved in such exalted circles. I recognised you from your picture in the *Journal*. Ancient world, isn't it? Your collectibles interest? My name's Alan, by the way."

Alan was a familiar enough type, a closet heterosexual pretending to be gay to further a profession in which gays excelled. He was full of refinement, fashionable tastes and bullshit. In normal circumstances, Luke would have given him the brushoff, but something inside him suddenly relaxed, and he said only, "This sort of thing has never turned me on."

"I could not agree more!" exclaimed Alan, not unexpectedly, with huge emphasis. "We only stock it because it has a certain mass appeal. Have you been downstairs?"

"No."

"Ah, now," said Alan, making animated gestures with his hands, "I think you may find a few *objets d'art* that are more in keeping with your taste. We've always tried to stock something that will appeal to a man of refinement such as yourself. Would you like to follow me, Mr. Webb? It would be an honour for me to show you what we have."

He minced towards an open staircase so thickly carpeted it would not have been out of place in a brothel. Luke hesitated, then followed.

The gallery's basement featured a limited number of items spotlit for dramatic effect: an Etruscan bronze of Minerva, an urn that might have been Sumerian, a cracked and badly executed marble of two Roman gladiators, a segment of mosaic floor, now tastefully framed, that depicted an erotic scene involving a woman and a goat, a bronze helmet and a half-life-size stone sculpture of a rearing horse.

"The trouble is," said Alan with a pained expression on his face, "the best of them are reproductions. Those gladiators are genuine, but would you give them house room? Crude. Crude. The horse is lovely, isn't it? Look at the workmanship of those genitals! But it's actually a copy. A sweet boy in Genoa turns out two of them a year. Hugely expensive but not, I fear, original. The helmet's quite interesting. The metal part has provenance to Roman Gaul, but the leather is actually Victorian—somebody decided to tart it up then, probably a collector. Of course that makes the leather more than a century old in its own right, so there are some who would say this actually increases the value. Are you interested in helmets, Mr. Webb?"

"No," Luke said.

"No, of course not," Alan agreed. "Your own collection is . . . ?" He hesitated, expectantly.

"This and that," Luke told him unhelpfully. Then, in a moment of pity, added, "I have a good many religious objects. A variety of periods—I suppose the most ancient are Assyrian. I, ah, try to avoid reproductions."

"Of course, of course. I would have expected nothing less. But don't you find these awful restrictions a bore? I mean time was when money talked with the Italians"—he rubbed his thumb and fingers together in the time-honoured gesture—"and everybody was able to trample over the Arabs, of course." He smiled gaily, then allowed the smile to fade. "Now the only people left to exploit are the Hindus, and even they can get quite bolshy. You don't have a thing for Hindu art, by any chance?"

Amused despite himself, Luke shook his head.

"No, I didn't think so," Alan said sorrowfully. "And yet, if you want the genuine article these days—I mean the genuine article of quality—the governments simply will not allow you to take it out of their countries anymore. I call it insular myself, but what can you do? I believe art belongs to the whole world, but did you read just last month about that poor woman who was jailed in Morocco? Some silly statuette she didn't even know was genuine. Morocco, I ask you! Most of their ancient art is on a par with knapped flints. But the civilised countries are even worse. It seems to me the only way a serious collector can add to his collection is by turning a blind eye to some of these irritating regulations." He stopped, watching Luke's face intently, then added, "And we wouldn't want to do that, would we?"

Luke, who'd seen it coming, kept his face expressionless. After a long moment, Alan said, "Mr. Webb, I have something that might interest you in our vaults."

The vaults proved to be a walk-in strong room down a lengthy corridor. They had a combination lock and steel door. "Would you mind turning your back?" Alan asked apologetically. "The combination . . ."

Luke turned his back, amused.

"Now, Mr. Webb," Alan said almost immediately, and Luke allowed himself to be led inside.

The vaults were obviously used purely for storage. There was no attempt at display, and many of the pieces lay in opened crates.

"These are not reproductions, Mr. Webb," Alan said firmly. "There might be some problems with provenance, but I think any reputable expert in the field would vouch for anything you might find in here. You'll appreciate that access is restricted to our more valued clients, Mr. Webb."

For "valued," read "valuable" or, more bluntly, "rich," Luke thought. With his face still carefully impassive, he said mischievously, "But I'm not a client, Alan. I've never bought from you before."

To his credit, Alan declined to react. Instead, he simply said, "There's a piece came in last month. It's . . . well, it's expensive, but very special. Very, very special. I've been holding it for someone such as yourself who appreciates beauty as much as he venerates antiquity."

He walked across to a cruciform crate standing upright like a coffin in one corner. He unwound the fastening, which was no more than a piece of twine. "Please do come over, Mr. Webb—I'd like you to get the full effect." As Luke stepped across, he opened the crate.

Luke froze. Inside, nestled against a bed of wood shavings, was one of the most stunning pieces he had ever seen—a half-life-size figure of Winged Isis, the mighty wings outstretched. The moon between the horns of her headdress was a milky sphere of rock crystal.

"Isn't she beautiful?" Alan exclaimed. "Egyptian, of course. Diorite. Very, very old. The diorite would tell you that, of course: they'd lost the secret of working it sometime in the Middle Kingdom. The quartz is extremely unusual. In fact, I think this piece may well be unique—I've certainly never heard of anything like it. We think it dates to the reign of the Pharaoh Sahure, and it might even be earlier, which makes it almost contemporary with the Great Pyramid. We know it was an altar piece. The workmanship is magnificent—you can see that. It seems to have been revered down the ages. The inscriptions at Philae mention a "Great Isis," and we've reason to believe it was this very piece. It was apparently brought there with enormous pomp by Nectanebo the Second, which means it was an object of worship as late as the fourth century BC." He half turned. "Please don't ask me for too many details of how—Mr. Webb, what's the matter? Are you ill, Mr. Webb?"

Luke was shaking like a spastic child. His jaw was slack, his mouth was open, spittle dribbled down his chin. His sightless eyes were fastened blankly on the Isis figure.

The Chronicles of Nectanebo: Two

The Gegum Sisterhood was strong a thousand years in Egypt by the time my glory dawned. It has been said they were established in the Twin Kingdoms by Queen Nefertiti, wife of the heretic Akhenaten and initiate head of the order in her native Mitanni. But this is a lie, as so much of Gegum history is a lie, fostered by the witch-nuns themselves.

In the matter of power, the Gegum did not act openly, but in secret and by stealth. Nor were their activities confined to Egypt. The Gegum convent extended far north into Palestine, Syria, Anatolia, Mesopotamia and perhaps even south into Nubia, although I saw nothing of them during my years of exile.

I have named only those countries where they held open convent. It was accepted that there must be many others where the convent remained closed and the order functioned unsuspected, even by the offices of the state. Because of this far-flung, part-secret spider's web, it was impossible to tell where Gegum interests lay. Their loyalty, of course, lay nowhere except to the sisterhood itself.

I had no more than a layman's knowledge of the Gegum at the time of which I write. I accepted (as all young men accepted, with fear and fascination) that behind the sober facade of ritual cooperation with the Temple lay the practice of dark witchcrafts, including a profound knowledge of the erotic arts. It was commonly believed that a Gegum nun could drain a man's seed more completely than a succubus, leaving him a withered husk. It was also commonly believed, among young men at least, that this must be the perfect way to die. Well though I knew Darius for so many years, I did not know his wife was Gegum. But, then, neither did he.

Darius married at the age of nineteen or twenty, I forget which. His bride was named Ankhesenpaaten, a woman older than himself by almost ten years. It was an arranged match, of course, cementing another of those interminable alliances between noble houses that have long complicated Egyptian politics. I understood from Darius he had not even seen his bride prior to the wedding.

I attended the ceremony in the tacit assumption that once the duty of the wedding night was done, Darius could return to the ways of his peers (an unimaginative mixture of dice, beer and whores, I regret to report). Ankhesenpaaten, for her part, would grow plump and placid on a generous allowance, awaiting the day when her new lord and master would have her with child.

It did not happen so: not any of it. Within a week, Darius was lovesick as a swan—for his own wife! It scandalised his former companions, myself amongst them. "But she is old, Darius," I remember saying (for I was of an age when a woman of thirty seemed positively senile). And he took me aside and gravely whispered bedroom secrets which suggested there might, after all, be something to be said for older women.

It is tempting to claim that thereafter I saw Darius become a puppet, but it would not be true. He sobered a little, as married men do, and his early fire mellowed into what I felt to be a genuine love for his wife. But this apart, he remained the same dear Darius he had always been. Pata—we both referred to her as Pata—in no sense came between us. I grew to know her well, and liked her. I caught no smell of witch at any time, not even when the betrayal occurred.

At this time, my plans to seize the throne were far advanced and my ambition an open secret. Tachos himself was in Syria, part of which he had occupied following the death of the old Artaxerxes, and was already experiencing the first of the problems Khonsu and I were determined to visit upon him: a portion of his army had deserted, pledging allegiance to my family cause.

Although I had not yet made any overt move, Tachos knew full well it was only a matter of time before I must challenge his claim to the throne. Now, faced with the first crack in the loyalty of his troops, disagreement with Sparta, opposition from the Temple and a war which had become a running drain on his treasury, it was clear Tachos must take firm, decisive action or lose Egypt by default.

I believed his most likely course was a withdrawal—at least temporarily—from Palestine. While the majority of his troops remained loyal, Tachos could then have marched directly back to Egypt and there put down the upstart who had dared to challenge his power at home. It is certainly what I would have done.

But Tachos did none of this. Instead he chose to move by stealth.

Darius's men came for me in the night. Their insignia—and the fact that their leader was personally known to the commander of my guards—was more than enough to gain them access to my villa. Once there, they killed several of my personal guard and entered my bedchamber to drag me naked from my slumber. I was beaten near senseless and carried to a desolate spot by the river, where three of the ruffians cast lots to determine which should have the pleasure of cutting my throat.

This decided, I was dragged to the riverbank, the better to dispose of my corpse. There was a boat waiting, by which they planned to escape. Barely conscious, I could make no use of my powers, which were, in any case, rudimentary at the time. Nonetheless, I realised well enough that destiny had carried me close to death, and the realisation gave me enough strength to break free of my captors and run staggering in the hope of escape.

It may be that my movement took them by surprise. I was far too weak to escape otherwise. Surprise, too, may have been what held them: not long, but long enough to allow me to disappear into the darkness. Knowing I had not the strength to run far, I discovered a bed of reeds and hid therein.

And therein I was found, only moments later, by one of the assassins, a burly man who had equipped himself with a short Roman sword. He might have called out, for his companions were only twenty cubits distant, but instead chose himself to dispatch me to the Hall of Judgement. I had neither wits nor weapon, but Hapi, the god of the Nile, walked the world that night and rescued me.

As Pharaoh's man swung his sword, time slowed for me so that every detail took on a singular clarity. First I saw the grim pleasure on his face change to pain and horror. Then the sword halted on its swing, and his body convulsed, twisting backwards on itself. A gurgling grunt erupted from his throat, then his mouth opened to emit a hideous scream. I saw that his left leg had been seized by a crocodile.

The sound of his terror attracted his companions. But while only moments had passed—much less time than it takes in the telling—my mind had cleared sufficiently to permit exercise of my powers. Thus, as they fell upon the crocodile to rescue their friend, they concluded I had fallen in the river and drowned. It was a small thing which would not withstand examination, but they were distracted by the reptile, which, in the manner of its kind, would not release the leg and took a long time to die. Thus, when the melee was done and they came to realise their foolishness, I was gone.

It may seem strange that I did not seek to alert my guards. But I had recognised the insignia of Darius on my would-be assassins, and so convinced had I been of his loyalty that, seeing it, I no longer knew whom I could trust. Besides, I suspected he might have sent sufficient forces to occupy the whole of my villa.

Thus I went to the home of a friend and sent word of what had occurred to Khonsu, who at once dispatched his own men to protect me while he inquired as to the extent of Darius's traitorous actions.

When it transpired that the assassination attempt involved but a handful of men, I returned to my own villa to decide on my next move. Within four hours, Darius was dead. Within four weeks, when news of the failed attempt reached the Palestine front, the remainder of Tachos's forces turned against him.

Tachos's sudden collapse was an unexpected bonus for me. Unopposed, I ascended the throne. Tachos and Darius passed into history.

Neither were bad men. In Tachos, my uncle gave Egypt a fool for a pharaoh, and had I not overthrown him, someone else assuredly would have. But Darius, as I discovered long after, was entirely innocent, even of foolishness. His retinue, when I questioned them as Pharaoh, told the story of his deepening obsession and horror of me, concealed to all but his private household. It was this obsession, this insane perception of me as a monster, that drove him to betrayal. And it was his wife Ankhesenpaaten, his beloved Pata, who laid the obsession upon him by a technique of Gegum witchwork with which I became personally familiar in later years.

Personal malice did not enter into Ankhesenpaaten's actions. She acted on orders from the sisterhood, who, for their own incomprehensible motivations, wished me dead at that time. The irony is that after I became Pharaoh, the Gegum accepted and supported me more profoundly than any man in history.

But that came too late for Darius.

FIVE

H e had to step over the body to move round the desk. The screen gave a view of the entrance door, and he saw with satisfaction that Gemel was in place. Taymur pressed the button that released the door lock and heard the buzz through the open intercom.

"Sandy, do you have the green file—?" It was a very tall young man in sweater and jeans, earphones hanging round his neck. He looked at Taymur. "Haven't seen Sandy, have you? Brown hair, nice eyes?"

Taymur made it a chest shot because of the distance, and the boy went down cleanly with a puzzled look on his face. There was very little blood.

Taymur stepped to the window and looked out. His men were running from the laundry van, making no attempt to hide their firearms. There was still no one else on the street, which was unfortunate. They had orders to shoot anyone they saw. It would have been good publicity.

Webb was not in sight. Taymur assumed he was already in the building. The men had been told to get him inside, under cover, before anything else.

He heard the vanguard in the stairwell seconds before the first of them appeared. They were wearing battle dress as befitted soldiers, although Taymur was aware the press would call them terrorists. But that was unimportant. As al-Hakim said, only results were important.

"Webb?" he asked.

"Soon," the man told him tersely.

"Secure the building," Taymur ordered.

SIX

Luke came to his senses in a cramped office with a cup of coffee in his hand. Alan hovered beside him in a flurry of hand-wringing and worried expressions. "Are you feeling better, Mr. Webb?"

"What happened?" Luke asked.

Alan blinked. "You seemed quite upset, Mr. Webb. Was it anything I said?"

Luke stared into his coffee, then lifted the cup. It was very strong and heavy with sugar, not at all as he liked it, but he drank it anyway.

"Shall I call a doctor, Mr. Webb? Frankly, you gave me quite a turn."

Luke rolled his tongue in his mouth to taste the coffee. It seemed like some sort of anchor to reality. He recalled . . . What did he recall? He recalled a bank vault full of packing cases and the figure of Winged Isis. He recalled dying in Nubia. He recalled the curious sensation of—

Dying in Nubia?

"A doctor, sir? Oh, please let me call you a doctor!"

"No doctor," Luke told him thickly. He turned to look into Alan's worried face. He'd never been to Nubia—he would be hard put to find it on a map. "Where is Nubia?"

"Africa," said Alan promptly. "It's next door to South Africa, I think. One of the black states. Mr. Webb, you're not well!"

Luke tended to agree. First the headaches and now this. Something was happening to him, and he didn't like it. As against that, he was definitely feeling better now. The weird, dream-like sensation was all but gone, the coffee was coping nicely with the chill in his body and his mind was growing clearer by the minute. He took another sip, looked back at Alan and actually managed a thin smile. "I'm sorry about that," he said. "My doctor has just diagnosed me as a migraine sufferer."

Alan was instantly relieved. "Ah, migraine! Mr. Webb, I am a martyr to it myself. Do you get the halo and the poor upset tummy? Perhaps you shouldn't be drinking coffee—they say it's a trigger."

"No, the coffee's helping," Luke said. He didn't for a moment believe he'd just had a migraine attack. But he needed to calm this idiot, and he needed to get away somewhere quiet and take time to think.

He made the effort to stand and discovered to his surprise that he was firm on his feet. Nubia, he thought. There were people round his bed and he could smell the resins carried by the embalmers who were waiting just beyond the door.

"There's nothing growing in your head," Helen Weiz had said. "You don't have an aneurysm or an embolism or an infection or an invasion of little green men from the planet Zog."

Nothing showed on the scans. So why could he remember he had died in Nubia? He drained the last of the coffee and set the cup down on the cluttered desk. "Thank you," he said firmly. "I feel much better now. I'm sorry I upset you."

"Not at all! Not at all, Mr. Webb. I'm just relieved you're all right. I mean you looked dreadful. Migraine does that, of course, but I'd no idea that migraine was the problem. I had visions of you dying right there in my vault." He shivered, as if the thought were too terrible to contemplate.

Luke fished a card from his pocket. "Call this number and ask for Sandra Spacek. Tell her to organise an independent inspection of the Winged Isis. Professor Donaldson or Sam Chatwin—either one will do. If they say it's genuine, I'll buy it."

Alan took the card with a look of confused joy. "Sandra Spacek," he repeated. "Professor Donaldson or Mr. Chatwin. I'll write that down so I remember. Thank you, Mr. Webb. You're buying a thing of beauty. And may I say how honoured I am to do business with you and how much I welcome your gracing my gallery and how I look forward, sincerely look forward, to seeing you again. You have no idea how—"

Luke edged his way onto the street with the words spilling over him like drizzle. "Hope your migraine will be better soon!" Alan called after him.

SEVEN

H e found a diner, took a table by the window, then ordered more coffee and possibly a doughnut as well since the waitress brought one with it. He drank the coffee slowly, staring at the traffic and the people moving on the sidewalk. His head was filled with the image of the Winged Isis.

"Anything else I can get you?" The waitress had materialised again, a bleached blonde with elfin looks. He suspected he was too well dressed for the place.

"Do you know where Nubia is?" he asked.

"Sure. It's in the Middle East. You know in the Sinbad movies? All those big black guys in the turbans are, like, Nubian slaves."

"Another coffee," Luke said. "Bring a pot."

The name Penfield crept into his mind. Sometime as far back as the thirties, a neurosurgeon named Penfield up in Canada had started pushing electrodes into his patients' brains. The idea was to find out what area of the brain controlled which part of the body. It turned out some parts of the brain didn't control the body at all; they controlled memories. When Penfield stimulated those parts, his patients remembered experiences in their past so vividly they seemed to be reliving them.

"There's nothing growing in your head."

But suppose Helen Weiz was wrong. Suppose the growth was so small the scans had missed it. The Foundation employed too many doctors for him to imagine the medical profession was infallible. Suppose there was a tiny growth pressing on a portion of his brain. Sometimes it caused headaches. Sometimes it worked like Penfield's electrodes and stimulated memories.

But Penfield's patients remembered real experiences, genuine incidents from childhood. They didn't have hallucinations about Nubia. As the waitress set down his pot of coffee, he slipped the cell phone from his pocket and dialled his private office. "Sandra?"

"Hi, Mr. Webb. I got hold of everybody. They're all very sorry blah, blah, blah, but it's okay. You can enjoy your day off."

"Thanks, Sandra. Now, there's something else I want you to do for me. Take a note of the name Wilder Penfield. Wilder Penfield, got that?"

"Got it, Mr. Webb."

"I think he's Montreal. Or was—I don't know if he's still alive. In fact, now that I think of it, I'm fairly sure he can't be. Anyway, assume it's Montreal—McGill University rings a bell. He did experiments there until . . . I don't know, the sixties, maybe. They involved stimulating the brain with electrodes. They're quite well known."

"I remember," Sandra said. "They brought back patients' memories, didn't they? All the tiny little details?"

He'd forgotten that Sandra had a master's degree in science, one of the reasons he'd hired her. "That's it. What I want to find out is whether any of the memories were false. Like, fantasies, hallucinations. I don't suppose you know?"

"No, I don't, but I can find out easily enough. There must be something on Google. Want me to ring you back?"

"Yes," Luke said and cut the connection.

He finished his coffee and walked to a bookshop, where he invested eight dollars in a pocket atlas. He went back to the diner and sat up at the counter.

"Just plain can't keep away from me," the waitress said and grinned.

"Did I ask you for a doughnut the last time?"

"Sure you did. Don't you remember?"

He didn't. He remembered ordering the coffee but not the doughnut. Christ, he never ate doughnuts.

"You want another one?"

He shook his head. "No, just more coffee."

"You should go easy on the coffee," the waitress told him. "Too much of it rots your brains." But she poured it for him just the same and left the pot.

Luke opened his atlas and checked the index to find Africa. When he turned to the relevant page, he couldn't find Nubia. The map showed Namibia, Botswana, Zimbabwe and Mozambique bordering South Africa but no Nubia. He checked the remainder of the map in case Alan had been wrong about South Africa, but Nubia wasn't shown anywhere. Could the waitress be right? Was it somewhere in the Middle East? He could do his own Google search, of course, but right now that would have to be on his phone, and the small screen gave him headaches. He was considering calling Sandra again when a voice said, "Look under Egypt."

Luke glanced up. The man in the chef's hat looked Jewish. "Under Egypt?"

"Beatrice told me you were asking about Nubia. Look under Egypt. You ever been to Egypt?"

Luke shook his head, flicking through the pages of the atlas.

"Me neither," the man said. "There—you got it there!"

The map showed Egypt, part of Libya, Sudan and Chad. He still couldn't see Nubia. "No Nubia," he said.

"That's because it don't exist no more," the man in the chef's hat said. "Goddamn Egyptians, you know what they did? Drowned it, that's what! But look here, see—"

A fat forefinger jabbed at the map. Luke bent forward. The area, to the right of somewhere called Ash Shamaliyah, was marked Nubian Desert. Luke straightened, feeling faint again. Something was happening to him. Something was—

—pressing on an area of his brain—

—making the world seem unreal. He took a deep breath to steady himself, wondering if he should call Sandra and ask for a car. But the deep breath worked; the coffee bar swam back into focus. The chef was a big man both ways: tall and fat. He had a healthy growth of stubble and an intense frown. "What do you mean, drowned?" Luke asked him.

"Drowned," the big man repeated. "Back in 1970. I was over in Israel at the time. Believe me, we knew all about it. The Russkies built a new dam for them down at Aswan. Nile backed up behind it to make a lake. They called it Lake Nasser after President Nasser of Egypt who died that year. Biggest friggin' asshole in the region. Lake Nasser is what used to be Nubia, except for that bit of desert. They drowned a whole friggin' country!"

"What did they do with the people?"

"Shifted them onto higher ground. So they said." The big man sniffed as if he didn't believe it. "That was Nubia. Hey, you wanna 'nother pot of coffee? On the house?"

The Chronicles of Nectanebo: Three

Following the assassination attempt that left me bloodied, shaken but alive, Khonsu came quickly to my villa to discuss our counter-move. The decision was by no means simple. That Tachos, ultimately, was behind the failed assassination neither of us doubted. But Tachos was in Syria, beyond reach. Thus, vengeance had to be directed against his instrument.

The most obvious move was a direct attack on Darius. My forces were in a state of readiness, since conflict with Tachos was expected soon. To dispatch a portion of them against Darius would have been easy. Yet I hesitated. To some extent, my strength depended on the willing support of others, priests and populace. I had this, so I thought, thanks to Khonsu, but it was support clearly directed against Tachos. Might loyalties waiver if I were openly to attack Darius, who was not himself without friends?

Another factor worried me. I had permitted Darius's men to escape (all but the scoundrel who fell afoul of the crocodile: his body had been pulled from the Nile with several important parts missing). That this was understandable I recognised. That it was a mistake, I was certain. Now Darius knew his attempt on my life had failed. Now he would be preparing for my countermove, fortifying his garrisons, calling on favours from friends. Speed might enable me to strike before he was ready, but this worried me less than the possibility that open conflict between us might spark a civil war, a complication I did not need and in all probability would not survive.

My other course of action was to fight stealth with stealth. Khonsu favoured this approach. The Temple knew where trustworthy assassins might be bought, and my priestly mentor was all for dispatching one or more to do to Darius what he had attempted to do to me.

It seemed something of the sort was my only real alternative, for with all my long love of Darius, I could not permit him to live. But I had little faith in the ability of any mercenary, however skilled, to reach him. Thus, I determined to do the work myself.

Khonsu was against it. He pointed out that more was at stake than vengeance. I was, after all, destined to become Pharaoh. I pointed out that the task required special skills. Although he knew what I meant, he remained unconvinced. In the end, I simply ignored his objections.

It was nearing dawn when I reached the estate of Darius. Already the place was a fortress: no party of ordinary assassins could have passed through such security. You may wonder how, then, I proposed to do so, and I can only tell you that I am Nectanebo. My powers were not then what they were destined later to become, but they were useful nonetheless. I remained concealed until I became familiar with the routine of the guard, then, in the brief moment when but one man was at the side gate, I made my move.

I knew from my observations what happened when legitimate entry was made. First came the challenge and response, then the identification: all normal military procedure. Then the guard called ahead for an escort. This was not standard procedure in any household I knew of. But for a simple system, it was astonishingly effective. It meant that you entered the estate under armed guard or ran the risk of death at the hands of the inner garrison.

I approached the solitary guard openly.

"Who goes?" he asked. He was not apprehensive. I was manifestly alone, and his companions were within sound of an alarm call.

"No one," I said softly, and reached out with my mind.

For a moment he stiffened, then a curiously bland expression descended on his features. "No one," he repeated. I walked past him, confident that he would not remember me.

It was only the first breach in the defenses. I was within the wall, but now I was a target for every wandering patrol. My powers were nowhere near sufficient to influence a group of men. I was, in fact, relying on something entirely different to bring me safely to Darius. We had been friends from childhood, and I knew his estate as well as I knew my own. I also remembered an incident which, I imagined, he had long forgotten.

In those distant, happier days, Darius and I had been playing a game of hide-and-seek within his family villa. It was my turn to hide, and Darius was seeking me.

Determined to discover the perfect place of concealment, I took myself to the oldest of the buildings and there, in an upper room, came upon a servants' privy. I might have left it without much interest had I not noticed the seat of easement was in poor repair and could actually be lifted out of its stone surround, giving access to the chute which carried waste matter down the outside wall into the garden beneath.

The mind of a small boy, as every parent knows, is a disgusting catacomb, and mine was no exception. At once I conceived a plan. I would remain in the privy until I heard the approach of Darius, then I would raise the broken seat, drop down into the chute and, pulling the seat back into position behind me, there hide until Darius completed his inspection.

In a short time, I had opportunity to put this foul plan into operation. I heard the approach of my friend, raised the broken seat and climbed quickly into the chute. I had some difficulty settling the seat behind me, but I achieved it before the privy door opened. Only then did I realise the filth and stench of my surroundings. By then, of course, it was too late: boyish honour was at stake. I held my breath and listened to the sounds of Darius moving about above. Then, suddenly, everything went dark.

I was a quick thinker and realised what had happened. Darius, or some other member of the household, had come to relieve himself.

It causes me no shame to admit that I panicked. In so doing, I lost my footing and the precarious fingerhold by which I hung onto the side of the chute. Thus, I learned it descended at a steep gradient into an ordure pit in the garden below. I might have broken my neck, or at least a limb. As it was, I fell cushioned by the wastes in the pit and bruised nothing more than my dignity.

The ordure pit had long been filled in now, and the privy was no longer used, but so far as I knew, the chute was never bricked off. I made for it now, reliant on it to give me access to the house. As it did. Time and disuse had rendered the passage sweeter than when I had made my first journey.

Within the house were only servants, who do not think or act like guards. Consequently, I found my way without difficulty to Darius's quarters. Of a truth, I did not expect to find him alone, but he was alone and sleeping, his witchwife gone I know not where. He was not, however, unguarded. Two brutes with swords stood without his door. To my joy, I saw one of them was the commander of the small group sent to assassinate me.

I became a statue, fighting fierce emotions. I could not afford to be anything other than calm. They had not seen me, but while only a short length of corridor ran between us, I could not traverse it unnoticed. I would dearly have loved to gut the ruffian who had beaten me, but I denied myself that pleasure in favour of a safer plan. From my tunic, I took the hollow reed and the poison darts I had brought with me. My assailant was the first to feel the insect sting on the side of his neck. His companion appeared to feel nothing at all. I waited. The darts are tiny, and the poison a mere drop of distillate from spider venom. It does not work quickly, and it is not always lethal. No matter: they slid to the floor, almost in unison, and I used their own swords to finish them off. Then I entered the chamber of Darius.

I still wonder to relate that he did not awaken even when I stood above him. I was glad. I did not relish what I had to do.

My feelings for Darius had been in abeyance since I saw his insignia on my would-be assassins. They remained in abeyance now; otherwise, I could not have done it. I killed him cleanly enough with a stab through the heart. But it was not enough that he die: it must be shown that Nectanebo had taken terrible revenge. Thus I mutilated him horribly.

In the course of this butchery, a wail arose in an antechamber. I went at once, fearful that the noise would draw more guards, and found a terrified slave girl with a child. She stared at me dumbly, eyes huge. I was covered in the blood of her master and must have looked like a fiend from the netherworlds. I cut her throat before she found her tongue, and she died in my arms like a lover.

I knew the child, the baby. He was Darius's new son, called in Egyptian Kanekht, although Darius preferred the Greek version, Arsames. I had brought gifts of spice and silver on the day of the birth, rejoicing with Darius at the arrival of an heir. I had bounced the infant on my knee and made avuncular noises. Even now it may have recognised me, for it ceased its wailing.

I stared down at him, and the thought passed through my mind that he who kills the father must always fear vengeance at the hands of the son. This child, so weak, so helpless, would someday grow to haunt me. My soul revolted in my breast at what I had to do. Yet it was necessary. I placed the point of the dagger on the small breastbone and pushed. Almost no effort was needed, so easily did little Kanekht die. Then I left the bedchamber to make good my escape.

EIGHT

He was back in the bookshop when the call came through. A couple of other customers glanced at him in disgust as he took it. Obviously cell phones weren't welcome here.

"Luke? Sandra. I got that information, and it's yes."

"Yes what?" Luke asked, keeping his voice low. He glanced at the other customers apologetically.

"Yes, some of Penfield's patients produced fantasies. One remembered every detail of a robbery that never took place. Also, there were loads of childhood memories that couldn't be checked. Might have been real memories, might not."

"Do you know anything about Nubia?" Luke asked her.

"Just what everybody knows," Sandra said. "It was flooded when the Egyptians built the Aswan Dam. The Egyptians didn't care, of course— the Nubians were always second-class citizens."

"If I wanted to learn more about Nubia, what category would I look under?"

Sandra knew his dislike of using his phone for the Internet. "You in a library, Mr. Webb?"

"No, a bookshop."

"In a bookshop, try under 'History' but you'd be better off in a library. Or I can get the information for you?"

Luke thought about it. There was a Carnegie library about a ten-minute cab ride away. "Why don't you chase up a few books you think I should read? But if I were in a library, where would I look?"

"Go to 'Reference' and get an overview," Sandra said promptly. "Then see if you can find any of the titles listed in the footnotes."

"Okay," Luke said.

He was in the library when his phone rang again. This time he got half a dozen dirty looks, and the librarian came directly over to whisper fiercely, "Cell phones aren't allowed in the Reading Room. Would you mind taking that outside?"

He clicked the button, said, "Hold on" and took the phone into the cloistered hallway. It was Sandra again.

"'Nubia was a region of ancient northeastern Africa between the Nile's First Cataract, the confluence of the White Nile and Blue Nile (near present Khartoum), the Red Sea and the Libyan desert. The ancient Egyptians occupied—'"

"What are you reading this from?"

"Britannica online. 'The ancient Egyptians occupied its northern area intermittently from about the twentieth century to the eighth century BC and strongly influenced its culture. In the late eighth and early seventh centuries BC, Nubia, known to the Egyptians as Kush, with its capital at Napata, ruled Egypt. In 671 BC, the Assyrians invaded Egypt and soon after drove the Kushites back into Nubia. The Egyptians destroyed Napata in 590 BC, but the Kushites established a new capital at Meroe and maintained an independent kingdom until about AD 350. In the sixth century AD, Nubia was Christianised, and it remained so until it was overrun by the Muslim Mamelukes of Egypt in the fourteenth century.' Then they drowned it," she added.

"Thanks," Luke said.

"Have you found a library?"

"Yes."

"Try Britannica for yourself," Sandra suggested. "That will give you the full story."

"Thanks," Luke said again.

In half an hour he'd discovered that Nubia was part of Black Africa and that Nubians were "darker in complexion than the majority of Egyptians"—a politically correct statement if ever he smelt one. But it tied in with what the waitress had told him, and she'd had to go no further than a Sinbad movie. He closed his eyes and tried to call up the memory of having died in Nubia, hoping against hope it would not trigger another attack. His head remained clear. But the picture he saw in his mind's eye, the picture of himself propped on a simple bed, was not a picture of a black man.

He opened his eyes and glanced at his watch. Why was he chasing fantasies? Why was he behaving as if the memory really was a memory? It wasn't a memory, any more than the headache was a migraine.

He left the library and hailed a cab. "Just drive," he told the cabby. "I'll think of where we're going in a minute."

The driver glanced at him suspiciously, but obviously decided he was too well dressed to be a crank. "It's your dollar, Mister," he said and pulled out into traffic.

Luke sank back into the seat and stared into the middle distance. He was thoroughly concerned now. Something was happening to him, and he didn't understand what. Worse, he didn't know what to do about it.

The sensible option would be to get back to Helen Weiz. She already knew about the headaches, and even though she'd misdiagnosed them, the new symptoms might put her on the right track. She could order more tests, more scans, if necessary.

It was the sensible option, but he was afraid to take it. It was stupid, but that was the way it was. Even though he'd faced her with the headaches, told her his worry about a tumour, he was afraid to tell her about this. Because this wasn't his brain, this was his mind.

The afternoon traffic was building so that after fifteen minutes the cab slowed, then halted in a jam. The driver drummed his fingers on the wheel impatiently. On impulse, Luke said, "Take me to Regis Bethany."

"When we get moving," the cabby nodded.

Strangely, he felt better at once. He'd already planned to visit Stanislav, and maybe he could ask to see one of the doctors there. He had no idea why this was better than facing Helen Weiz again, but it was. Besides which, he didn't feel ill now. There had been no headache all day, and the memory of the blankness that had overcome him in the gallery was receding.

The cab lurched into motion again, and Luke thought, *Is it really so weird?* He'd been looking at ancient artifacts. Winged Isis was Egyptian. Maybe . . .

A name returned to him. He called Sandra. "Has some character named Alan been on to you?"

"Art and antiques? He says you're buying a piece—is that right?"

"If it checks out," Luke said. "Philae: ever hear of it?"

"Temple in Egypt," Sandra said promptly. "For double the money, ask me another."

"A pharaoh named something like . . . is it Nectanebo?"

"I lose," Sandra said. "Never heard of him."

"Can you check him online? I'll hold."

"Sure thing, Boss."

He waited, listening to the distant sound of a computer keyboard. Sandra came back. "First or Second?"

"Sorry?"

"There are two of them. Nectanebo the First or Nectanebo the Second? Which one do you want?"

"I don't know," Luke said. "Was one of them connected with Philae?"

"Hold on . . ." More keyboard noise. "That would be Nectanebo the Second. He added to the temple there."

"What can you tell me about him?"

"Not a lot. Last native Egyptian pharaoh, didn't seem to do much except lose a war against the Persians. That cost him the throne. He had to flee to—hey, he went to Nubia! Small world. Died there in exile."

Got it! "Thanks, Sandra." He cut the connection. He sank back in the seat with a flooding of relief. That was it for sure! Somewhere or other, maybe years ago, he'd read about the Pharaoh Nectanebo, then forgotten him. He was still feeling fragile after yesterday's migraine attack—Helen was right, it was migraine; that many scans would never have missed a growth no matter how small. When Alan had mentioned the name Nectanebo, the memory had pushed right up. He remembered reading that Nectanebo had died in Nubia. That was all there was to it. It was so simple!

"You want to get out or what?" the cabby asked.

"Sorry?"

"We're at the hospital. That'll be eighteen bucks."

Luke climbed from the cab, reaching for his wallet.

NINE

There were three studios. Two of them had the usual three-camera setup, the cams on dollies so they could be moved around. There was provision for a sound boom, but mostly it was lapel mikes with built-in miniature radio transmitters so there wasn't a trailing wire. You could create a set in these two studios with minimum expense and not much effort. Tacked drapes went a long way, and props didn't need to be anything fancy. Lighting was simplicity itself: floods and the big umbrella reflectors still photographers used. There was an elevated control room behind darkened glass where the producer watched and gave orders through a mike that linked with phones worn by the camera crew and a deaf-aid earpiece worn by the presenter. Apart from the sound gear, there was only a bank of monitors and some chairs in the producer's box. There was no live feed from these studios. For a show, all you did was record. The editing was done afterwards.

The third studio was smaller and even simpler. It was a fixed cam space—just two cameras this time, no dollies, one head-on, the other to the side. The set was a permanent news desk backed by a board that featured the ACB logo in red and gold. The important thing about this studio was that it did carry the live feed into the networks, and that made it more valuable than platinum to Taymur.

He looked around slowly, noting every detail. Gemel was at his side now, a rock of a man with broad, Semitic features. Taymur knew that together, the contrast in their appearance created a particular air of authority that would be useful in the hours ahead.

There had been no further killing, which was good. Now that the building was secure, he needed hostages to generate the dialogue that would precede the inevitable SWAT attack. Taymur had no doubt the city would authorise an attack. That had been standard policy in terrorist situations for over a year now. Nor did he doubt he would die in the attack, as would Gemel and his men. But that was not important. Only results were important. The thing he had to do for al-Hakim and the cause was buy the time to guarantee those results. That was where the hostages came in. The more hostages there were, the more drawn out the dialogue could be. A gradual release of prisoners could stretch that aspect of the situation into days if need be.

"God willing, we will execute Mr. Webb here," he told Gemel.

TEN

An unfamiliar duty nurse glanced up from her computer screen. She must have been new to the job, because she asked coolly, "Can I help you?"

"I'm here to see Mr. Regis," Luke told her.

The nurse favoured him with a professional smile. "I'm afraid Mr. Regis isn't—" Her colleague, a plump black girl, swiveled to whisper something into her ear, then grinned at Luke and swiveled back. The nurse's eyes widened. "I'm terribly sorry, Mr. Webb—I didn't recognise you. You can go straight up. Do you know the way, or shall I call somebody to . . ."

"I know the way," Luke said.

Stanislav's rooms were on the second floor, a special suite that included its own operating theatre. Luke ignored the elevator and took the stairs to convince himself he was fit despite the headaches and the blackouts.

There was a dragon lady in nurse's uniform sitting guard on the corridor that led to the suite, but she recognised Luke at once and waved him through. He passed the time of day with the two security men guarding the door, both of whom recognised him as well, then pushed the door open.

His grandfather had a woman on the bed. He seemed to be drawing her into a passionate embrace while she kicked shapely legs and struggled in an effort to get free.

"Good God!" Luke stopped in the doorway, grinning broadly. Looked as if Stanislav had made a dramatic recovery. Then he noticed that three lights on the monitor machines were flashing red.

The woman on the bed pulled herself free, and he recognised her as Patsy Kennet, Stanislav's personal nurse. "Help me here!" she hissed urgently. Stanislav was without his breathing mask. His eyes were glazed, but he was flailing his arms wildly.

Luke's paralysis broke, and he ran to the bed. "What's happening?"

"Idiot took off his mask, and now he's gone into crisis! Help me hold him."

Luke grasped his grandfather's wrists. The old man was far stronger than he'd imagined, but he managed to hold him. The nurse pulled the mask back over his face, then made some hurried adjustments to the monitors. Luke felt Stanislav relax a little.

"He should be okay in a moment," Nurse Kennet said breathlessly. "Hopefully there won't be any permanent damage."

Luke released his grip. To his relief, Stanislav stayed put. "What just happened here?"

Nurse Kennet favoured him with a disgruntled look. "What happened is he has a mind of his own, but that won't be news to you, I'm sure." She glanced at the display and made another adjustment. One of the red lights turned green. "Your grandfather's on a continuous drip of medication to help him over this bad patch. The gas-oxygen mixture through the mask is part of the cocktail. For some reason, he took it off. The balance was affected, and he went into crisis." A second red turned to green. "He should be fine in about ten minutes."

"I am fine now," said Stanislav Regis's voice, amplified by the electronics in the mask. "Is that you, Luke? I cannot be sure of anything just now—when the mask comes off, I seem to hallucinate."

Join the club, Luke thought wryly. Aloud, he said, "It's me, Grandfather."

"I would not believe everything that Patsy tells you," Stanislav said. Even after all these years, his voice still carried a hint of an accent, and he spoke with the precision of someone who was not using his native tongue. "For one thing, this is not a 'bad patch.' I am getting on with dying. In fact, you could make the case that I am already dead—I certainly could not survive without those tubes and this damn mask. And for another thing, I did not take it off 'for some reason.' I took it off to find out what would happen."

"What did happen, Mr. Regis?" Patsy Kennet asked him.

"I thought you were an angel, Patsy. An angel come to take me off to heaven. That is why I grabbed you—do not pretend you did not enjoy it, because I certainly did."

"Just don't make a habit of it," Nurse Kennet said. She glanced back at the monitor as the third red turned green. "Are you going to behave yourself if I leave you alone with your grandson?"

"I expect I will," Stanislav said. "Do you think you could find a nurse who is not too liberated to bring the boy a coffee?"

"Sure."

As Kennet closed the door behind her, Stanislav said, "I am glad you came, Luke. I wasn't sure God would spare me long enough to see you again."

"What's this about God sparing? Are you feeling ill?"

"I am not feeling ill," Stanislav said. "But without the help of the medical profession, I am quite certain I should be feeling dead, so naturally the subject is on my mind. You are an intelligent young man. What do you think happens to a man when he dies?"

"He goes to heaven and plays harps," Luke said.

"That sounds more like hell. But the question was serious."

Serious but uncomfortable, coming from somebody so close to death. As he often did in conversations with his grandfather, Luke fell back on detail. They both shared an appetite for hard facts. "The trouble is deciding when he's dead. You can take a successful electrocardiogram anytime up to three minutes after the heart stops. If you drop pilocarpine into the eyes, the pupils will still contract after three hours. You can get a viable arterial graft from the body as much as seventy-two hours after the heart stops beating, and we all know that nails and hair keep growing for weeks." He shrugged, hoping to shrug away the whole question and replace it with a question of his own. "So at what point does death actually take place?"

Stanislav didn't fall for it. "You are avoiding the issue," he said easily. "Let me rephrase it: Your heart has long since stopped beating. Your body has begun to rot. Your family has cremated you. Your bleached bones are picked clean by buzzards. Your brain is microbe food. There is no doubt whatsoever about your status. What, in such circumstances, do you believe may have happened to your consciousness?"

Luke's discomfort increased. His mouth felt dry. He looked up to discover the spreading wings of Isis above his grandfather's bed.

The Chronicles of Nectanebo: Four

Of my powers:
It was widely assumed, even by those like Khonsu who should have known better, that my powers resulted from my studies of the Hermetic Arts. This was not the case.

I was born a normal child, exhibiting no unusual characteristics. In my thirteenth year, however, there occurred an incident that was the harbinger of my future.

There was a childhood game of which I was inordinately fond called Phoenicia. The game may have been based on some ancient conflict, for it involved two "armies" and a "rout."

As I recall the rules, the armies were not evenly divided: one was permitted to have no more than five members, each separated from the others at the beginning of the game. The second army could be of any size, at least in theory: in practice, we preferred to play with its numbers twice that of the first.

On the call of "rout," the second army would attempt to seek out and capture the members of the first. These players, in turn, were supposed to seek out and join with each other. A capture might only be effected if the Searchers were double in number those found. Thus, two Searchers might capture a solitary member of the first army, but four were required if two members of the first army had found each other, six for three and so on.

On the occasion of which I write, I was still alone, crouched in what remained of a disused corn store and convinced, correctly, that the Searchers were almost upon me.

The door of my hiding place was flung open. Only one boy was there, which meant that I could not be captured. But his companions were so close I could hear them calling to one another.

Caught in such circumstances, one should run, but the sounds of the opposing army convinced me that to run now would be to run directly into them. The boy who had found me, named Ram, a dark child with piglet eyes, stared at me in that familiar moment of incomprehension before he realised what he was seeing and raised the alarm. Foolishly, I closed my eyes, shutting him out, and screamed in panic, *I am not here! I am not here!* The scream was in my mind and did not leave my lips. I heard the door close and opened my eyes again in darkness. He did not raise the alarm.

I shall not pretend this incident set me to thinking, for it did not. I quickly forgot it, and it remained forgotten until a mounting pressure of similar evidence convinced me that I could (sometimes) influence the minds of others.

My newfound ability was, to say the least, uncertain, prone to fail completely at those times when I tried hardest to make it succeed. Yet I accepted that it happened, and, in time, I came to discover the rules that governed the ability.

I was able to influence someone only when I could look him in the eyes: action at a distance was then impossible to me. I could influence no one older than myself. (But this changed completely when I became an adult.) Only a simple influence was possible: I might, for example, persuade Ram he had not seen me when in fact he had, but I could not persuade him he had seen someone else. Such simplicity is not so great a drawback as one might imagine. Puberty was upon me when I first discovered this ability, and I used it to considerable effect in seduction during those turbulent years. The secret (which still puzzles me even now) was to persuade the girl that I was harmless, like a small, furry animal.

My talent remained secret. Even then I had sufficient instinct to realise that general knowledge of what I could do must bring me trouble. In later years, however, I came to realise I was not unique.

I have said that my powers did not arise from my study of the Hermetica, and this is true. But there were aspects of the Hermetica which enlarged the scope of my abilities through training. The art of prophecy was, in its discipline of the mind, one such aspect. Mekhenesis was another.

According to Khonsu (who did not, I may say, believe the literal truth of this tradition), the art of mekhenesis was taught by Thoth of the Ibis Head to a priest of the Serpent Cult in times of great antiquity. I quickly came to see how closely it resembled my childhood talent for the influence of minds.

Mekhenesis means the taking away of responsibility. The technique by which it is applied is simple enough: a matter of speech and gestures which anyone might learn in minutes. But for those with the gift, this simple technique achieves marvellous results.

Through this art, the will of a man is set in abeyance so that he becomes malleable in the hands of another and will obey orders like a slave, though he be a freeman or even an aristocrat. But this is the least of it, for through mekhenesis a man may be persuaded to believe that which he knows cannot be true. Thus, if shown a flower and told it is a serpent, he will evince fear and attempt to flee. More miraculous still, if told the serpent has bitten him, he will sicken like one suffering from the venom and may even die unless given an antidote; or is at least told he is being given an antidote.

In the course of my training in the healing arts, I was taught the mekhenistic technique and used it with success on my very first attempt. The application took nearly an hour. The next time I attempted it, I saw that much of the hour was not needed, for my subject—a young woman who assisted in the Temple—achieved the state much sooner. This caused me to experiment, and soon I discovered I could induce the mekhenistic trance in moments.

I quickly abandoned the lengthy induction procedure altogether, and instead I would stare at my subject fixedly, voice some arbitrary command (such as "Be calm" or "Sleep") and the trance would follow. Although not always. Here I saw at once the similarity to my inborn power. The same feeling of certainty that allowed me to influence the minds of others would allow me to engender the mekhenistic trance in an instant. I came eventually to conclude the two abilities were in fact one: aspects of a single power.

Thus, in my youth, my powers had already begun to manifest to a small, but definite degree: a seed taken by the Gegum and nurtured into a monstrous tree.

ELEVEN

"Are you all right, boy?" His grandfather's voice reached him from a great distance.

Luke made a massive effort, and the room swam back into focus. Winged Isis no longer smiled down at him from above the bed. He licked his lips. "I'm not sure. I've been having . . ." He searched for words that would not alarm Stanislav. ". . . . odd bouts lately. Helen thinks they may be migraines."

"Helen does not know her ass from her elbow," Stanislav grunted. "She still half believes the cure for everything is chicken soup. They maintain a flashy front, but most of these Jews have the intellectual capacity of a houseplant." Like many East Europeans of his generation, he was openly anti-Semitic. Curiously, it had never affected his recruitment policy for the Foundation. "Do you have a headache?"

"Yes." It was true. His headache had returned, although not severely.

"Would you like me to call for Nurse Kennet to bring you a tablet?"

Luke shook his head. "No, I'll be fine. I'm fine now, really." He could talk to a doctor before he left. He *would* talk to a doctor before he left.

Stanislav took him at his word. "We were speaking of death," he said, "and like so many people of your age, you have scarcely given it a thought. But I do not have that luxury. I am long past my three score years and ten, so death may come to me at any time. I have spent much time in research. There are many published works on near-death experiences. Even some serious papers. Now here is the curious thing. You would expect a consensus. But there is not a consensus. There are contradictions . . ."

Luke nodded. In his childhood, the priests at Heliopolis had instructed him that the sun god Ra traversed the heavens each day in his glorious solar boat. Upon death, the righteous ascended in their soul bodies to join his celestial crew and travel with him throughout eternity. Some among mankind would journey further after death, said the priests, travelling through the void eventually to join the Imperishable Ones, the circumpolar stars. But this fate, unlike the ascension to Ra, was reserved for the great on Earth.

"If you look at the old literature," Stanislav was saying, " and some of the modern writings, come to that, it would seem that on death you find yourself outside your body, sometimes floating near the ceiling. You feel normal, even well. You may believe yourself to have been miraculously cured of your illness. But you cannot communicate with anyone. They ignore you. They mourn for the death of a body lying on the bed, a body that looks suspiciously like you. Eventually you realise this is—or rather was—your body. You attempt to reanimate it, but in vain. You watch it be buried or cremated. You wander the world as a ghost. But eventually you undergo a second death. Is that not a strange concept, Luke? Yet the idea of a second death is a myth that arises in many cultures. An old, old belief . . ."

Luke's heart was thumping. It was happening again. But Stanislav, in full flow, did not notice. "As against that nonsense, everybody nowadays seems to be experiencing the tunnel effect. You come out of your body and travel through a dark tunnel towards an area of light. Sometimes you are met by deceased friends or a great religious figure of your faith—Jesus Christ, or Moses or Mohammed or whoever. These entities then lead you into the light." He coughed behind the mask. "This experience is absolutely consistent in modern reports, but you cannot be certain this is not an artifact of modern communications. The books have sold in the millions, there have been television discussions, radio talks . . . you cannot be certain. But then again, you have similar descriptions of the tunnel and the light hundreds of years old in the literature of Buddhism, particularly Tibetan Buddhism. Are we talking merely about psychological states? You appreciate the dilemma." He looked directly at his grandson for the first time. "My word, your headache is bad. Let me call for the nurse."

It was passing, but he had to talk to a doctor. Using every ounce of his willpower, Luke held his voice steady. "I'll find a doctor on my way out. And, actually, if you don't mind, I think I might—" He began to push himself up from the chair.

Stanislav said, "I should like you to stay just one minute longer, Luke. I have something important to say to you."

Luke sank back into the chair. He could feel sweat on his forehead.

"Whatever may happen to me when I die, which I shall discover soon, in any case, I think it is important to organise what happens to the Foundation in my absence. You know it has been willed to your mother?"

Luke nodded. "Yes."

"You know she does not want it?"

"Yes."

"Have you not wondered why I should leave the Foundation to your mother who does not want it and not to you, who has the same sort of mind as myself and even now works within the structure of the Foundation at a high level?"

Luke said nothing. All he wanted was for Stanislav to finish so he could get out and see a doctor. His headache, though steady, was still not extreme, but these visionary flashes, these insane pseudo-memories—

The old man said, "I have decided to change my will. Your mother shall be well provided for, but I wish for you to own and run the Foundation I created. I must warn you there may be legal complications."

Luke didn't care. He didn't care if he owned the Foundation. He didn't care if there were legal complications.

"There is a problem with your birth," Stanislav said. "I have sworn to Harriet that I would never tell you this, but Jack Webb was not your father."

It was no surprise. His mother's marriage had lasted less than three years, every one of them a nightmare, so far as he could gather. Who could blame her for taking a lover? But what did it matter? Jack Webb had never had any claim on the Foundation. Or if he had, he was dead now. What did it matter?

"I am sorry," Stanislav said suddenly. "It is obvious to me that you wish to go. Find a doctor and get a pill. It is perhaps just as well that I do not tell you the whole story now. I wish to make my peace with Harriet about it, and it would be better if she were here for the telling. You go now; ring me when you are feeling better. We will arrange a proper meeting with your mother."

With no idea at all what his grandfather was talking about, Luke stood and stumbled gratefully from the room.

TWELVE

He found a young doctor who gave no indication he was impressed by the grandson of the man who owned the Foundation that paid his salary. If anything, he managed to convey the impression that he had far more urgent things to do. But he conducted Luke into a cubicle, sat him on the bed, then perched beside him before pulling curtains round for an illusion of privacy.

"Your own physician says it's migraine?"

Luke nodded. "Yes, but it isn't just a headache."

"Migraine isn't. You can have disturbances in the field of vision as well as nausea and vomiting. You can have extreme sensitivity to light and sound. You can have a decrease in tactile sensitivity, particularly in the facial area, sometimes to a degree where it mimics a stroke." He stared at Luke, then reached for a pad and began to write a prescription. "Try these," he said. "Several of my patients find them very good."

This wasn't working out. "Dr."—Luke read his name-tag—"Anderson, this is not nausea or vomiting or disturbances in my field of vision. This is something . . . something . . ." He suddenly gave up and reached for the prescription. The headache was dying down again, and he knew, without a shadow of doubt, that he was never going to discuss his mental symptoms with this arrogant young clown. "Thank you, Doctor. I'll have this filled at once."

He'd been planning to call another cab, but when he reached Reception, the nurse who hadn't recognised him earlier almost ran across the foyer to catch him. "Excuse me, Mr. Webb," she said breathlessly, "there are press outside."

"Press?" Luke echoed foolishly. It was all he needed. His dislike of publicity was well known, but the media still hounded him. Usually at times like this, when all he wanted was to crawl away somewhere and die. He wondered what had set them off. "What do they want?"

"I don't know, sir," the girl said. "But I took the liberty of ordering you a car. It's waiting for you in the basement car park if you don't want to talk to them. You can go out that way." She indicated the elevators.

Luke leaned across and kissed her on the cheek.

There was a uniformed chauffeur waiting as he stepped out of the elevator, although not Phil, his usual driver. "Mr. Webb," he called. "Over here." He had a slow, South Carolina drawl.

The car was an overblown Ford, not one of the usual Mercs, and as he reached it, Luke had a sudden feeling of unease. The thought occurred to him that sometimes the less ethical members of the press pretended to be something they weren't in order to get an interview. But this man didn't look like press. There was a lot of hard muscle underneath the uniform. "Do you have ID?" he asked the driver casually.

"Sure thing, Mr. Webb." The man smiled broadly at him. Then something hit him from behind, and, before he could react, he found himself bundled into the back seat of the car. Rough hands pulled a black sack over his head and drew the fastenings so tightly round his throat that he gagged. Luke kicked out reflexively. There was a hard blow to his stomach, then he was flung back in the seat as the engine gunned and the car leaped forward.

THIRTEEN

Taymur picked up the phone.

"We have him." The voice sounded excited.

"Problems?" Taymur asked.

"None, sir."

Allah smiled on them. "How long?"

"Until we reach you? Five minutes, maybe seven. There is not so much heavy traffic."

Taymur cradled the phone. Now there was much to do.

The Chronicles of Nectanebo: Five

O n the day of my coronation, the Gegum Sisterhood (who had so recently ordered my assassination) sent me a gift.

It was a marvellous artifact, a graven hardwood chest, two cubits square by one cubit deep, set upon a platform and, when in use, oriented to the cardinal points. Arising from the corners of the chest were magnificent representations of marvellous creatures, one to each corner, holding within their claws an ivory egg. Below them were four large frogs, staring upwards, open-mouthed. The workmanship was superb, but the ingenuity of the device was almost magical, for it had use as well as ornament: it was designed to predict earthquakes.

For a pharaoh, such information is extremely valuable, for it permits help to be quickly dispatched when the focus of a quake is in the more distant reaches of the kingdoms.

Such, then, was the gift of the Gegum. It came with the blessing of the Abbess Lipta, delivered by a retinue of graceful acolytes headed by a sister of the Azure Robe, who had a gift of her own for me that evening.

It was customary (and less risky) to accord any Gegum on official business the status of an ambassador. But Mitanni, Syria or Nubia had never produced an ambassador remotely resembling Ruuth Beni Bar Jain, a Hebrew by race and Egyptian by nationality: if, that is, a Gegum could be said to have any national loyalties.

I was fascinated by Ruuth. She delivered the gift with a pretty speech and the graceful suggestion of a discussion of "mutual interests." I was nothing loath and extended a suggestion of my own that the discussion might take place over a meal. She accepted as though dining with Pharaoh was the most natural thing in her world.

I confess I had plans for seduction even then. I have mentioned, I think, the prevalent mythology that the Gegum were adept beyond all others in the erotic arts. It was the day of my coronation, and I could think of no better time to test the truth of this legend. But I was in no way prepared for what actually happened.

Had my experience been greater, I should never have entertained Ruuth alone. For all dealings with the Gegum, a battery of advisers is strongly recommended, and even then one should count one's fingers afterwards. But I was newly come to my glory and saw her only as a beautiful woman to be flattered, cajoled and conquered.

I remember much of our conversation even now. There was little strain in it, beyond my building sexual tension, since I had not then learned the Gegum connection with Darius. I began by speaking of inconsequential things, as befits a man engaged on flirtation, but quickly found myself, without quite realising how or why, engaged in a discussion of affairs of state.

It is obvious to me now that the sisters were interested in how I planned to run the kingdoms: in my foreign policy, for certain, but in subtler (and far less understandable) matters such as the laws governing funereal monuments, grain taxes, which of my twin crowns I should choose to wear for Temple worship and (predictably) my attitude towards the sisterhood. Ruuth questioned me with such skill that I did not even realise I was being interrogated.

I answered her as best I could, for in many of the matters which interested her, I had no policy at all, which is to say that my policies were not yet formulated. She directed the conversation towards sport, an activity traditionally patronised by Pharaoh, and introduced me all at once to the most clearly distinguished of all Gegum characteristics: love of paradox.

"It is strange, Lord, is it not," she said thoughtfully, "that our intellect confirms the fleetest warrior in Egypt could not win a race against a tortoise."

"My intellect confirms nothing of the sort, Lady," I told her. I was already relaxed by wine and wondering how I might persuade her to end this conversation and retire with me to the royal bedchamber.

She smiled lightly. "Ah, but think on this, Pharaoh, which I had from a Greek Sister a year or more ago. These Greeks have a tradition that their fastest warrior, Achilles by name, was once matched in a race against a tortoise. Since Achilles was so fleet and the tortoise so slow, the creature was given a head start of one-tenth of a stadium. Both began their race at the same time, of course, on the command of the Marshal of the Games. Naturally, the fleet Achilles quickly reached the point at which the tortoise started, one-tenth of a stadium distant. But by then, the tortoise, slow though it was, had moved a small distance forward. Achilles raced to the spot where the tortoise now was . . . but again the little reptile moved forward a short distance. And so it was throughout the race, for each time Achilles reached the spot where the tortoise had been, the creature had moved a little further onwards until, inevitably, it won the race."

I stared at her. Her eyelids half closed like the hood of a cobra, and she smiled. It was nonsense, but I could find no flaw in her logic. Later, as we lay together, I set aside my pride and asked her the meaning of the paradox. She shrugged lightly as if it was of no importance, but then said, "Paradoxes teach us that even when our minds persuade us something is impossible, it may yet be done."

There was naught to disappoint me in the manner of our coupling. The lips of her vagina were purple rather than pink (a Hebrew characteristic, she told me, indicative of pure blood), and she had developed extraordinary muscle control within it. She was skilled in the discovery of pleasure nerves and held me at a height of arousal greater and longer than any other woman I had ever known. I was not so crass as to inquire whether her skills derived from Gegum training, although I suspected they did.

For my part, I did my best to please her, withholding my climax until she had achieved her own and attempting to induce in her the mild state of mekhenesis which would increase her pleasure. Ruuth realised at once what I was doing and, far from resisting, cooperated fully.

Afterwards, she questioned me gently about my ability. I spoke to her of the healing arts and how the mekhenistic state was obtained. It did not occur to me that she might know far more about the subject than I.

In probing my aptitude for mekhenesis, she discovered (though I told her none of it) my budding power to influence minds. It was this discovery that earned me an audience with the most remarkable Gegum of them all.

FOURTEEN

A rookie named Jansen caught the call at the precinct house closest to the studio. He sat on it, inexplicably, for fifteen minutes. Then, in his own time, he asked two cops named Gebler and O'Rourke to take a look since their car was in the neighbourhood. Gebler, who was driving, hauled ass into that miserable side street, saw the laundry van, saw Taymur's black Ford—both empty—and for no reason at all got a prickly feeling up the back of his neck.

"Something's wrong," he said.

O'Rourke, a nervy black guy with the weirdest name in the force, said, "That kid don' know his ass from his elbow; how come they give him a mike and let him mind the shop?" He reached for their own mike to make the call-back but bypassed Jansen and asked for Sergeant Gould, who packed nearly thirty years of experience and knew his ass from his elbow even on a windy night.

"What was the call?" Gould asked.

"Jansen just said there was some trouble at ACB, break-in or somethin', I dunno."

"What the fuck's ACB?" Gould asked.

"TV studio," O'Rourke said. He actually knew the place. He had a younger brother who delivered pizza to it all the time.

"ACB Television?" You could hear Gould frowning across the airwaves.

"It's a production company, man," O'Rourke said. "They make stuff for the networks. Don' you never read the small print?"

"You think I got time to watch television?"

Gebler, who had driven the car out of the street and was circling the block, reached across and took the mike. "Gebler, Ed. I don't like the look of this one."

"How come?" Gould asked at once.

Gebler hesitated before answering, then didn't really answer at all. "Listen, Ed, I'd be happier if you got back to the kid and found out exactly what was called in. I mean, exactly. I got a bad feeling here, don't know why." By "kid," he meant the rookie Jansen. Gould knew that. Everybody in the precinct called Jansen "the kid."

"Stand by," Gould said and cut the connection.

Gould's desk was in back of the building, and while he could have talked to Jansen on the phone, something told him this would be better face-to-face, so he walked. On the way, he got stopped by the captain, who wanted to talk about some charity thing. Result was that a few more minutes went by. Meanwhile, back on the street, Gebler had finished circling the block and was cruising the side street again.

As he did so, something fell out of the sky, something with arms and legs, and struck the asphalt maybe thirty, forty feet in front of him.

FIFTEEN

"Shit!" Gebler hissed as he hit the brakes.

"Hey, man, what the matter with—?" O'Rourke's protest cut short as he saw the body.

The cruiser snaked to a stop with feet to spare. Gebler killed the engine, and both cops were out of the vehicle before it had stopped shaking. The girl was a mess. Her skull had exploded like a rotten melon, and there was brain tissue in a streak across the road. Her body was slim and looked young, but that was all you could tell. Her face didn't really exist anymore.

"Christ!" breathed Gebler softly. From the skin tone and the muscle condition, he estimated a girl in her mid-twenties, max. He had a daughter around that age.

O'Rourke said, "Holy fuck, where'd she come from? Jump off the roof or what?"

Gebler looked up and decided it was this building, this TV studio, that was giving him the creeps. One of the high windows was open, dark behind it so it looked like a blind eye. "Off the roof, out a window, something like that," he told O'Rourke. Except what was bad enough to make a young girl, a girl in her twenties, throw herself off a roof or out a window? And how come she did it from a building that had just called in trouble?

O'Rourke, who hated blood and sometimes barfed at brains, backed off hurriedly, then climbed into the cruiser to call it in. Gebler, holding his breath against the smell of meat, gently tugged down the girl's skirt so her panties wouldn't still be showing when the photographer arrived. He noticed she was wearing one of those pouches round her waist that so many of the kids wore these days. He flipped it open, found eighteen dollars and change, a driver's licence and some papers. The licence identified her as Alexandra Turner with an address on the east side. He counted from her birth date and found she was twenty-one years, three months old.

A letter in the pouch told him she'd been employed as a receptionist by ACB Studios for just eight days.

The Chronicles of Nectanebo: Six

The Gegum Abbess Lipta was the most remarkable woman I have ever known. Even the act of dying is less vivid in my mind than our first meeting.

It was a measure of her arrogance that she summoned me, Pharaoh of the Twin Kingdoms, to attend upon her when the Hebrew sister Ruuth carried back tales of my potential. It was a measure of my fascination with the sisterhood that I consented.

Egypt is a vast country which geographers have divided into four main sectors: the Nile Valley, which is the most fertile and consequently the most densely populated part; the Western Desert, in which nothing grows beyond the oases and only nomad tribesmen live; the Eastern Desert, with its limestone and sandstone plateaux and its scattering of coastal villages; and the Sinai Triangle, which points like an arrowhead into the Red Sea.

My people were widely scattered, of course—the most primitive of the desert tribes paid me obeisance when they remembered (or were reminded)—but as Pharaoh, I thought of my country as the Nile and its alluvial plain, seven hundred and fifty miles of fertile civilisation surrounded by the desolation of a wasteland. The great cities of Egypt were on the Nile. The great temples of Egypt were on the Nile. The grain fields of Egypt flanked the Nile. All commerce, save for a few camel trains, flowed with the river. Why, then, would the Gegum chose to establish convent headquarters in the Sinai?

The order had more accessible convents: at Memphis, Karnak, Heliopolis, Itj-towy, Tanis, Sais and the island of Elephantine. But all bowed towards the northeastern wasteland of the Sinai where for centuries there lurked the great essential convent of all Egypt. Few people of importance outside the sisterhood had ever seen it. I certainly had not until my summons came. The fortress was so remote that there were some (and by no means all fools, either) who considered it a myth.

Sinai . . . the place was a wilderness: two indented plateaux, guarded by an approach of parallel dunes, some of them 100 cubits high; and the south, where the convent was established, a rugged hellhole of sharply serrated mountains. There were no established towns here in the days of my glory and only the barest scattering of coastal villages. Nomads roamed the central plateaux and the mountains.

The entire wedge was a place of ill omen, a haunt of spirits and ethereal creatures from the nether planes. The Hebrews believed their god lived there, belching and farting on a mountain top. Travellers' tales spoke of weird vapours which rose up from the rocks and ignited in the heat of the sun, burning any vegetation or creature that might be caught up in them. Much of the area was rainless at any season. The most common living thing was a scorpion.

My journey took close to four brutal months.

Like all Egyptians, I was an occasional citizen of deserts and respected the splendour of our western wasteland in particular. But this was a desert like no other, an empty infinitude of dull, dead colours, swept by a great cold wind and crushed by a sombre sky.

Within a day, I was seized by a sort of melancholy terror that was to remain my constant companion until eventually banished by the sight of the convent itself. My mind ceased to function with its usual clarity, as if I had eaten some narcotic plant. This was due in part to the extraordinary limpidity of the air, which endowed unusual depth to perspectives and imposed an alien quality to every scene. Distances receded to infinity. Mountain chains interlaced themselves like the work of insane Titans. No vegetation softened these bitter contours, nor ever had. One felt oneself witnessing the world as it was at the creation, and the effect on the mind was disturbing indeed.

On our departure for the delta, the priests at Sais had sacrificed for good weather and made a mess of it so that towards the end of our journey (having lost seventeen good slaves and four excellent freemen to scorpion or snakebites, falls, illness and, in one case, what seemed to be simply terminal exhaustion), we climbed two days through snow.

This was the worst of it. There was not a man in our party who was not valley-born. Most had never seen snow and treated it either with terror or, far more dangerously, as an interesting novelty. Soon we were losing men to frostbite. (One idiot actually walked barefoot.) Beyond this, we suffered a tempest and much thunder and lightning, so that one could understand why the Hebrews believed their bad-tempered god lived hereabouts.

Eventually it ended. A member of our vanguard returned to report the convent was in sight. I hurried ahead and saw tall ramparts and cypress trees against the backdrop of a chill, silent, sinister and empty mountain. Nefri, our guide, nodded at my unspoken question and smiled with that spontaneous gaiety of a child who has come home.

Trembling with cold, we reached the gigantic walls, their summit lost in swirling snow. There were no great gates such as would certainly have adorned a fortress of this size at Karnak. Instead, we were admitted through a little ironclad door, which closed behind us with an armoured clang.

Two more such doors led into a vaulted tunnel through the first rampart. We emerged into an opening too narrow to be glorified with the name of courtyard and approached the second rampart, in which I could see neither gate, door nor opening.

Our guide set to making a curious sound, somewhere between a whistle and a trill, and at once huge baskets were lowered on stout ropes from above. My personal scribe, a pompous man named Rhen, took exception on my behalf, claiming Pharaoh was not to be hauled like a sack of corn. But I waved him to silence, intrigued by this novel form of transportation, and was soon rising upwards in the basket: an experience I enjoyed and might have found positively addictive had it not been for the biting cold.

Having passed the second rampart (we were lowered down the distant side in the same manner as we had ascended), our party crept up some flights of rough, broken stairs hewn from the rock and hence to our quarters, a self-contained hostel for visitors.

Thus far we had seen no Gegum other than Nefri—the baskets had been hauled and lowered by dour, handsome, muscular men: slaves, servants or possibly just household pets of the order. Now, suddenly, the witches were everywhere, silent, graceful (and in many cases astonishingly beautiful) in the formal robes worn on state occasions.

It is possible to determine Gegum rank by robe colouring, although I did not then know the whole key. White was an acolyte, azure an initiate, saffron a mistress of poisons. Tavern talk had it that a russet robe marked a sexual adept, but I saw none wearing russet (nor saffron, to my relief). The majority wore white, although most had braiding of a different colour, the significance of which I did not know. They brought us hot—and exceedingly pleasant—herbal infusions as an immediate ally against the biting cold, then carried in lighted braziers and dainty offerings of food. With the food came jugs of a heady distillate of wine, the finest I have ever tasted—and the most deceptive. I sipped it carefully but even so experienced a lightness in the head that, while by no means unpleasant, was no state in which to meet an abbess.

A dark woman wearing white fringed with purple introduced herself as Bardas Lo Garman (an initiate name by the sound), an envoy of the abbess. She led me through a tangle of passages and stairways, not to Lipta as I had imagined, but to a private bathhouse, steamy with an underlying scent of herbs. With the aid of two other Gegum women, she undressed me completely, showing neither embarrassment at nor interest in my exposed genitalia, then assisted me down the granite steps into the heated pool.

It was a magnificent antidote to a filthy journey, and I sank into the water gratefully, closing my eyes and allowing the heat and the herbal infusions to leech away aches and tensions. I was vaguely aware that

Bardas Lo Garman and her two helpers had joined me naked in the pool, but if they had it in mind to offer Pharaoh erotic sport, I disappointed them, for it was as much as I could do to remain awake long enough to leave the water and stretch on a convenient pallet. I slept for I know not how long and awoke well refreshed in a different chamber with fresh clothing from my luggage laid out and Bardas on call to help me dress.

I had lost all track of time and hurried to prepare myself for whatever formalities lay in store, wondering vaguely where my retinue was quartered. I was presentable—if only just—when a timid knock announced the hesitant arrival of an old, arthritic crone to my chamber. She stood just within the door, like one preparing to flee, eyes downcast lest they be dazzled by the splendour of her pharaoh.

Even now it pains me to admit I took her for a cleaning woman, a sister grown old in the service of the order and now useless for anything other than the most menial of tasks. Something in her stance suggested she was in pain, and certainly she seemed fearful of me. I went at once to reassure her, for I dislike unnecessary discomfort in others.

"Mother—" I began respectfully, one hand outstretched. Then her eyes came up to meet mine, and I knew I was mistaken.

SIXTEEN

When the phone rang, Taymur waited for the ninth pulsing tone before lifting the receiver. "Hello," he said calmly.

The voice on the other end displayed an interesting mixture of education and authority. "Who am I speaking to, please?"

Oddly, he had not expected them to ask his name. It was perfectly predictable, yet it had not occurred to him. For perhaps a second he wondered if he should give it but then realised it did not matter at all. He had no police record in America, so there was no psychological profile on file to trap him. And while he meant to play for time, he knew that in a day at most he could be dead. "My name is Anwar Taymur," he said softly. "By the will of God, I am a citizen of Jumhuriyat MIsR Al-'Arabiyah." He took a slow, deep breath, then translated, "The Arab Republic of Egypt."

"Jeff Parrinder," the voice said. "Critical Incident Response Team. It seems we have a situation on our hands."

Taymur noted the easy, almost friendly tone, the diminutive use of the first name—Jeff, not Jeffrey. He noted how Parrinder said "we" so that right from the outset they were together, seeking a solution to the "situation" in which they found themselves. It was all standard procedure in terrorist negotiations. "You could say that, Mr. Parrinder."

"Can you tell me what's going on in there, Mr. Taymur? Are you in charge?"

"What is going on in here, Mr. Parrinder, is that representatives of the Sword of Allah have taken control of this building, its facilities and personnel." For reasons not at all clear to himself, Taymur found he was smiling. "And, yes, in answer to your second question, I am in charge."

"I understand you are also holding Luke Webb of the Webb Foundation," Parrinder said, coming to the nub of things early.

"That is so," Taymur said. He allowed the words to hang in the air, happy for the moment to allow Parrinder to lead the conversation.

"Is Mr. Webb okay?"

"If by 'okay' you mean is he uninjured and in good health, yes he is. He is not particularly happy to be held captive, and in that sense he is not at all okay. The others here have not been harmed with—"

"We have a dead girl out here, Mr. Taymur," Parrinder broke in.

"I was about to say, 'with two exceptions.' They were casualties of our assault on the building. We deem it unfortunate."

To Parrinder's credit, his voice remained calm as he said, "You threw her out of a window?"

"No, sir," Taymur said softly. "I shot her. It was only her body that I threw out of the window."

"You shot her personally, Mr. Taymur?"

"Personally," Taymur confirmed. Their conversation was being recorded, of course, but that did not matter. Only results mattered.

There was a pause of five heartbeats before Parrinder said, "You said there were two exceptions."

"I was also forced to shoot a young man. Personally. Others in the station have identified him as David Wood. He was a sound technician."

"What did you have against Mr. Wood?" Parrinder asked. A slight edge had crept into his voice.

"Nothing. As I told you, Mr. Parrinder, both Mr. Wood and the young woman you have—I understand her name is Turner—were unfortunate casualties of war."

"I wasn't aware we were at war," Parrinder said coldly.

Taymur decided to turn the screw. He reached down with a well-manicured hand and cut the connection. Then he cradled the phone.

SEVENTEEN

"Bastard hung up on me," said Parrinder to no one in particular. "Mr. Parrinder, can you please tell me what the situation is in there?"

"Who the hell are you?"

"Press, Mr. Parrinder. Julie Bear."

"Get this woman out of here."

"Mr. Parrinder—"

"This place is going to be crawling with the media in a minute. Make sure nobody, but nobody, comes within a hundred yards. This is a hostage situation."

"Yes, sir."

Parrinder was partnered with a woman named Tess White. She was standing by his side now, scanning the scene with intelligent eyes. Paramedics were loading the broken body of Sandy Turner into the ambulance that would take it to a nice cool morgue. Uniforms from the NYPD had sealed off both ends of the street. Around the corner, out of sight of any window of the building, were two unmarked vans housing the SWAT team. The boys—and one girl—were on a low level of readiness. The drill was always talk first, action later. There would probably be a great deal of talk. At this stage, the team was only in place as insurance.

"How'd you feel about talking to him?" Parrinder asked.

White shook her head. "Dagger of Allah?"

"Sword. What's that got to do with it?"

"Moslem extremists. Bet your shirt they're Fundamentalists. They think women are for fucking and breeding. What's his name? Anwar? I doubt Anwar would pass the time of day with me." She shrugged. "Ring him back."

"Think so?"

"Sure. He's only playing footsie. They all do it at the start of the nego-tiations. You know that."

Parrinder punched the redial button on his cell phone.

It went better after that. Inside an hour, Parrinder had satisfied himself that Luke Webb really was unharmed. After some back and forth, Taymur creatively suggested that since he was in a television studio, he should put Webb in front of the camera. Parrinder stalled long enough to talk to some technical people about how they could keep the show private—the last thing he wanted was Webb displayed on the networks at this stage. When he found it was possible, he called Taymur back and told him to go ahead. Minutes later, he was looking at a black-and-white image of Webb on a portable monitor. He looked dazed but otherwise okay.

After that, they talked about what Taymur wanted. It was predictable enough. The Sword of Allah was some sort of nutcase religious group with a grudge against the Government of Egypt. They had links with the Taliban, Al-Qaeda and God only knew who else. Their idea was that since the people of Egypt couldn't be trusted to run their own affairs, the current government needed to be replaced by an Islamic state where God would run things for them. Since the Sword wasn't getting very far in Egypt, despite God's personal support, somebody had decided to export the struggle to the United States. They believed the U.S. Govern-ment could be persuaded to put pressure on Egypt to allow Fundamen-talists—Taymur called them "men of God"—more say in the running of the country.

Parrinder listened with his eyes closed, filing away the relevant facts in his mind, not at all concerned with the political naiveté since he suspected there would be worse to come. There was. Taymur told him that, "as everyone knows," the American administration reacted only to media pressure and public opinion. Thus, he had seized a television studio and now wished to broadcast to the nation. It would have been funny if two people hadn't already died.

Parrinder framed his reply carefully. "Mr. Taymur, you have to understand that I have no control over what the television networks broadcast—not even the president himself can tell them what to do. How—"

"I do indeed appreciate that, Mr. Parrinder," Taymur's smooth voice interrupted. "But I suspect that if you, or the president, or someone else in authority requested them to carry my broadcast, they would do so. Why would they not? Have I not seized one of the richest and most powerful businessmen in the United States? Am I not holding a further twenty American citizens? Is this not news, Mr. Parrinder? I assure you I shall not take up precious air time. I have prepared a message with sufficient impact that it may be brief."

"I was going to say, Mr. Taymur, that while I can't absolutely guarantee the networks will carry your broadcast, I would imagine they would be favourably disposed to a request. As you say, the situation is newsworthy." It was the understatement of the century. There wasn't a news channel in the country that wouldn't carry a sound bite from Taymur at this minute, whether they were asked to or not. If Taymur really was prepared to keep it brief, he didn't need Parrinder for that at all. But fortunately he didn't seem to realise it. "The only thing is, Mr. Taymur, I have to answer to my superiors, and they will want some sort of quid pro quo." He wondered suddenly if Taymur would recognise the expression and added quickly, "Something in return. Something to show . . . good faith on your part."

"How might I demonstrate that?" Taymur asked.

"By releasing your hostages," Parrinder said, moving into the first substantive negotiation of the day. Very much to his surprise, Taymur agreed to release the first of his studio hostages at once. The girl stumbled from the side door of ACB Studios less than five minutes later. She was weeping, but they were tears of relief.

She was unharmed.

EIGHTEEN

"'I have to answer to my superiors!'" Tess White mimicked. She looked at Parrinder with her head to one side.

"Don't knock it when it gets results," Parrinder said. The siege was less than two hours old, and already he had one hostage release. That was nice going in anybody's book. Tess could mock him all she liked. It was his name in the morning papers.

But despite his understandable elation, there was a mouse nibbling at the back of his mind. Something about Taymur's reactions worried him, although just at that moment he couldn't say why.

The Chronicles of Nectanebo: Seven

She was not, perhaps, seven thousand years old, although I never sought to discover her real age. Although she sometimes affected to walk with a stick, Lipta had two sound legs. Her only physical peculiarity was one I had never heard spoken about: those feral eyes, which danced and glittered like cold flame, were of different colours, one steel-blue, the other blue-green. The difference was slight, but definite, and the effect disturbing.

She was, of course, neither frail nor arthritic. I lived to see her kill a warrior with a kick to the throat, and she could tumble like an acrobat during the interminable morning exercises all Gegum undertook. But her real power was no more physical than my own. It resided in her mind.

I felt drawn to her at once, oddly for me since I make friends seldom and then slowly. Even more oddly, she was drawn to me, as she told me long afterwards. At the time of our first encounter, nothing of it showed, and she played her games with consummate skill, the better to manipulate me.

Thus, in my quarters in this desolate fortress, I met the Gegum abbess and believed for a while that she was a frail old woman, confined to her convent by the weakness of her body, overjoyed that her Lord and master, the pharaoh, should deign to call upon her. My stupidity was astonishing.

It is strange how clearly I recall that first meeting, for there was little substance to it. Lipta played the obeisant crone, I the condescending king. We spoke of my journey, and she (who had caused it!) sympathised with its rigors. She congratulated me on my ascent to the throne and placed the entire Gegum order in my service—a lie to end all lies and one I did not take seriously even then.

She inquired as to the quality of the welcome my party had received from the Sinai sisters, as if she did not already know every detail and nuance of it. She asked after my health. She mentioned, as an aside, an afterthought, a matter of no importance whatsoever, the Hebrew Gegum Ruuth and managed subtly to suggest that any one of a dozen sisters would be honoured to share my bed that night if I so wished.

In this, at least, she was genuine, for she wished desperately to learn more of my embryonic powers and calculated (probably correctly) that a woman in my bed would be an ideal siphon for information. Innocently, I thwarted this ambition, on the first night at least, for the journey had exhausted me and the bath relaxed me, and though I had slept already, I had not slept enough and wanted nothing more than to retire alone. It was all one to Lipta, who, sensing my mood, took care not to outstay her welcome and left, promising to entertain me formally the next day.

This she did, first during an audience at which we discussed weighty matters of state, next during a tour of the fortress and, finally, that evening, at a banquet. I was surprised at her grasp of Egyptian politics, puzzled at how current she was on affairs of the court (since news of what is happening takes time to travel and should have taken much time to travel to such a godsforsaken outpost as this isolated convent. Yet she knew it all.).

I found the tour of her fortress doubly impressive. Lipta had by then decided to abandon her pretence of geriatric weakness and became my guide. I swiftly discovered the convent was a history book in stone, originally a fortress outpost of some pre-Akkadian empire. Its walls bore the scars of ancient wars. The Gegum had been in residence for more than a thousand years, or so she assured me, and I had no cause to doubt her. Though they had not builded the great keep, they had achieved an engineering feat as impressive in its own right: the construction of a series of tunnels that crawled like warrens through the bowels of the mountain for a distance measured in stadia. These tunnels, centuries old, had become funeral catacombs for dead sisters and archives for those records built up by the Gegum order age by age.

Lipta was an exceptional guide to these gloomy corridors, which she seemed to have mapped mentally, for she led me through the most confusing mazes without a hint of hesitation. Assuming (correctly, as it happened) that my Egyptian blood would give me an interest in funereal arrangements, she showed me the catacombs first.

They were remarkable: row upon row of withered women, their skin turned to leather, sightless eyes staring out towards eternity, each dressed in the robes of her rank and propped (unceremoniously, it seemed to me) against the walls of the tunnels. They were not embalmed. Lipta explained that the Gegum did not accept the Temple doctrine of the mummy, but the dryness of the air and something in the chemical composition of the mountain caused swift dehydration and preserved the corpses as effectively as any bandaging.

The degree of preservation was extraordinary. She was able to show me the body of the first abbess. This tiny woman, left indecently naked now that her robes had crumbled into dust, was blacker than my friend Khababasha, wrinkled as a dried fig, tougher than the leather of my sandals, but still upright in her niche after one thousand, seven hundred and sixty years.

If I was fascinated by these ancient corpses, I was overwhelmed by the Gegum archives. The weight of knowledge stored in these tunnels was almost beyond human comprehension. The documentation far predated the fortress itself, for the origins of the Gegum Order were lost in the mists of prehistory, and the sisters had carried records here which were ancient when they first occupied the keep. All had been stored in the tunnels, and the atmosphere which so successfully preserved the corpses stood guard over these ancient documents as well.

A team of some forty sisters of scholarly bent was perpetually engaged in cataloguing and arranging this vast store. It was, Lipta assured me, an unending task since new records were added more quickly than the old could be processed. I was curious as to the substance of these newer records but somehow never quite got round to asking her about them. I doubt she would have told me then, in any case. Later, when she came to trust me as she had seldom trusted any man, I learned that much of the material was concerned with bloodlines (my own included). There were also reports of alchemical experiments.

Lipta wore saffron when she presided over the evening banquet, my first hint of her sense of humour. But my entourage and I survived the meal. Later, fortified by wine, I accepted a young Gegum acolyte named Mitta into my bed and was lulled by breasts and loins and tiny, skilful hands into ecstatic oblivion.

NINETEEN

Nightfall marked a heightened danger. If a SWAT team were ordered, this would be the most likely time for it. Taymur was as confident as he could be that no such order had been given, but he placed his men on heightened alert all the same. It was no more than prudent, even though he had, in his own estimation, controlled the situation admirably throughout the day. Parrinder had his first hostage released with the promise of more to follow. That, if nothing else, should postpone an attack.

Furthermore, Taymur's demands had been far from unreasonable. Parrinder would try to get as much as he could for nothing, then, when Taymur dug his heels in—probably after the release of one most hostage in the morning—he would begin, however reluctantly, to make arrangements for the broadcast. By then, Taymur would be ready.

"How long does it take to flay a man?" he asked Gemel.

Gemel shrugged. "It may be done quickly or slowly. If quickly, no more than half an hour."

"How long will he live once the skin has been removed?"

Gemel shrugged again. "The American is young and strong. He might endure many hours. Perhaps even days if he received transfusions."

Taymur nodded. It was no more than confirmation of what he already knew, but he found his comrade's words a comfort just the same. Once the timing of the broadcast was set, the flaying could be done quickly. It would increase the impact if Webb appeared before the cameras while still conscious, so his agony was apparent. Then his execution, violently and quickly, before network technicians had time to cut the broadcast short. The images would live forever in the American psyche, a constant reminder of the Sword of Allah. If it was God's will that he and his men were martyred by a SWAT team, it would compound the message.

Taymur decided he would speak to Luke Webb first thing in the morning. He wanted to assure him it was nothing personal.

TWENTY

The broadcast was set to catch the early evening news shows, following not one but three more hostage releases at intervals throughout the following day. Parrinder was well pleased. There had been no bloodshed since his arrival on the scene. Luke Webb was safe, and four of the twenty-one captives had now walked free unharmed. When word came down from his superiors that he was to accede to Taymur's demand for air time, he suspected pressure had been applied by the Regis Foundation. By and large, he approved. Acceding to the demand would have been his own call anyway, although he would probably have held out longer. As it was, he forced Taymur to agree to a three-minute time limit on the broadcast, which meant the networks snapped it up without a moment's hesitation.

After the broadcast, Taymur promised the release of the remaining hostages, including Webb. Parrinder didn't believe he would deliver, but he was certain he could predict the sequence of events thereafter . . . and control them.

Once Taymur had his moment of television glory, he would demand safe passage out of the country, bartering the remaining hostages to get it. Parrinder would promise safe passage but demand that all the hostages be released first. This would be rejected, of course, but it was Parrinder's estimate, based on Taymur's past behaviour, that some more of them might walk free.

ACB Studios was a flat-roofed building, which meant, almost certainly, that Taymur was thinking of a helicopter lift for his men and himself to the nearest airport, where he would demand that a plane be standing by to take them . . . where? Back to Egypt? Parrinder doubted it. It was more likely to be some godforsaken destination like Libya or Iran with no extradition treaty and little love for the United States. If that really was the plan, Parrinder estimated that, with hard negotiation, he could obtain the release of all but a handful of hostages, perhaps even all except Webb, before the transport helicopter landed. Taymur would have to take at least one hostage with him—and surely he would select the most important hostage—as a guarantee of Parrinder's good faith. But more than one or two would be superfluous and possibly difficult to control, so it would make sense simply to release them. Parrinder thought he might even manipulate that by claiming only a small chopper could be brought into service in the time available.

How would it go then? There could be no question of permitting Taymur to escape, of course, not after his admitted murder of two U.S. citizens. Even pressure from the Regis Foundation wouldn't change that. So a SWAT operation was inevitable. The only question was the form it would take.

Parrinder's first thought had been an attack on the building. His team was still on standby for that eventuality. But now he was beginning to wonder if a different approach might be more productive. Why not allow Taymur to think all his demands had been met? Why not carry it through as far as the helicopter pickup? With the broadcast behind him and everything apparently going smoothly, Taymur might relax a little. And even if he did not, the transfer from the chopper to the plane would be his most vulnerable point. The SWAT team could hit him then. SWAT personnel could even be hidden in the waiting plane.

He reviewed the plan in his mind. Luke Webb's safety had to be his first priority, but Webb would be far safer in the open, where he could be seen, than held somewhere inside the ACB building. As a plan it had a lot going for it, not least of all its flexibility.

Parrinder was fairly sure he could sell it to his superiors. He was absolutely certain it would allow him to maintain control.

All in all, Taymur was proving a bit of a pussycat.

TWENTY-ONE

"All is in place," Gemel said.

Taymur glanced at his watch. It was time. "Is the link open?"

Gemel nodded.

Taymur checked the four television sets banked together in the room. They were actual sets, not monitors, each tuned to a different channel. This was his guarantee that events would be broadcast without editing or technical trickery. "Will they put us on air as they have agreed?"

He was musing aloud to himself rather than asking an actual question, but Gemel answered anyway. "Insh Allah," he said. God willing. The Americans would keep their bargain or they would not. Nothing more could be done. It was in the hands of God.

"You are prepared, Gemel?" Taymur asked.

Gemel turned his head slowly towards the surgical instruments laid out on the smaller of the two tables. A strange light entered his eyes.

It was all the answer he needed. Taymur turned to the armed men stationed at the door. "Bring in the American." All the hostages were American, but he did not need to specify which one he meant.

Luke Webb seemed dazed, as he had seemed dazed from the moment they had taken him. Apart from the first few moments in the car, he had made no attempt to struggle or escape, had put up no resistance at all. He made no resistance now as the men, on Gemel's order, removed his clothing.

Taymur watched with muted curiosity. Webb was younger than he was by several years and well, but not heavily, muscled. He had substantial genitals. He was not a conventionally handsome man, but his skull was elongated, and his face was quite striking. Ironically, he might even have been an Egyptian, one of the old race ruled by the pharaohs.

There was still no resistance as the men spread-eagled him across the second table—he actually closed his eyes, as if planning to sleep. Because of the nature of the operation, he could not be tied down, and because consciousness was required for the broadcast, he could not be drugged. Thus, two men were delegated to hold his arms and two more to hold his ankles, with a fifth standing by to secure his head if necessary. This was the moment Taymur had believed would be most difficult. However passive Webb was just now, he would surely not remain so when Gemel began to cut the flesh from his living bones. But his screams, his pleas, his struggles would be in vain. His destiny was fixed. His suffering would be a sacrifice to the greater good.

"Flay him!" Taymur ordered.

Luke Webb opened his eyes as Gemel reached for the scalpel.

The soldier holding Luke's right hand, a thickset Egyptian named Mahmoud Molokya, released it, stepped back and unslung his automatic weapon.

"What—?" Taymur began, meaning to ask what was the matter. He felt no concern: Mahmoud was a loyal and reliable member of the organisation. If there was something wrong, he could be relied upon to deal with it.

Mahmoud shot Gemel through the head, then swung to spray the room with bullets. Taymur watched with horror as his men went down, then watched with astonishment as Mahmoud turned the weapon to cut a bloody swath across his own stomach. The chest wounds Taymur had himself sustained did not hurt at all, but his knees weakened, and he slid to the floor. As the light began to dim, he saw Luke Webb climb calmly off the table.

Book Two: Resurrection

TWENTY-TWO

Janet stared at the envelope with a premonition of unease. It had the clinic logo—a discreet lowercase embossed *d*—on the top left-hand corner and her name, Dr. Janet R. Winters, immaculately typed in the centre. The precise centre. She was convinced that if she took a ruler, the white space to the left would exactly match the white space to the right and the white space above would exactly match the white space below. It had to be from Hooper. He was the only anal-retentive in the building with access to a secretary.

She tapped the envelope on the knuckles of her left hand, then threw it on the desk where she'd found it.

Janet walked over to the window and stared out. It was raining. People seemed uncomfortable with their umbrellas, as if they'd forgotten how to use them. There was a lot of business for taxis. She glanced back at the envelope. It was really stupid not to open it, but then again, she'd always had a tendency towards denial under threat.

Or was it regression? She felt quite a lot like a little girl now, powerless, helpless, wanting somebody bigger, older and preferably male to come and meet the threat for her. It was something Hooper called out of her, and she suspected he knew it. That was probably why he'd risked—

She went back to her desk and opened the envelope, then found herself holding the folded paper without reading it. What was she doing? She began to take slow, deep breaths to reduce her heartbeat and forced herself back to an adult perspective. She was thirty years old, well-qualified, experienced, good at her job. She was not rich, not famous, but she was okay.

She unfolded the paper. It was a letter of dismissal.

The Chronicles of Nectanebo: Eight

I awoke alone, assailed by a fear that gripped my stomach like a vice. The room was not entirely dark, for several of its high windows remained uncurtained, permitting a filtering of desert starlight. Nonetheless, I was unable to see other than the roughest shapes and shadows. Within them, I was convinced, danger lurked.

There were (or should have been) guards upon my door, but I did not call for them. If there was an intruder in my chamber it meant, almost certainly, that the guards were dead. Besides, I had been Pharaoh for a short time only and had not formed the deadly habit of reliance on others. Thus, regulating my breathing so that I appeared to sleep still, I reached with slow caution for the short sword concealed beside the bed.

My subterfuge was in vain. A hand gripped my wrist, but gently, and the voice of a woman whispered in my ear, "Be still, Nectanebo."

It was not the voice of Mitta but, rather, a mellow soprano, pleasing to the ear, which I did not immediately recognise. Then the hand released my wrist and touched my chest near the throat in a certain way, and recognition dawned as memory flooded. "Ruuth!" I exclaimed, not at all displeased, yet puzzled, for I had believed my first Gegum lover to be still in Karnak.

"Hush, Lord," Ruuth ordered in tones which caused my belly to constrict and fire erupt within my loins. Mitta was young, enthusiastic and pleasing, and I had left my seed within her body no more than an hour or so before. But Ruuth had skills as yet unlearned by any acolyte. Her body exuded the heady fragrance of lust; her voice held special promise of dark desires and satisfactions.

As was the habit of a lifetime, I had been sleeping naked. Ruuth pulled back the covers and slipped silently beside me in the bed. I turned towards her, but she said with urgency, "Do not touch me, Nectanebo: I come to minister to you tonight." Nothing loath, I lay back, already stiff with anticipation.

"Feel," said Ruuth. "And learn . . ."

Her knowledge of the body's neural pathways was unmatched in my experience. Her hands traced patterns across my breast, stomach, inner thighs and testicles, which caused my erect organ to throb with a desire that fell just short of pain. I felt her breasts brush me briefly, nipples erect. Her cool hand curled around my organ, and she stroked it lightly so that I emitted an involuntary groan of pleasure.

"Remember, Nectanebo," she whispered, "desire is of the mind." Her hand left my penis and began again the delicate traceries across my breast. This time, it seemed to me, a tingling energy emerged from her fingertips and flowed in channels through my body, causing me more pleasure than I could ever have imagined possible.

"Turn, Nectanebo," she whispered. I turned obediently, lying like a dead man on my face while she began a curious manipulation of my spine, which, to my astonishment, caused fearsome creaks and cracks, without, however, causing pain. She then scratched along the verte-brae, starting from my neck, and immediately a glow of warmth spread outwards through my body.

Encouraged by the gentle pressure of her hands, I turned again. At once she straddled my monstrous erection, massaging the tip with a rotating movement of her vaginal muscles. I reached for her—and knew at once this was not Ruuth! She had the same hard, well-muscled body, but her breasts beneath my hands were differently formed, her erect nipples longer.

"Who are you?" I hissed.

"Hush, Nectanebo," she bade me. And, in truth, I had more to mind at that moment than her identity, for her unbelievable control of her inner muscles was drawing me towards a fiery climax, then permitting me to cool, again and again. I was half mad with excitement and frustration.

Just when it seemed I must ejaculate, she dismounted from me and began to chant softly in my ear. The effect was indescribable. My body, already light, now seemed almost to float, buoyed up in the air as the bark of a cork tree is buoyed up in water.

This was witchcraft, pure and simple. I knew it, and I did not care. The intensity of my experience was climbing far beyond anything I had ever known before: not with my wives, not with Mitta, not with Ruuth, not with anyone. I was a sunburst of shimmering excitement, a magma of pleasure, malleable as clay in the hands of an expert potter.

There was a momentary stab of pain, then fire erupted, fountaining upwards in a volcanic torrent along my spine. I do not speak figuratively. The witch ignited something in my genital region which burned and glowed and raged and clawed its way upwards through the centre of my body.

I screamed. The agony was indescribable, yet with it came an ecstasy as intense. I could not say whether I wished this thing to stop, but there was no stopping it, in any case. The torrent reached my brain and exploded in a silent flash of intense light which left me momentarily blinded. I had not climaxed. My erection was as strong as ever. Yet my whole attention was locked within this new thing, an experience far more intense, more pleasurable than sex; an experience that now took control of my entire body.

I was beyond movement, helpless as an infant. The fire still poured along my spine, but painlessly now, a constant torrent that showed no sign of diminishing or stopping. When it reached my head, it passed through and beyond to cascade like a fountain of brilliant blue-white light which surrounded me like some monstrous egg.

It seemed to me that I grew gigantic, so large that I filled the world and stretched beyond it into the realms of Nuit, where stars crowned me and my legs bestrode planets. I threw back my head and laughed with joy, and the sound of my laughter filled the universe. My climax came upon me, and torrents of semen erupted white-hot from my monstrous penis to create galaxies.

In time, of course, I shrank and became again no more than Pharaoh, son of Amon Ra, a god encased in mortal flesh. Yet the fountain of fire and light within my spine remained, with a roaring in my ears that threatened to disrupt my sanity.

My mind pulsed. I can think of no better word to describe what I experienced. Expanding, I became one with the universe. I was Nectanebo in a growing plant, in a hunting beast, in a brooding rock. I was the world at creation's dawn. I was a woman in the agony of birth. I was the child she delivered, the seed that gave it life. I was an army in battle, an eagle in flight. Contracting, I was Nectanebo changed, with fire along my spine and a roaring in my ears, Nectanebo trapped in his dark bedchamber within a witches' den.

I could no longer measure time, but it was still night when the sound faded from my ears and the raging torrent in my spine slowed to something more akin to a fast-moving river. My perceptions were changed, sharpened to a preternatural degree. The breathing of my companion seemed like a hurricane, her voice, when she spoke, like a howl of agony. It was ecstasy, but an ecstasy too much to bear.

"It will pass, Nectanebo," she told me in a whisper that echoed across the mountaintops of Sinai.

"Who are you, witch?" I screamed at her in torment. "Who are you that has done this thing to me?"

She made me no answer, but an errant moonbeam caught her unawares, and while her face remained in shadow, I saw the gleam of feral eyes.

TWENTY-THREE

"You're early today, Dr. Winters," the nurse said pleasantly. "Your mother's down by the lake. Such lovely weather. She does so much like to make the most of it."

"Thank you," Janet said.

As she walked down the broad, shallow steps, she was struck, not for the first time, by the sheer beauty of the grounds. They had been established in the eighteenth century when the owner of the estate was the Earl of Hartford, but even in those days, Janet doubted they were better tended. The broad sweep of manicured lawns carried to a screen belt of mature trees. It was almost impossible to believe you were still in London. In most areas of the grounds, you couldn't even hear the traffic.

Her own clinic—she still thought of it as "her" clinic despite the fact that she wasn't going back—strove to keep up appearances in a surround of garden that was a fraction the size of these grounds . . . and failed miserably. The difference was money, of course.

She found her mother on a bench by the lake, a slender, grey-haired figure who still managed to look elegant in spite of everything. There was no wheelchair beside her, which was a good sign. She was wearing her lilac silk suit, which was another.

"You're early today," she said as Janet sat down beside her. She smiled. "I was planning to meet you at the front door and surprise you."

Janet leaned over and kissed her lightly on the cheek. "You're looking better, Mother." Close up, even her skin tone had improved.

"I'm in remission!" Emma Winters told her daughter, smiling broadly. "It started yesterday after you left. I'm sure your visit had something to do with it—you always cheer me up. I improved over the evening, and this morning I felt so good I actually fancied bacon and eggs. Ate most of it too. I'm tired, of course: not much energy. But that's only to be expected, isn't it?"

"What do your doctors say?" Janet asked. Multiple sclerosis, or MS, was characterised by remissions, but this one seemed a little fast. As against that, her mother had been unremittingly ill for nearly three years now, so a remission might be due.

Emma dismissed her doctors with an airy flick of her hand. "Oh, you know what they're like—they're more cautious than you are. Circumspect, they like to call it. "Too early to say" . . . "Best wait a little and see" . . . "Hopeful signs" . . . She cast her eyes exasperatedly to heaven, then looked at Janet and smiled. "But I know my body, and I'm definitely feeling so much better it isn't true. It's a remission, all right. Better find me a good man so I can enjoy it."

"Robin Crawley sends his love," Janet said, then bit her tongue. Robin was an old friend of her mother's and was also Janet's solicitor. Janet had called him to find out if there was anything she could do about the dismissal. She hadn't meant to mention the visit to her mother, especially not now when there was a chance of a remission. Worry always hampered progress, and Emma would worry if she discovered Janet had lost her job.

"What were you doing with Robin?" her mother asked at once. "You're not in trouble, are you?"

"Nothing I can't handle," Janet told her.

But her mother didn't leave it, any more than Janet had imagined she would. "What is it?" she asked simply.

"Darling," Janet said, "it's nothing—nothing at all for you to worry about."

"If it's nothing at all, I won't worry," Emma said sharply. "On the other hand, I have a habit of imagining the worst."

"It's a problem at work," Janet said stiffly.

"Have you been fired?" her mother asked.

It was a relief to tell her, far more so than talking to Robin. When she'd finished, Emma said, "Are you in the market for advice?"

"In spades."

"Let it go and move on," her mother told her bluntly.

"Let Hooper get away with it?"

"Get away with what?" asked her mother. "You had an affair. You dumped him. He may or may not have been spiteful in his recommendation—you'll never prove it either way. But the board wouldn't fire you just on his say-so."

Janet stared at her. "What's that supposed to mean?"

"It's supposed to mean that there's some other reason."

"Like what?" Janet demanded.

"Don't get angry with me, darling. I'm not the one who fired you. They may be dissatisfied with your work, but since you're an excellent psychologist, I doubt that. At the same time, they may disagree with your decisions, or some of them. Or it may have nothing to do with you at all and they're just having to make cutbacks. I don't know. But whatever the reason, the only sensible thing you can do is let it go and move on. You've had as good training as I have—you should certainly understand that."

Emma Winters's training was as a Jungian analyst. She'd been a good one before the MS had taken her out of the scene. Janet wondered if she'd been as hard on her patients as she was on her daughter. Frowning, she said, "So you don't think I should sue?"

"I certainly don't," Emma said. "Start going to the courts and, before you know it, you're making a career of it. You're boring your friends to death and worrying yourself into an ulcer. What does Robin think?"

"He's against it too. He thinks they might try to drag up my past, make a thing of my love life."

To her surprise, her mother began to smile, then laugh. "Your past?" she echoed. "I'm sorry, darling, but you don't have a past! If Hooper introduces your love life in evidence, he'll put the judge to sleep!"

Janet glared at her, then relaxed. After a moment, she began to smile. "I suppose you're right," she said ruefully. "It's not exactly tabloid material, is it? I got myself sort of confused about that talking to Robin."

"He used to have that effect on me," her mother told her dryly. "But, frankly, in my opinion, you have to put this whole sorry episode out of your head and look for another job." She pushed herself off the bench. "See, I can stand. If you let me lean on your shoulder, I can even walk back to my room, where I'll bully the sister into bringing us some tea and scones. Tomorrow, with luck, I'll be able to walk by myself."

Janet took her arm. As usual when her mother voiced an opinion, she made life sound so simple.

TWENTY-FOUR

It still sounded simple on the tube. All she had to do was find another job.

That bit wasn't simple, of course. But at least she could get the papers tomorrow, contact an agency, put out a few feelers. It would give her the impression of being in control, however false that might be. She sat back and closed her eyes. At least money wasn't an immediate problem. She still had something left of her father's legacy, and since she had never been a spendthrift, there were even some savings from her salary. Add in her severance pay, and she could manage very nicely for a while.

Of course, if she couldn't find another post in a reasonable time, things might start to get tricky. But since she was applying positive thinking, that was something she was quite prepared to forget until it actually happened.

The phone was flashing when she walked into her flat, but she ignored it. What she wanted now, more than anything else, was a shower. She headed for the bathroom, pulling off her blouse.

She ran the water hotter than usual and allowed it to soak away the tensions of the day. By the time she came out of the shower, she was planning to call her nearest Japanese restaurant and order takeout. It was an extravagance under the circumstances, but their food was wonderful, and at least getting takeout was less expensive than actually dining there. She also planned to break open the reserve chardonnay at the back of the fridge. Getting sacked wasn't all bad. It gave you a sense of freedom.

The phone rang as she wandered into the living room.

For a moment she was tempted to let the machine pick it up—she was really in no mood to talk to anyone just now—but then the thought occurred to her that it might be a job offer. She was reaching for the phone when she realised just how stupid that thought was. Only a handful of people knew she'd been sacked, and none of them was in a position to employ anybody. But by then it was too late; she already had the phone to her ear and was saying, "Hello?"

"Am I speaking with Dr. Winters? Dr. Janet Winters?"

"Yes." The voice was male and unfamiliar. It had one of those soft, reassuring American accents that reminded her of Alistair Cooke.

"Dr. Winters, this is Adrian Abbot. I was wondering if you'd decided whether to meet with me."

She didn't know any Adrian Abbot. "I'm sorry?"

"Adrian Abbot, Dr. Winters. From the Regis Foundation? I wrote to you five days ago. I was purely wondering if you'd come to a decision yet. About meeting with me? Please don't think I'm being pushy, but I'm actually booked on a flight back the day after tomorrow, so time is sort of running out for me."

Janet blinked. "Mr. Abbot—"

"Adrian, please."

"Mr. Abbot, I'm afraid I don't know what you're talking about. I haven't received any letter from you." She was cautious—most women living alone in London necessarily were—but he didn't sound like a crank or a heavy breather. To soften it, she added, "It may have gone astray in the post, but . . ."

"No, it was delivered by hand. I used a courier service—it's standard Foundation policy for something like this: we don't trust the post." He hesitated. "Unless the courier was unreliable. I'm not all that familiar with London couriers—I just picked one from the Yellow Pages."

An uncomfortable suspicion was forming in Janet's mind. A hand-delivered letter would have ended up with Bernice at the reception desk. She would have left it on Janet's desk if Janet wasn't in her office, which, most of the time, she wasn't. If she hadn't seen Janet immediately afterwards, she might well have forgotten to mention it. There had always been a lot of papers on Janet's desk, and five New Year's resolutions to the contrary, she wasn't always efficient in dealing with them. "I'm sure they were perfectly reliable, Mr. Abbot," she said hurriedly. "I expect there's just been some sort of mix-up. Why don't you just tell me what was in the letter and we can take it from there?"

"Not a lot, actually," Abbot told her. "It purely introduced the Regis Foundation—I don't suppose you've heard of the Regis Foundation, by any chance?"

"Afraid not."

"No, it doesn't seem to be known at all in Great Britain. It has a high profile in the States—some parts of the States, anyway. Essentially it's a research foundation. Established in the fifties by the late Stanislav Regis. It's administered by a privately owned family trust now. It . . . does research. Well, it funds research projects. Anything and everything—very catholic in its tastes. That was a policy established by Mr. Regis himself. What more can I tell you? Anyway, I've got a suitcase full of PR material if you're interested, but you can take my word for it they're great people—I've worked for them since I left college."

"Why did you think I might be interested in the Regis Foundation?" Janet asked cautiously.

"Well," Abbot said, "the thing is, we've got an offer for you. I was hoping we might meet and discuss it. That's what else was in the letter."

"What sort of offer are we talking about?"

"A job offer."

Janet felt her heart jump, but she fought down the rising excitement. In her experience, life was never that easy. You simply weren't fired from a job one day and offered another the next. A sudden thought struck her. "How did you get my number, Mr. Abbot?"

"From Susan Hardiman," Abbot said without elaboration.

"Did she suggest me for the job?"

"No, the principal of the Regis Foundation suggested you. I think she saw your paper in the *Clinical Psychiatry Quarterly*. But Ms. Hardiman told me she thinks very highly of your work and would be happy to act as a referee. Dr. Winters, forgive me, but this really isn't something we can discuss in any detail over the phone. I realise you may not be in the market for another job"—he hadn't heard, Janet thought—"but I really would appreciate the opportunity to meet you face-to-face and explain what we have to offer."

She was no longer able to fight back the excitement, although now it was mixed with a sort of delighted confusion. "Well . . . yes," she said. "Yes, of course, I'd . . . I'd love to meet with you. When? I suppose it'll have to be tomorrow since you're flying back . . . Does tomorrow suit?"

"Dr. Winters, would you mind if we met tonight? My people back in the States want an answer as quickly as possible. And apart from that, you may have questions I can't immediately answer. I think tomorrow would be cutting it too close."

She had no serious doubts that the man was genuine, so she said, "All right—tonight. Where and when?"

"Have you eaten, Dr. Winters?"

She thought of the Japanese takeout and the bottle of chardonnay. "Not yet."

"Then why don't you join me for an early dinner? Somewhere convenient to you—name a place you like, and I'll find it—at the Foundation's expense, of course. Would that suit you?"

"Do you like Japanese food, Mr. Abbot?" Janet asked.

TWENTY-FIVE

Abbot was younger than Janet had expected, late twenties at most, but very much the academic in jacket, slacks and horn-rimmed glasses. He rose from his seat as she approached and extended his hand. "Dr. Winters, I am really grateful you agreed to see me."

"Nonsense," Janet said. "I adore Japanese food." It came out exactly as she wanted: light and easy, as if she received job offers every day.

"Good," he said. "Good." He held out her chair. "Can I order you a drink while you're looking at the menu?" He waved to an inscrutable waiter before she could reply. "I suppose it'll have to be saki. I love Japanese food, but I have to tell you I hate saki."

Janet smiled. "They'll bring you anything you want—they're quite civilised here."

"Vodka martini? Do you think they can stretch to that? With crushed ice? Nobody seems to have heard of crushed ice in London."

"You can always ask."

When the waiter went off, he turned back to her. "You want to know more about the Foundation?"

Janet shook her head. "No. I have to apologise to you, Mr. Abbot. Your letter did arrive safely—it's just that I hadn't actually opened it. I have now, though, so I know a little about your Foundation." She'd found the courier package among the papers she'd moved from her desk. Among other things, it contained a printed brochure. Abbot's letter was on Savoy notepaper, which suggested the Foundation wasn't miserly when sending representatives abroad. "What I would like is more details about your offer."

"Yes, of course," Abbot said. "Just one thing: can we drop the Mr. Abbot stuff? I know you British prefer things formal, but it makes me nervous. Please call me Adrian. I'll keep calling you Dr. Winters if you like."

"You'll do nothing of the sort!" Janet smiled. "My name's Janet."

The waiter reappeared with their drinks. "Do you want to order now?" Janet asked.

"I'll just have what you have," Abbot said.

"I don't know what I'd like yet."

Abbot waved the waiter away. "Now," he said at once, "here's the offer you can't refuse. Hopefully. Dr.—Janet, I'll be up front. I've been sent here to headhunt you. We've read all your papers, and the way you think is just—" He made a gesture with both hands. "And your clinical experience reinforces that. Anyway, the point is, you don't have to sell yourself to us: we know you're perfect. Do you object to working in the United States?"

"The job's in the United States?"

"Yes. Does that present a problem?"

Janet blinked. Stupidly, she hadn't considered that the job might be in America. So many American companies had British subsidiaries she'd somehow assumed that if the Regis Foundation was recruiting British staff, it was for some British project. "I'm not sure," she said. In theory, she could work anywhere she wanted—she had no husband, no children, no dependents. But there was her mother. "My mother's got multiple sclerosis—she's in a nursing home." Emma might be in remission now, but she wouldn't stay that way.

"Yes, we know."

"Do you?" Janet asked, surprised.

Adrian Abbot volunteered no explanation. "There are two possible solutions. The first is you fly back to visit her, say twice a week. The Foundation will fund it. The other is that you bring your mother with you. The standards of private health care are very high in the States. The Foundation will fund that too. Your choice."

Janet stared at him, astonished. He looked hardly old enough to be making high-level decisions that could cost his foundation thousands of dollars.

"What do you say?" he asked.

Janet licked her lips. "Let me think about that," she said. "You haven't told me what the job is yet."

To her surprise, a shadow crossed his face. "Ah, now we come to the tricky bit. I can't tell you what the job is."

Janet waited, then realised that was it. "You can't—? I don't think I understand you."

"No, I don't suppose you do. This is going to sound peculiar. The work we need you for is . . . delicate. It's in your field, of course, but I'm not in a position to give you details of what you'll be doing."

Janet smiled, laughed a little, then stopped. "Oh, come on!"

"No, that's the way it is." He looked at her seriously. "If you take the job, you'll be required to sign a nondisclosure contract."

"You really expect me to take a job in a foreign country without even knowing what it is?"

"America's not a foreign country," Abbot said. "Not really. Look at the Special Relationship. Look at your television any night—you probably know more about the U.S. than I do."

Janet shook her head. She was beginning to see why they'd sent Abbot, young though he was. "Is this national security or something? Some sort of subcontract from the government?"

"No."

"You must be able to tell me something about it."

"I can tell you it's well paid." He named a figure that was three times her salary at the clinic, even after she made the dollar conversion.

"What?" Janet exclaimed.

He named the same figure. "That's the first year, of course. After that, it's negotiable upwards. Plus your accommodations are paid for. And your car."

"Car?" Janet echoed.

"Your choice up to a hundred grand. I'm afraid they're all automatics in America. You British prefer stick shifts, don't you? Can't get them over there. Unless you pick a sports car. You could have a sports car."

Janet stared. She had never owned a sports car. She had never believed she could own a sports car.

Abbot said, "I appreciate money isn't everything, but you can negotiate a six-month contract, see if you like the job. If you don't, you can always come home—subject to nondisclosure, of course. If you like the Foundation as much as I think you will, you can stay on."

"For how long?"

"That's up to you."

After a long moment, Janet said, "Where would I be working? New York?" She'd noticed the headquarters of the Regis Foundation was in New York.

"Arizona," Abbot said. "Tell you what—why don't you plan a little trip across, see the facility, meet the people, maybe get a better idea about what you'd be in for? No obligation, and we'll pick up the check. Give you something to base your decision on. I don't know, maybe you'll persuade my boss to tell you more than I can."

The waiter materialised at their table. "May I take your order?" he asked politely.

"I haven't decided yet," Janet said. But that was just about the food.

TWENTY-SIX

Janet had only the most fleeting impression of Phoenix before catching a connecting flight to Tucson. She had only a fleeting impression of Tucson as well, which was a pity, given that it was featured in so many of her favourite songs. But she doubted she'd have appreciated it much anyway, since by now she'd entered the unreal state of grey exhaustion brought on by jet lag.

Somebody met her at the Tucson airport and bundled her onto an aircraft that surprised her by taking off straight up until she realised it was a helicopter. Although she'd never been in a helicopter before, she actually dozed, then slept until a hand shaking her shoulder dragged her reluctantly back to consciousness.

"Time to get out, Dr. Winters," a voice said in her ear. So she got out and walked across the tarmac, vaguely aware that somebody had an arm around her shoulders, holding her crouched so she would not be decapitated by whirling blades.

There was a limousine waiting with deep, comfortable back seats so that she fell asleep instantly. She dreamed that somebody helped her check into an hotel where the room was air-conditioned, the sheets were cool and clean and the mattress was as welcoming as a lover.

She woke to sunlight, wondering where she was. It had the feel of a hotel room. There was an oversized television set at the bottom of the bed, and she could see a bathroom through an open door. She found her watch on the bedside table and discovered it was almost noon. As she completed the long swim into consciousness, she saw an envelope beside the watch. Her name was written on it in a cramped, careful hand. She tore it open. The single sheet of paper inside was a Regis Foundation memo sheet. The message read:

Dear Dr. Winters,

Welcome to the United States and Arizona in particular! It's a long haul, but I hope you will find it all very worthwhile. You looked pretty shattered when you arrived, so I thought it best to let you sleep over in town before bringing you out to the facility.

I've arranged to have a car call for you at the motel at 3 p.m. tomorrow. (Or today, I suppose, since you'll be reading this in the morning.) If that's a problem, call the local number listed at the head of this sheet. If not, I'll look forward to seeing you again.

Meanwhile if there's anything you need, call reception at the motel and charge it to Regis. We run an account there, and they're pretty good for small-town boys.

Yours sincerely,

Donald R. Wright

Janet pulled herself out of bed and headed for the bathroom. Her body still felt like lead, but her head was mercifully clear. There was no bath, of course—Welcome to America!—but the shower controls looked like they belonged at Cape Canaveral.

By the time she emerged from the shower (which doused her in a perfumed spray at the touch of an amber button), she was feeling not just human but positively energised and more than a little hungry. She was also excited. She would be at the Regis Foundation's Arizona facility that afternoon. With luck, she might even discover a bit more about the job she was being offered.

She lifted the phone and dialled reception. "This is going to sound silly, but where exactly am I?"

"Easy Rider Motel, ma'am," a male voice told her as if guests got confused every hour of the day.

Janet said, "I was also wondering about the name of the town."

"Nogales, ma'am. The town's called Nogales. Only round here folks think it's a city."

The motel restaurant was functional and clean. The waitress looked Spanish but didn't have the accent. "Hi, honey, you're the new gal out in the facility—right?"

"Thinking about it," Janet nodded, amused.

"My name's Donna. Bet you're a doctor—right?"

"I am, as a matter of fact."

"I'd like to be a doctor, but I never had the brains. Don't know what it's like back where you come from, honey, but over here doctors make a fortune. You'll never meet a poor one. You hungry?"

"Starving," Janet told her.

By the time Donna brought dessert, which featured ice cream, whipped cream and caramelised sugar as well as bananas and honey, Janet knew her well enough to ask, "Do you know much about the Regis facility?"

"Know it's over thataway," Donna said, jerking her head in an indeterminate direction. "You figuring on walking?"

Janet smiled. "Not today. I was wondering if you knew what they did there."

"Sure do, honey. Is this a test or what?"

Janet shook her head. "No. They've offered me a job, but they won't tell me what it is until I get there."

Donna laughed. "That's them all over. That's them for sure! Whole place is supposed to be a big-deal secret, even got their own security setup, but you can't keep nothing to yourself in a place the size of Nogales. They're doing research into plants out at the facility. That's what it's all about—food crops you can grow in really dry conditions, like the Sonora. Won't talk about it because that sort of thing could be real big money now the world's getting hotter and all. Hey, bet you thought I thought you was a medical doctor, eh? Well, I didn't. You're a plant doctor, ain't you? What do they call it? A botanist? You won't be short of stuff to do out there, honey. You'll have more odd plants to take care of than you can shake a stick at."

Janet stared at her, wondering what on earth a botanical research facility wanted with a doctor of psychology.

TWENTY-SEVEN

Donald R. Wright turned out to be a balding, middle-aged man whose face looked familiar because, so he assured her, he had met her at the airport the afternoon before.

"I have to tell you, Janet, you looked a mess," he remarked as they shook hands in his office. "Not that I blame you. I can't stand flying myself, avoid it when I can. No room, rotten food and the jet lag kills you. You're looking much better now. Good sleep?"

"Yes," Janet told him.

"Good," he nodded. "The Easy Rider's not the Ritz, but it's comfortable. We use it quite often. What are your first impressions of our little facility?"

"I was a little taken aback by all the security," Janet told him honestly. "Is it true your perimeter fence is a hundred miles long?"

"Must be something like that," Wright nodded carelessly. "Who gave you the figure?"

"My driver."

"Who did you get?"

"Somebody called Joachim."

Wright said, "Great character. If he says the fence is a hundred miles, I believe him. I'm afraid the security is an unfortunate necessity. The work here is very experimental, but it has large-scale financial implications. Until we take out patents, security is the only way to safeguard our investment. It's a heavy investment as well."

"I understand you're experimenting with arid-environment food crops," Janet said.

"Joe tell you that as well?" Wright asked easily. "Very naughty of him."

"As a matter of fact, I heard it at the motel."

Wright still looked relaxed. "It's supposed to be a secret, but you can't really keep something like that under wraps. We try to stop people talking about it, but you know . . ." He shrugged. "Anyway, let me give you the guided tour. You didn't fly all this way to listen to my security worries."

The guided tour was impressive. The Regis facility isolated in the Sonora Desert was more like a small town than a research centre. It had shops, restaurants, a recreation centre that included a cinema and swimming pool, administrative offices, research labs and even its own community police, who, Wright assured her, were separate entities from the security people.

"We've got about eight thousand people working here one way or another," he said with a hint of pride. "That puts us in much the same league as a small midwestern town. They don't all live here, of course, but what with dormitory overnights and so on, you don't often have less than six thousand in residence at any one time. That many people take some looking after. When the facility was set up, we considered a dump truck full of plans on how to do it and finally settled on running things on a straightforward civic model, right down to our own sheriff. We have community housing and community activities to try to develop a community spirit. For all intents and purposes, this is a small town in the middle of the desert."

"Except it's owned by the Regis Foundation."

"Except for that, yes," Wright agreed. "Let me show you your accommodations. This is where you'll be for the duration of your stay and where you'll live if you decide to join us."

She had expected an apartment. Something newer, probably a little larger, certainly better appointed than what she was used to in London. What she got was incredible. The accommodation was a small villa set in its own grounds on the edge of town. There was garage space for two cars, a swimming pool in no way smaller than the municipal pool she'd seen earlier and tasteful period furniture throughout. There was even a piano—a piano!—in the lounge.

"There's somebody who takes care of your garden," Wright said. "When all the water has to be piped, it's a bit tricky to try to do it yourself. Besides, you probably won't have time. You've a Mexican maid to look after the house, and you share a cook, which just means you get her every day but you have to negotiate meal times. If that doesn't suit, you can use your meal allowance at one of our restaurants. The place is yours rent-free as long as you're with us. Did Adrian tell you there's a car? You get to choose your own, so I can't show you. You also get to choose your own entertainment centre—TV, stereo, that sort of thing. We used to have them installed before we moved people in, but these days, you know, everybody has their own taste, so now . . . Anyway, your personal computer's in the office. You don't get a choice there, because it's linked to our intranet. And the Internet, of course, although I doubt you'll have much time for surfing. There's tennis and golf if you're fond of sports and—"

"Don," she interrupted quietly, "does everybody who takes a job here get this sort of place?"

He grinned at her happily. "Only the ones we want really badly."

Her suitcase was sitting in the middle of the largest bed she'd ever seen. Janet leaned against the doorpost. "Let's just talk about that now," she said.

"Sure," Don said. She thought he looked a little apprehensive.

"Secrecy aside, this is a botanical research facility?" Janet said.

He nodded. "Yes."

"What do you want with an amnesia specialist?"

He glanced at his watch. "Mrs. Webb will be flying in this evening. I thought you might meet her after dinner. She's by far the best one to explain."

"Who's Mrs. Webb?" Janet asked.

Don looked mildly surprised. "Mrs. Webb owns the Regis Foundation."

The Chronicles of Nectanebo: Nine

The meeting in Sinai was my first encounter with the Abbess Lipta but not, of course, my last. I had occupied the throne less than two years before there came another summons, couched in the diplomatic niceties of "the Abbess begs" . . . "would be greatly honoured" . . . "implores the mighty Pharaoh" . . . and similar such wordy nonsense. It was a summons nonetheless, not to the Gegum convent, but to a place in its own way just as strange.

We walked together in the ruins of Akhet-Aten, following a line that roughly paralleled the old King's Way. Nothing remained now, save for a track. Time had converted the Pleasure Palace into a jut of granite blocks half buried by the sand. Not even a depression marked the great artificial lake.

"Do you feel an affinity with this place?" Lipta asked me in that abrupt way of hers.

I shook my head. In fact, the ruined city made me a little nervous, as if it were peopled by ghosts, and part of me imagined I could still catch the whiff of heresy and was suitably repelled. I had not yet walked the Gegum Way, although my friendship with Lipta had certainly blossomed. "Why do you ask?"

She was staring out beyond the ruins to where sunlight glinted on the placid surface of the Nile. "I thought you might be Akhenaten returned," she said shortly, an edge of irritation in her voice, as if I should have known.

I stopped. "The Heretic?"

To my surprise, she said, "Oh, it's heresy that troubles you now, is it?"

"He banished the gods. All but one." I looked around me. "And they took their vengeance."

"You think a man should walk in fear of the gods?" Lipta asked, scowling.

"Of course." It was orthodox doctrine. I was still naive enough to imagine that since the Gegum took part in Temple ritual, they must believe in Temple teachings.

"You're a god, aren't you, Pharaoh?" There was just the barest hint of emphasis on the final word.

I was sufficiently wary to see the danger signs and began a careful answer: "One must separate Nectanebo the man from Nectanebo the pharaoh, Abbess. I was, of course, born of woman like any other man, and, as such, mortality is my inheritance. But once Destiny directed me to assume the mantle of Pharaoh, I assumed at the same time the function of divinity which—" I stopped this pompous nonsense eventually. She was laughing.

"Akhenaten was one of ours," she said eventually, still smiling.

"One of yours?"

"The sisters initiated him. The first man in history." By sisters she meant the Gegum Order.

I was staggered, as much by the implications as the information. "But how could you condone his heresy? How could you support—" A sudden realisation dawned, and I stared at her. "It was not his heresy, was it?"

She shook her head. "Gegum. All of it. The One God Aten. The demolition of the temples. Everything. Nefertiti was Gegum, of course, which made it easier." Nefertiti was Akhenaten's queen.

"But why?" I asked, appalled.

Lipta shrugged. "Presumably the abbess of the day had her reasons." It was as close as she ever came to explaining Gegum motivation. She looked around her, eyes glinting from beneath the abba hood. "A disastrously mistaken move, of course. The change did not outlive him by a single day. Look at this. All the grandeur, and what's left? A few crumbling blocks and a dried-up aqueduct." An overstatement, but it made the point. "All the same, the sisters still consider this city sacred soil." It was a lie, although I did not find it out until much later. The sisters considered nothing sacred. Except possibly their own accursed schemes.

She was in unusually talkative mood, for only a little later she said, "I am reminded of a corpse." And later still, as if following an inward caravan of thought, "Have you yet learned what they will do to that fine body of yours, Pharaoh, when you die?"

I frowned. "They?"

"The embalmers, Nectanebo. Do you know the arts of the embalmers?"

I did not, nor wished to. Like all Egyptians, I was fascinated by death. Like most, I preferred to avoid its details. But Lipta pressed on remorselessly. "Since you are Pharaoh and incarnate son of Amon-Ra"—there was not a hint of irony in her voice—"you will naturally receive the best treatment available. First, they will split your nose and insert a tube upwards: this they will use to introduce solvents into the skull cavity. When your brain has part liquefied, they will draw it out through your nostrils with an iron hook. This complete, they will call the dissector."

She smiled, and something twinkled in her eyes. She reached out and touched my naked abdomen above the apron. "He will cut here, Pharaoh, using a knife of Ethiopian stone." She drew the tip of her finger along the path of the incision, holding me with her eyes, and it was all I could do not to flinch from the imaginary blade. Still smiling, she withdrew her hand and took four agile, dancing steps backwards, like a little girl at play. "And he will run away!" she exclaimed, pleased by her own dumb show. "And the dignified embalmers will pursue him, hurling stones and imprecations and curses for the injury he has done to Pharaoh."

She returned to my side and took my arm as if for support while we resumed our stately walk. "Then they pay him and get on with the job."

Despite myself, I was developing a horrid fascination for this grisly monologue. When she remained silent, I prompted, "What do they do next?"

She looked up into my face like a lover. "They remove your entrails, Nectanebo. Liver and lights. Cubit after cubit of intestines—all out and dropped into the nearest canoptic jar. Then they flush out the cavity with palm wine and stuff scented aloes up your arse."

She sighed and turned her gaze to distant horizons. "You are then soaked in natron for seventy days and bandaged. The priests tell me this process creates a suitable vehicle for your ka should it ever wish again to walk on Earth. I've often wondered what sort of life you would lead without your bowels or brains and your backside full of aloes."

She stopped abruptly and turned, reaching up to place a finger on my lips. "Shall I tell you a secret, my ambitious friend? The sisters do not believe there is an afterlife. None. None at all. No Halls of Osiris. No Judgement. No flights to the stars. Nothing but an endless sleep, devoid of dreaming." Again the hand withdrew. "So take what you are offered, Nectanebo, and fear nothing, for in the end you will come to nothing but a shell for aloes."

"You really believe that?" I asked her.

"I believe I shall live again," she told me briskly, breaking the mood. "But that is not official order teaching, merely a vision of my own." Our respective retinues moved with us, but at a discreet distance so that our words could not be overheard. She looked at me archly. "So, too, shall you live again, Nectanebo. Are you not Pharaoh and immortal? Perhaps we might even resurrect together and gambol like spring lambs." Lipta signalled, and two stunningly attractive women flowed towards us bearing bowls of melon seeds and nuts. A third followed closely with a skin of wine and two ceramic goblets. Lipta helped herself casually to some seeds, presumably to indicate they were free from poison, then waved her hand vaguely in invitation. "A morsel, Pharaoh? Or some wine?"

I shook my head. "Neither, Abbess." Since my dramatic sexual experience in her convent, I had to be extremely careful what I ate. Several types of grains made me feel bloated and ill for days. Meat of any sort was emetic. I was cautiously expanding the varieties of food I could still enjoy but so far had not attempted melon seeds. I had no wish to do so now and risk vomiting before half the court. Wine, and especially the light, pale wine favoured by the Gegum, was perfectly palatable to me, but solid instinct told me I would always need a clear head with this woman.

"I shall have some wine, Anek," she told the woman with the wine-skin, apparently unconcerned by any threat I might represent. When her goblet was filled, all three withdrew. Lipta sat on a convenient boulder, perched on its edge like a black crow.

"We were interested in Rameses, you know—the second Rameses. He seemed to have great potential, but ultimately he betrayed us."

"How so?"

"He used the sacred wisdom for his own ends, for his own aggrandisement. The ultimate sin. We cursed him and withdrew our support, which is much the same thing. For all of his faults, Akhenaten was far more successful. At least he never betrayed the world of spirit."

After a time, I asked her, "What made you think I was Akhenaten returned?"

"Parallel circumstances," Lipta said.

I hesitated, wondering if I had missed something. I could see no circumstances parallel between the career of the Heretic and myself. "What circumstances, Abbess?"

"The sisters have decided to offer you initiation," Lipta told me blankly, as if this were something outside her control.

TWENTY-EIGHT

The woman who came round the desk was in her early fifties but could easily have passed for forty-five. She was smaller than Janet with the sort of figure that carried no superfluous fat. The real surprise was that she was dressed so casually—jeans and a T-shirt with not a hint of a bra. She had an open face, not exactly friendly but somehow reassuring. All the same, Janet noticed Don Wright treated her with a deference that bordered on wariness. "Mrs. Webb, this is Dr. Winters."

"Thanks, Don. We won't keep you." The woman shook Janet's hand as he closed the door. "Good of you to come all this way to look us over."

"There were inducements," Janet said, smiling. She mistrusted first impressions, especially her own, but she found the woman likeable. There was a directness about her that was appealing. Her eye contact was firm but lacked the implied challenge of a power player. Janet guessed the men in her organisation might find her difficult. She had all the confidence that came from a great deal of money and a great deal of power, but her looks didn't quite fit. That sort of combination threw men—or at least the sort of men who became business executives. They could never quite get rid of the impression that here was somebody who needed looking after. In Janet's professional opinion, Mrs. Webb was very capable of looking after herself. She wondered what Mr. Webb was like.

"Yes," Mrs. Webb said easily, referring to the inducements. "I wanted to make sure you came. They treated you well?"

"Astonishingly," Janet said. "I can't believe the accommodations." Then, because her instinct was to like this woman and she valued frankness, she added, "You know you could buy anybody in my field for half of what you're offering."

"I don't want anybody in your field," Webb said. "I want you." She smiled lightly. "You'd probably like to know why."

"Yes, I would. It's obviously not for whatever you're doing at this facility. I'm no biologist."

"No, you're not. You're a clinical psychologist and a specialist in amnesia. I've been watching your progress for some time now."

Janet blinked. "I don't understand."

"You published a piece in *Archaeology Today* about human mindset in the ancient world—"

"That was years ago!" Janet exclaimed, astonished. The paper had been accepted shortly after she had qualified as a doctor—a speculative piece with more popular appeal than scientific foundation.

Mrs. Webb shrugged. "You made the case that it's hard for us to understand the ancient world from written records because even in translation, words have come to take on a whole new emphasis. In some cases, even a whole new meaning. That's what you said, wasn't it?"

"Yes," Janet said. "I'm amazed you remember after all this time. It wasn't a particularly important paper. It wasn't even all that original."

"Don't put yourself down," Mrs. Webb told her. "You write very accessibly for an academic. That's the sign of a clear mind. Do you remember what you said about the term 'Greek warrior'?"

Janet nodded. "Yes."

"So do I," said Mrs. Webb. "It was what stuck in my head. You said when we read a term like 'Greek warrior,' we conjure up a heroic image. We get a mental picture of a noble figure living a life of brave deeds. But, in reality, he was just an old-time G.I. You didn't say G.I.—that's American. I forget what you did say."

"I think I may have said 'Private.' It's much the same thing in the British Army."

"I was taken by the piece," Mrs. Webb said. "I kept a weather eye out for anything else you'd published. It hasn't been a lot, and you sure publish in some weird places, but it gave me a picture of the way your mind works."

"I'm afraid the obscure journals are the only ones interested in my ideas," Janet murmured. She felt immensely flattered. It was almost all she could do to stop herself from sounding kittenish.

Mrs. Webb shrugged again. "That's because you're an original thinker. In my experience, the important scientific journals reserve space for papers that preserve the status quo, not the ones that challenge it. Was the piece in the *Clinical Psychiatry Quarterly* the last thing you've published?"

"Yes."

"Some interesting insights," said Mrs. Webb.

With an urge to take the initiative, Janet said, "I gather you own the entire Regis Foundation, Mrs. Webb. That's obviously a full-time job. I'm surprised you have the time to trawl through . . . well, things like the *Clinical Psychiatry Quarterly*."

Mrs. Webb smiled thinly. "My guess is you're also surprised I have the interest."

"Frankly, yes."

"I think you'd better sit down. Take the couch. You can put your feet up—I won't mind if you kick off your shoes. This could take a little time."

Janet sat down on the leather couch but kept her shoes on her feet. She watched Mrs. Webb sink gratefully into an armchair opposite. She looked small, even vulnerable. "I'm tired," she told Janet unexpectedly. "I have so much money now I've lost count, but I spend my days doing things I don't really want to do." She saw the expression on Janet's face, read it her own way and added, "I was left the Foundation by my father. My maiden name is Regis. I never wanted the damn thing, and now I don't know how to get rid of it." She sighed. "Still, money is power, so they tell me. It lets you get things done." An absent look came into her eyes. "Sometimes it even lets you fix past mistakes."

Janet waited. She had no idea what was going on, but experience taught her listening was the only way to learn.

Mrs. Webb said, "My father, Stanislav Regis, was Latvian—'Regis' is the Anglicisation of his name. He decided most Americans wouldn't be able to pronounce it, and he was right on. Do you know much about Latvia, Dr. Winters?"

Janet shook her head. "Not a lot."

"My father claimed it was the asshole of the universe. I visited it in 1983, and actually it didn't seem too bad. Small country, something like two and a half million population, but industrialised and reasonably wealthy. But my father couldn't wait to get out of it. He emigrated to America as a young man. Do you know the American saying 'You can take the boy out of Kansas, but you can't take Kansas out of the boy'?"

Janet nodded. "We have a similar saying in Britain."

"My father was like that. He may have loathed Latvia, but Latvia shaped him. Traditionally there's always been an emphasis on education there, particularly in the sciences. Nobody knows this, but Latvia has the highest ratio of doctors per head of population in the whole world. My father's father was a tailor. His mother was a schoolteacher. But Latvia turned my father into a scientist, and he stayed a scientist until the day he died. I've never known anyone with so much curiosity about what makes things tick. Or about people and what makes them tick. You'd have liked my father, Dr. Winters."

"Yes, I'm sure I would have," Janet murmured.

"Most intelligent immigrants into the States try to get set up in business, make their millions. My father wasn't interested in money. What he wanted was the chance to do scientific research. The irony was that he made his millions anyway. He took a job with one of the big chemical companies and stumbled on a chemical reaction that stopped plastic from getting brittle at low temperatures. Doesn't sound like much, but it had some practical implications in the defense industry. Those were the days when the idea was that you sent rockets over the pole to nuke Moscow. Anyway, he had the sense to patent the discovery in his own name. His employers were very annoyed, even took him to court, but he had a sympathetic judge and held onto the patent. That was the foundation of his fortune."

"So your father was a research chemist? The Regis Foundation is essentially a chemical company?"

"Not even slightly," Mrs. Webb said. "My father started his career as a research chemist, but he had the sort of mind that wanted to poke into everything—he used to repair old clocks as a hobby. He used chemical money to set up his foundation, but it was established to fund research in any area that took his fancy. By rights, he should have lost every penny he ever made, but somebody up there was looking after him. He just got richer and richer. The Foundation got bigger and bigger."

"Where did you fit into all of this?" Janet asked curiously.

"That's what I set out to tell you. Father insisted I train as a scientist. I hated the idea at the time—I wanted to be a painter—but he was right. When I got a little older, I realised I loved science. I also realised I'd inherited my father's mind. I love to poke into odd areas of human knowledge. You come to my home, you'll find a library of scientific textbooks and subscriptions to half the scientific publications on the planet. I can't read as much as I'd like, but I read enough. That's how I came upon your work."

"I'm impressed," Janet said truthfully. "But what aspect of my work interested you enough to offer me a job?"

Mrs. Webb didn't answer her directly. "My people will have told you that you have to sign a nondisclosure agreement if you're to work for me. How do you feel about that?"

Janet shrugged. "I'm not used to such agreements—they're not very common in Britain—but if the work has some sort of security aspect, I suppose it may be fair enough."

"So you don't object?"

"Not really. I mean, not on principle. To be honest, I'm just nervous about accepting a job I know nothing about. Confidentiality is no problem—that comes with my profession whether we sign papers or not—but I don't even know if I can handle the job."

"You can," said Mrs. Webb firmly.

Janet smiled disarmingly. "I think I'd like to decide that for myself."

Mrs. Webb's head jerked away to stare through the window. "I told them it was bullshit," she said mildly. She turned back to Janet and smiled. "The trouble is, I've far too many men working for me. They're useless when it comes to judging human nature." She stood up abruptly. "I told them legal agreements don't work unless you're dealing with an honest woman and if you're dealing with an honest woman they're not necessary. This isn't security, Janet—it's personal. You could hurt me a great deal by shooting your mouth off. Suing you afterwards wouldn't change that."

Janet watched her, not understanding.

Mrs. Webb said, "Luke Webb is my son." She stopped, watching Janet's face intently. "You obviously haven't heard of him."

Janet shook her head.

"You know, I think that's something of a relief. After a while, you start to believe New York's the centre of the world." Mrs. Webb smiled. "If you were a New Yorker, you'd know about Luke. Eligible bachelor. Wealthy. Heir to the Regis Foundation. He's never been a playboy, and he doesn't court publicity, but they write about him all the time. They used to write about me like that once, although I never had the looks to become a real celebrity. Now I only get in the papers if I spend a million on something stupid." She looked back out the window, but thoughtfully this time.

Janet searched her face for any indication of regret, any thirst for the recognition that was slipping away, and found none.

Mrs. Webb came and sat beside her on the couch, drawing her feet up underneath her like a little girl. "Luke is having trouble with his memories. I want you to help him."

The Chronicles of Nectanebo: Ten

Rena, my Gegum Combat Mistress, would sometimes engage me in lessons that I considered to have nothing to do with combat. Some bewilder me even now.

"Love," she told me, "is that state which exists when a sentient creature instinctively places the welfare of another before its own. From this definition, it follows that animals may experience love, as in the relationship of a lioness for her cubs. It further follows that the object of love need not always be a living being but may be an object, a country or an abstraction such as duty."

We were streaming sweat following almost two hours of continuous activity within the training hall of the Gegum Convent at Elephantine. It was a measure of our respective expertise that she could still talk, while I, bent double with exhaustion and sick of stomach, could only listen.

"Once the reality of love is recognised," Rena said, "it becomes clear that the most dangerous of all warriors is she—" she caught herself and added, "—or he who loves profoundly."

It was not at all clear to me, but I was too breathless to question her, almost certainly the reason why she chose this moment for the lesson.

"It is equally clear," said Rena, lapsing into another of the paradoxes of which all Gegum seemed inordinately fond, "that love is to be avoided by a warrior at all costs."

Initiation into the Gegum Order was a far cry from the ritualised ordeals of the Egyptian Mysteries. It involved several years (the actual number purposely vague) of training in philosophy, history, witchcraft, prediction, esoteric anatomy and the art of war. This for a male initiate, of which I was one of only two in the order's whole existence: Gegum women learned also the arts of command, poisoning, sexual enslavement, mob control, wooing (by which I understood the art of causing another to love you) and a most odd form of inwardly directed mekhenesis which might be used to control fertility or procure abortion.

My Combat Mistress, Rena, was quite the most stunningly lovely creature I have ever seen, surpassing those Gegum who lay with me, surpassing their convent sisters who did not, many of whom were beautiful and all of whom could create an aura of sexual attraction with the certain instinct of a striking cobra.

To the Gegum, the art of war derived exclusively from personal combat: tactics and strategy learned face-to-face might be writ large, according to this theory, and applied to the clash of armies. In Weapons Combat—dagger, sword, lance, club and bow—I was taught to examine my reactions to the weapon and to note how it performed in differing circumstances, to recognise that no weapon is universally useful but has merit only in relation to the conditions.

In this way, so the Gegum assured me, my abilities as a general would become instinctive. By knowing the bow, I would know the placement of my bowmen. By knowing the sword, I would know the placement of my swordsmen. And so on.

Not even the Gegum could make me a great general (or if they did, Artaxerxes was greater), but it is certain they made me a better general than I was before.

Unarmed combat training created for me alone among initiates a unique problem. In practice, the beautiful Rena was accustomed to wearing no more than a brief cloth of linen about her loins, and more than once, the wavering of my concentration earned me a blow or kick. Although I have long had only limited interest in the skills of personal combat—preferring always to use my mental powers once I developed them—Rena was not at all unhappy with my prowess. She believed a certain physical type with a specific muscular and skeletal development was ideal for Gegum training in this art, and it was a type to which, fortuitously, I belonged.

She was further intrigued both by the differences and similarities involved in training a man. Thus we related well, she and I, and I learned much of the manner in which these women could so easily maim, cripple and kill those who failed to retain their affection.

The subjects of witchcraft and esoteric anatomy combined to influence the development of my powers. The mind, I discovered, is a labyrinth . Over centuries of study, the Gegum had charted more of it than any individual or institution I know. Furthermore, as I quickly found out for myself, they recognised that the subtle channels of body and mind were, in fact, inextricably interlinked so that manipulation of one invariably involved manipulation of the other. In this, I was a star pupil.

My Craft Mistress, Abet Xu (an odd Egyptian name which translates as Month of Spirits), was an old woman with a ready wit which to some extent disguised her profound insight and knowledge. Although she did not have my powers, she understood them well enough and bent her whole attention towards coaxing them into full flower.

She never feared me, even when she succeeded beyond both our expectations, and was, indeed, so confident that she would permit me to practice upon her, invading and controlling her mind until the pathways became instinctive to me. She had, of course, her own abilities, and when I embraced her soul to capture it (an experience of greater intimacy than lovemaking), I felt always that I succeeded on sufferance.

Of all the gifts the Gegum gave me, this—and this alone—was marred by tragedy. For Abet Xu died before she could teach me the manner in which I might control large bodies of men at a distance. It was a power I might have used to save Egypt, but it was never granted me. Two other witches took up my training, but none could match Abet Xu and did little more than clarify a few remaining details. It is a token of Abet's influence that I sorrowed more for the old woman than I did for my own mother.

So it went on my visits to the convent at Elephantine, where Lipta now resided in order to supervise my training. Philosophy . . . history . . . prophecy . . . witchcraft . . . anatomy . . . and the seemingly unending art of war.

Back in the present moment, Rena approached me. "Again," she said. I shook my head, too exhausted to speak. "Tired already, Lord Pharaoh?" she asked with just the barest hint of derision. Uncaring, I nodded. Her eyes locked on mine, and it may be that she took pity on me, for her face softened.

In the wordless silence, it came upon me that we were alone in the hall and that the doors were locked, as they were always locked when Pharaoh trained. Her breathing deepened, and still staring deep into my eyes, she reached out and placed my right hand gently on her naked breast.

My reaction was visible and instantaneous. She dropped her gaze to my tented loincloth, and for one glorious moment I knew beyond all doubt that she must rip it from me. But the hands that moved at reptile speed were warrior's hands, and in a confused moment, I found myself thrown down and bruised upon the ground.

"The lesson, Nectanebo," Rena told me, "is that there is always something in reserve." And took her leave of Pharaoh with a secret smile.

TWENTY-NINE

S o the mystery wasn't such a mystery after all. A wealthy New York socialite had some sort of amnesia problem and needed professional help. Any one of a dozen American psychologists could have provided it, but she had been selected precisely because she wasn't American. If the poor sod had broken his leg, they'd have had no hesitation in calling in local specialists, but anything connected with the mind, anything at all, suggested incompetence to handle his own affairs. When those affairs involved billions of dollars, people suddenly got security conscious.

Janet said, "Of course I'll help him. At least I'll try."

"I appreciate that. Thank you."

Janet took a deep breath. "I think it's a pity your people pretended there was some sort of ongoing job for me here, not least because it was quite unnecessary. Once I've had an opportunity to examine your son, I can give some indication of how long his treatment is likely to take and, indeed, whether treatment is likely to be successful. I don't wish to alarm you, Mrs. Webb—"

"Alarming me isn't all that easy."

"—but not all amnesia cases are amenable."

To Janet's surprise, Mrs. Webb didn't take up her last comment. Instead, she said, "Treating my son may take longer than you think. But even if I'm wrong about that, I want to tell you nobody tried to screw you around. This may be a botanical research facility, but the Foundation has other interests. There are clinics that could make full use of your expertise. I have to tell you they're not in Arizona, but I don't suppose you'd object to working in New York."

"I'm not quite sure why I'm not in New York now," Janet said. "I assume your son is there."

"No, he's here. He's less well known here than in New York." A curious shadow crossed her face. "Besides, he prefers the climate."

"I see." Janet took time to think, then said, "Look, why don't we leave things open? I need to see him—obviously—to get a feel for the problem. Once I've done that, we can talk again if that's what you'd like—"

"It is."

"Okay," Janet said, "that's what we'll do." Her own eyes flickered towards the window. It was dark by now, but streetlights had come on, just like in a town. What a strange place this was. She was almost sorry she wouldn't be working in it. She looked back at Mrs. Webb. "Was it some sort of injury?"

"I'm sorry?"

"Some sort of injury," Janet repeated. "A blow to the head or something of that sort? We'll need scans to find out the extent of the physical damage, if he hasn't had them already."

"No injury," said Mrs. Webb woodenly.

Janet frowned. "Unusual." She looked at Mrs. Webb. "I'll need scans anyway—to rule out the possibility of a tumour. That's not likely in someone of his age, but we need to rule it out. I don't suppose you have the facilities here, but we can always—"

"We do have the facilities here," Webb cut in. "There's a fully equipped hospital on-site. It's small, but it's got every goddamn gadget known to man. I tell you, Janet, doctors in this country can spend money faster than my father. If you want Luke scanned, you can have him scanned, but he doesn't have a tumour."

She said it with such conviction that Janet almost believed her. Denial of life-threatening conditions was common enough among mothers worried about their children. Janet decided not to push it any further for the moment. "Well, as I said, I shall need to see him before anything else. Can we arrange for that in the morning?"

Mrs. Webb said, "I'd prefer you to see him tonight."

THIRTY

To Janet's surprise, the villa was more modest than her own. Mrs.
Webb drove her to it personally in a small blue car that came as
a relief after the oversized limos. A plump woman in a nurse's uniform
opened the door.

"How is he?" Harriet asked at once, and Janet read the worry in her
voice.

"He's relaxing by the pool, Mrs. Webb," the nurse said. "He seems
much less withdrawn." She cast a friendly glance in Janet's direction. "I
think he's looking forward to meeting Dr. Winters."

They walked inside. The villa was sparsely furnished in a style Janet
couldn't immediately place, although it felt oddly familiar. For some
reason it made her uneasy.

Mrs. Webb said, "I assume you'll want to see him on your own?"

"That would be preferable," Janet nodded. Something in the other
woman's tone prompted her to add, "Is there a problem?"

"No. No . . . it's just . . ." Mrs. Webb looked disturbed. "Oh, I don't
know. I haven't really told you anything about his condition. Sometimes
I wonder if I'm handling any of this."

"I think you're handling it extremely well," Janet said reassuringly.
"Frankly, I prefer to make my own diagnosis. It's sometimes easier to start
with a clean slate." All the same, the appearance of the nurse made her
wonder if she was the first doctor to see Luke Webb . . . and if not, what
the previous diagnosis had been. She decided to bring it out in the open.
"Have you had Luke examined before?"

Mrs. Webb hesitated, and for a long moment Janet had an almost
overwhelming intuition that she was trying to decide whether or not to
lie. Eventually she said, "Yes. Yes, I did."

Janet waited. When Webb said nothing more, she remarked mildly,
"It might be useful for me to know the results."

The nurse said, "I'll leave you to it. Unless you want me for anything more, Mrs. Webb?"

"No, nothing more, Lucille." She watched as the nurse walked out of the room, then turned back to Janet. "What were you asking me?"

Janet said firmly, "It might be useful for me to know the results of the last examination. In fact, it might be useful for me to know as much as possible about the last examination—who made it, what was their diagnosis, whether they gave you a written report." The business between Mrs. Webb and the nurse was interesting. Lucille obviously knew something about the last examination, or at least knew Mrs. Webb wouldn't want her in the room while she was talking about it. Yet the nurse must know about Luke Webb's condition: she wouldn't be his nurse if she didn't.

Mrs. Webb stared at her for a long moment, then seemed to come to a decision. "You're right, Dr. Winters—I've been patronising you. It's not like me, and I apologise. Of course you need to know everything. Let's sit down for a moment, and I'll tell you. After that, you can decide whether you still want to see Luke."

Janet sat. Whether she still wanted to see Luke? This was becoming more and more intriguing. She also noticed that Mrs. Webb had moved to the more formal "Dr. Winters." Up to now it had been "Janet," although she had made no attempt to give Janet her own Christian name. Janet waited, curious to discover how much further Mrs. Webb was prepared to go. Whatever had happened to her son was obviously very worrisome.

"When Luke . . . ," Mrs. Webb began, then stopped. She seemed to be having trouble deciding how to put it. "When Luke started to develop his . . . his symptoms, I suppose you'd call them. When this happened, it didn't occur to me at first that it might be a problem. I mean, a serious problem. It just seemed . . . you know . . . interesting."

Interesting? Janet felt herself frowning again. Your son starts to develop amnesia, and you find it interesting? Unless it wasn't exactly amnesia. It might be some sort of condition that involved amnesia to a greater or lesser degree. Christ, it might be something really nasty like early-onset Alzheimer's. No joke at any age, but at thirty . . .

Mrs. Webb was talking again. "There's no shortage of medical doctors in the Foundation. The first examinations were purely physical. Luke's had every scan you're likely to order, Dr. Winters, and then some. That's how I know he doesn't have a tumour. You can order more if you like, but I can't see that his condition will have changed. Whatever. Luke's a fit, healthy physical specimen, no problems there—everybody told me so. Next step was obvious."

"You have psychiatrists in the Foundation." Janet nodded.

"Not as many as medical doctors, but some. Good people, too, and I wouldn't have to worry about their discretion. We pay them more to work for us than they would earn in private practice. Nobody wants to lose that sort of income by shooting off his mouth. Besides, we select our personnel carefully. They just aren't the type." She closed her eyes briefly. "I'm burbling. I suppose I don't really want to tell you this."

Janet said quietly, "But you've started now."

Mrs. Webb drew in a deep breath, releasing it explosively. "The man I picked was Paul Schaeffer. He—"

"I think I've heard of him," Janet interrupted. "Didn't he publish something on . . . what was it? . . . Pseudo memories? Or memory implantation? Something like that?"

"You got it in one," Mrs. Webb told her. "I don't know if it hit Britain, but there was a fashion in the States a few years ago for remembering you'd been sexually abused in childhood. Dr. Schaeffer was one of the first to blow the whistle on the fad. Sure, some kids get touched up, some even raped. It happens. But Schaeffer showed that in a whole slew of cases, the memories were phony. They'd actually been implanted by the therapists who thought they were trying to help their patients dig up some buried trauma. He carried out an experimental study that proved you could persuade people to believe all sorts of fantasies about their past. You probably read the published results. He wrote several papers."

"I think you're right," Janet said. "It rings bells. So Dr. Schaeffer saw your son. What happened?"

"The examination went badly. Luke almost killed him."

"What?" Janet exploded.

Mrs. Webb sighed. "You see why I didn't want to talk about this? Paul Schaeffer's in his mid-sixties, overweight and has a heart condition. There was some sort of argument. Luke pushed Schaeffer, and Schaeffer went into cardiac arrest. Fortunately all of this happened in one of our facilities—New York, this time—so he was only minutes away from medical attention. Even so, it was touch and go whether he would survive. They stabilised the heart, but he was in a coma for nearly a month. He's still not back at work. There's some doubt he ever will be."

"Good God!" Janet exclaimed.

Mrs. Webb stared her straight in the eye, and when she spoke her voice was pleading. "My son is one of the kindest, most gentle human beings you are ever likely to meet," she said.

The woman was protesting too much. After a long moment, Janet asked, "But he attacked Dr. Schaeffer?"

"No. Even according to Schaeffer it was an accident." She shook her head. "I'm sorry. I should have told you about this right away."

"Yes, you should have," Janet said.

"It's just . . . you know . . ."

"It's just that you wanted me to see him. You're worried about your son's condition, you think I may be able to help and you were frightened I might refuse."

"That's about the size of it. Are you going to refuse?"

Janet thought about it. She wasn't sure how far she trusted Mrs. Webb's version. Maybe it was an accident, or maybe Luke was more violent than his mother wanted to admit. Janet didn't relish dealing with a violent patient now, but if she were honest, she was thoroughly intrigued by the case. She was intrigued by the secrecy, by the money, by the whole ambience. It also occurred to her that she might be a little less easy to injure than Dr. Schaeffer with his weight problem and his heart condition. All the same . . .

Mrs. Webb said, "I brought up my boy to respect the old-fashioned values. I don't think he would harm a woman if his life depended on it."

Janet suspected Mrs. Webb hadn't imagined her son could harm a middle-aged overweight psychiatrist either, but she let that go. She stood up. "Where's the pool?"

THIRTY-ONE

There was a smell of chlorine. Low, indirect blue lighting reflected on the surface of the pool. Janet's footsteps echoed, and her nervousness increased. She could not see him at all, then there was a movement to her right.

"Luke? Is that you?"

"Am-a asta en heqt ses a mu em abter hru pef setem-k ren-a." The voice was soft and masculine and strangely familiar.

"I'm Dr. Winters," Janet said. "I'm here to help you."

He emerged from the shadows. "I know who you are," he said in English.

He was wearing a short, open bathrobe over swimming trunks, and his body was superb. He had the sort of clean muscle definition that was mainly the prerogative of athletes but without the heavy bulk that came with weight training. She tore her eyes away with some difficulty, feeling adolescent and silly.

"What language were you speaking just now?" she asked to cover her confusion.

"Egyptian."

"Arabic?" It hadn't sounded like Arabic.

He hesitated fractionally, then shook his head. "Not Arabic—Egyptian. The tongue of ancient Egypt."

Luke Webb had one of the most interesting faces she had ever seen. Not handsome, but striking and extremely—

His skull was curiously elongated and shaven almost to the scalp. The planes of his face were as well defined as the muscling of his body. His mouth was wide, with thick, sensual lips. His eyes had an Oriental slant, with a curious fold at the edge. It was impossible to tell their colour in this light, but they seemed pale. He must have taken after his father. There was not a hint of his mother in his looks.

—sexual, if she was honest with herself. Behind the sexuality was a distinct scent of danger.

"I didn't know anybody could speak ancient Egyptian now."

"Only a few of us."

"You must be very well read," Janet said. "I know there are scholars able to read hieroglyphs, but how do you know the pronunciation? Or do you just guess?"

He shrugged, vaguely.

When she realised it was the only answer she was going to get, Janet said, "What did it mean?"

"The phrase? In English it is rendered, 'Behold, I have eaten the bread of sorrow and I have drunk the water of affliction since the day that thou didst hear my name.'"

It wasn't that he had an accent—or, rather, it wasn't that he had an accent other than the cultured American she might have expected. But he constructed his sentences almost like a foreigner, almost as if, however well he knew it, English was not his native tongue. She wondered briefly if he'd been brought up in another country. She knew his grandfather had come from Eastern Europe. Perhaps Luke had spent his early years there as well.

She turned her attention to what he had said: "Behold, I have eaten the bread of sorrow and I have drunk the water of affliction since the day that thou didst hear my name." It had the feel of a quotation. "Where's it from?"

"An old text."

"I hope we don't find it appropriate," Janet said, trying a smile.

To her surprise, he smiled back and said easily, "I'm sure we won't." The careful construction was gone. For an instant he was speaking like a native-born American.

Janet set the small puzzle to one side and said, "I gather your mother has spoken to you about me?"

"My mother believes I'm in need of therapy."

"But you don't?"

"I'm in need of help. That's not the same thing."

It was a promising start. Many patients were in denial about their problems. "I'll try to help you," Janet said gently. "Your mother tells me you are having trouble with your memory."

"My mother's misled you. Or possibly you've misunderstood what she was trying to tell you. Or perhaps she was just afraid of telling you more than a part of the truth. I suspect the last of these is the most likely. Do you enjoy swimming, Dr. Winters?"

Janet blinked. "Yes, sometimes," she said, taken aback. Was he about to invite her to use the pool?

"So do I," Luke said. "Very much, in fact. For a long time I had little opportunity, but now—" He gestured towards the pool and smiled. "So much water so far from a river. I swim at every opportunity. Have you ever thought what it must be like to grow old?"

The conversation was losing her. She shook her head. "I try not to dwell on it."

He nodded, then said seriously, "Imagine an old man, a very old man—eighty years or more—with all the weakness and infirmities of old age. Then imagine that, miraculously, he regains his youth. One day he awakens in a strong, young body. Imagine the joy and the freedom. That is how I feel when I swim."

It was sometimes useful to give patients their head, encourage them to follow their instincts and observe the result. Janet said, "Do you want to swim now?"

"Your company gives me everything I want. It's like meeting an old friend."

This was not what she expected. She caught sight of two poolside loungers and suggested, to cover her confusion, "Let's sit down."

They sat down side by side. He drew the short robe carefully around his body and tightened the belt. There was something about his close proximity that made her feel . . . uneasy. Before she could take charge of the conversation, he said, "Dr. Winters, what is your opinion of far memory?"

Janet frowned. "Far memory?"

"Is that not the term? I think I read it somewhere. By 'far memory' I mean recollections of past lives."

Why the interest in past lives? Harriet Webb had used the term "memories" in the plural. "Trouble with his memories"—something like that. It hadn't registered on Janet at the time, but it did now. Was it possible this man was beginning to remember what he believed to be past lives? No wonder his mother was embarrassed to say too much. At the same time, Janet knew quite a few people who accepted reincarnation and believed they could remember how they had lived before. Many of them were cranks, but one or two seemed sensible enough.

To give herself time to think, she asked, "Are you familiar with a psychological process known as regression?"

Luke stared at her thoughtfully, then shook his head. "No."

"It goes back to Freud," Janet said. "As you probably know, he thought many emotional problems were the result of childhood traumas. He believed that if a patient could recall the trauma, healing would take place. So he developed techniques that would allow them to return to their childhood—in other words, to regress. He used hypnosis at first but later abandoned it in favour of psychoanalysis. Today there are a number of ways to bring about a regression, including drugs. That's what I mean by regression."

"I understand."

Janet began carefully to construct her reply to his original question about far memories. "There are some psychologists who believe personal memories don't start at birth but in the womb. I'm not sure I'm one of them—it's difficult to see how such memories would be carried when the brain stem isn't even formed. But leave that to one side. Regression techniques certainly do produce what appear to be intrauterine memories. I understand that when the techniques are pushed to their limit, some people produce what purport to be memories from beyond the womb—as you say, of past lives. Whether they actually are past lives is another matter entirely."

"Do you believe they are?"

Janet hesitated, then said, "No."

"If they are not past lives, what else could they be?"

Janet shrugged lightly. "Fantasies created by the unconscious. People who lead dull lives might find some comfort in the belief they were once Julius Caesar or Cleopatra."

"So if I believed I once lived as, say, an Egyptian king, that would, in your opinion, be a compensatory mechanism?"

Janet opened her mouth to say yes, then closed it again. She was finding it more and more difficult to retain her professional composure, and since she had vowed to be honest with herself in this area, she knew the reason why. She found Luke Webb sexually attractive. In fact, she found Luke Webb very sexually attractive.

She forced her mind back to his question. After a moment's thought, she said, "Luke, I understand you are an extremely wealthy man. Your position in the family that controls the Regis Foundation would arguably make you as powerful, if not more powerful in some respects, as any king of the ancient world. You have the equivalent of subjects in your employees and the equivalent of a court in your immediate advisors and helpers. You can travel further and faster than any ancient king, do things he could not even dream of doing. It's frankly quite difficult to see a compensation mechanism in there."

"I was thinking much the same thing myself," Luke said. "But if it's not a compensation mechanism, then what is it?"

"I suspect you want me to say the memories may be genuine, but I'm not a psychical researcher, so I'm not qualified to answer."

To her surprise, Luke said, "I have no need for reassurance, only information. Am I right to say there are people who don't so much recall memories as experience the sensation of a whole other person sharing their body?"

Alarm bells went off in Janet's head. The question was put casually, but Luke Webb was obviously speaking of his own experience. If so, he could be in a great deal more trouble than she had imagined. She decided to play straight but move carefully. "Some people do experience the sensation you describe, although not always in relation with past-life memories." She hesitated, then went on, "To be frank, not often in relation to past-life memories."

She waited, wondering if she'd gone too far, but he only said thoughtfully, "Perhaps, as a doctor of psychology, you could explain to me how such sensations arise."

Janet took a deep breath. "I'll do my best. You know, of course, that your personality is not the whole of you."

Luke nodded. "The consensus seems to be that it's an interface constructed to allow one to interact with the outside world."

Janet glanced at him in surprise. It was the first time she'd heard the term "interface" used in this way, but it exactly defined what most psychologists believed. "Yes," she said, "that is . . . that is perfectly right. But in constructing our persona, certain aspects of what we are have to be suppressed."

"Like murderous rage or the instinct to take a woman for whom one lusts," Luke said. He smiled.

"Well, there are less dramatic examples," Janet said. "But the point is that suppressed aspects can sometimes constellate into subpersonalities in the unconscious. In certain circumstances, these subper—" She stopped, suddenly angry with herself for failing to follow her instincts. He had asked her an important question, and she was treating him to a course in psychobabble. "Oh, shit!" she said. "Let's stop dancing around this. Are you experiencing a second personality sharing your body?"

Without a moment's hesitation, he said, "Yes."

She quickly reviewed his earlier questions and saw the pattern at once. "And is this second personality that of an ancient Egyptian king?"

The pale Oriental eyes were looking calmly into her own. "Oh, no," he said. "The second personality is that of Luke Webb."

The Chronicles of
Nectanebo: Eleven

There is a story told of ancient days when the Pharaoh Sneferu ruled. It appears this king, who was father to Khufu, whom the Greeks call Cheops, was subject to fugue. On a day in summer, falling into low spirits, he called on his court to find some means whereby his heart might be lightened.

Failing in the more usual remedies of song and gossip, the nobles called on the assistance of the wisest man in Egypt of that day, a priest and writer of books, one Tchatcha-em-ankh. The priest advised the king thus:

"Go, Majesty, to the lake near the palace and there sail upon it in the boat which I have had prepared for thee."

So the king went to the great ornamental lake and there discovered a craft unlike any other, graven with the forms of fabulous beasts and leafed with beaten gold. The paddles of this craft were of ebony, inlaid with gold, and in place of oarsmen were twenty female virgins, the most delicately beautiful in all of Egypt. Tchatcha-em-ankh had caused these young women to be dressed in netting, like that of sea fishermen, so that the most intimate aspects of their bodies were at once concealed and revealed.

When the king entered the boat, these nubile women manned the oars and sang sweetly to him while they rowed him hither and thither. And Sneferu, watching the fluid movement of their bodies beneath the netting, became aroused, and with arousal, his heart, too, rose up.

Whatever the morals hidden in this folktale, I could never hear it but that I extracted only one wonder from it: where did Sneferu find the time to go boating?

I have never doubted the story to be true, yet the whole picture painted of a pharaoh and his court remains incredible to me. Where were the petitioners who claw for the ear of the king every waking moment of his day? Where were the crises, minor and major, which beset any court and demand immediate attention? Where was the stultifying ceremony, the audiences, the public appearances, the sacrifices at the Temple, which eat time like a ravenous tiger? Sneferu may have found the hours to stimulate himself with near-nude virgins: I never could.

It was in my middle years that I first noticed my perception of time had changed. I sometimes think it was this, as much as armed might and strategy, that won Artaxerxes the battle of Pelusium. I simply could not focus my mind swiftly enough on all the details necessary to save the day.

Ironically, it was not a great battle. But ultimately it proved the only vital one. For Pelusium was the key to the delta. When Pelusium fell, the delta inevitably followed. The collapse of the delta aroused universal shock, all the more profound for the speed at which Artaxerxes's men began knocking at the gates of Upper Egypt.

By rights I should have died then. I did not realise the fate of my country was sealed until it was too late to save the realm and almost too late to save myself.

With Pelusium and the delta under his control, Artaxerxes swept onwards like a tidal wave. That he was still wary of me I have no doubt, for he took great pains to hunt down and slaughter any messengers who might have carried news of our massive defeat before him. I was in my palace at Karnak, a fact that seems to have been known to him. Obviously he wished me to die there, for he sent a swift detachment ahead of his main force with, I have no doubt, orders to separate my head from my body and stake my heart. They might have done it, too, had not the warning trumpets sounded.

I fled to Nubia.

It is easy in the telling but was far less so in the actuality, for Nubia lies south of Egypt and the route I chose to reach it lay through territory which the Persians now controlled. It was a calculated gamble. On the one hand, there was the element of surprise: who could imagine I would flee towards the enemy, rather than away from him? On the other, there was the simple risk of recognition—my likeness was on coinage and statues everywhere. But by my private calculation, the risk was smaller than it seemed. The common people never see the pharaoh as he really is: they see a god, and this weaves an illusion of greater height, greater strength and beauty—the regal nimbus, as Khonsu once referred to it. In searching for Pharaoh, the common people, Egyptian or Persian, will always (quite unknowingly) look for the nimbus and, failing to find it, will not find the king. Besides, I had long held the power to cloud men's minds, and as a last resort, there was always the Gegum.

In any event, all three factors aided me. Once, in the robes of a merchant, I stood beneath my own statue by the ferry to Elephantine and none recognised me. Indeed, I grew so accustomed to passing unrecognised that many days later, passing through some crude Persian entertainment set to amuse the soldiers, I almost failed to see the signs of danger. Almost . . . but my fine-honed sense of survival rescued me. I obliterated the memory of our meeting from the mind of the man who recognised me. My servant Ani, wisely mistrustful of sorcerous power, crept back and slit his throat.

But this, and one or two other encounters like it, were small incidents, easily handled. There came a day when news reached us that Artaxerxes had somehow got wind of our route and sent a force of cavalry to cut us off.

We were not, you will appreciate, a fighting band. We were a small, disguised contingent, travelling light. Our strength was in the innocence of our appearance. Once that was gone, we were virtually defenseless. Even my powers would be of little moment. I could control one or two men, perhaps even three, but a large force was beyond me.

Thus, with cavalry ahead and, we had to assume, more of Artaxerxes's forces advancing from behind, the desert on one side and the Nile on the other, our position was desperate: it was a matter only of time before we would be captured and killed. I prayed daily to Ra, to Horus, to Hathor, but it was Isis who rescued me. At the time of our greatest extremity, she directed my steps towards a secret Gegum convent. Once there, of course, the witches took care of everything. Within days, I was clear of danger and on the road to Nubia. It is my understanding that Artaxerxes's men chased phantoms for weeks after.

THIRTY-TWO

There was a tall, boyish, fair-haired man with Harriet Webb. "This is Bernstein, Dr. Winters," she said by way of introduction. "I've been thinking of marrying him."

Bernstein shook hands. "I'll leave you to it." He smiled, heading for the door. "I need time to adjust to that little announcement."

Mrs. Webb said, "He's secretly delighted—it will make him rich." She turned to Janet, her face sobering. "Well . . . ?"

Janet took a deep breath. She hated being the bearer of bad news, and the news she had was the worst. "I think you'd better sit down, Mrs. Webb."

"That bad, huh?" She sat down nonetheless, watching Janet expectantly.

Janet sat down herself, pulling the chair around to face her. After a moment, she said, "Did Dr. Schaeffer give you a diagnosis of your son's condition?"

"He told me Luke was psychotic," Harriet Webb said without hesitation.

"You didn't tell me this."

"I didn't want it to influence your own conclusions."

Janet said, "Luke is ill, Mrs. Webb. Frankly, he's very ill. Are you familiar with the concept of multiple personality?"

"Schizophrenia?"

"No, it's not schizophrenia. Strictly, schizophrenia is a condition in which the patient lives wholly or partially in a fantasy world, losing his grip on reality. There are aspects of this in Luke's illness, certainly, but the main problem is a severe personality fragmentation."

"Janet, you'd better explain that to me," Harriet Webb said.

She was taking it too calmly. Janet was certain she'd been told it all before, presumably by Dr. Schaeffer. Which meant Janet was being called

161

in for a second opinion. Possibly Mrs. Webb hoped Janet's specialisation in amnesia might lead her to a different conclusion. Except that this case was a million miles away from amnesia or any of its complications, and Harriet Webb must know that, must have known that when she had given her people orders to recruit Janet. This was making no sense at all.

Janet said, "Has Luke experienced any major trauma recently—prior to the development of his symptoms, that is?"

"Why do you ask?"

Janet sighed. "Mrs. Webb, personality fragmentation typically arises out of serious, prolonged abuse in childhood, usually sexual. The child is unable to withstand the abuse and equally unable to escape from it. So she—or he—splits off a second personality, or even a series of personalities, whose job is to occupy the body while the abuse is going on. The original personality hides behind them and so survives. At least in a manner of speaking. The problem is that once split off, the secondary personalities are not easily reintegrated. The child grows up and functions like a person possessed by spirits. The differing personalities then manifest in response to prevailing circumstances. The patient is no longer an individual but a revolving door."

"Luke wasn't abused in childhood," Mrs. Webb said mildly. "I would have known."

"I'm not suggesting he was, Mrs. Webb. I assume his symptoms had a late onset; otherwise, you'd have looked for help much earlier. That's why I asked you about recent trauma. Something's caused his problem."

"Luke was a kidnap victim, Dr. Winters."

Janet noted the change to the more formal mode of address, although she wasn't sure whether to interpret it as increasing respect or increasing annoyance. But at least now they were approaching the heart of the matter. "Was he held long?"

"Some days."

"Abused by his kidnappers?"

An odd expression crossed Harriet Webb's face. "They were preparing to kill him."

Janet shifted position in her chair. "Mrs. Webb, I don't specialise in personality fragmentation, and if you take my advice, you will call in someone who does. I only know that split personality will normally result from trauma. Perhaps for a sensitive individual it would be enough to be held and threatened. God knows, kidnapping in itself is abuse enough without looking for anything more."

"What form does the split take, Dr. Winters?"

This was turning into a game. Janet said, a little brusquely, "You must know this already, Mrs. Webb."

"Perhaps I do. But I really would value your observations. Please?"

The woman could be disarming when she wanted. Janet stared thoughtfully into the middle distance. One thing was certain: her career as a consultant to the Regis Foundation was over before it had even started. She did not have the expertise to treat Luke Webb's condition. The best she could do was offer her diagnosis—and she had no doubt at all about her diagnosis—then bow out gratefully, collect her fee and leave the treatment to someone better qualified.

She pulled herself back from her reverie. "Luke's condition could be worse, Mrs. Webb. At the moment, so far as I can see, he is experiencing only two alternating personalities."

It caught the other woman's attention at once. Harriet Webb said quickly, "Can there be more than two?"

Janet nodded. "Oh, yes. Fragmentation can be very extreme indeed. Back in the early eighties, I think, a woman from New York State named Trudi Chase presented herself for treatment. Her psychiatrist discovered she had ninety-two different personalities."

Harriet Webb blinked. After a moment, she said, "She must have been a gibbering wreck."

"She was holding down a perfectly responsible job so far as I know," Janet said.

There was a lengthy silence. Eventually Harriet Webb said, "Luke isn't like that."

Janet took it as a question. "Luke is aware of two inner selves. One of those, so far as I can tell, is the original Luke Webb—your son, the boy you watched grow up. The other is a powerful fantasy figure."

This time Harriet sighed. "The Pharaoh Nectanebo."

So now it was out in the open. Mrs. Webb knew all about her son's condition. It never ceased to amaze Janet how far people would go, how many different professionals they would call in, how much money they would spend in order to avoid facing an unpleasant truth. She nodded. "Yes."

"Does Nectanebo strike you as a personality fragment?" Harriet Webb asked.

"Perhaps the term 'fragment' is misleading. Mrs. Webb, you must remember that in cases of this type, each personality is a fully developed, complex unit with its own set of memories and behaviour patterns—even its own set of friends, in many instances."

"Isn't an Egyptian pharaoh a bit unusual?"

"Yes, it is," Janet agreed. "As against that, these personalities are created for a purpose. Trudi Chase had one personality called Miss Wonderful, who functioned as the perfect hostess. She had another called Ean, who was a philosopher and poet. They both served to express elements of the original self. But she also had a personality called Mean Joe Green, a tough who protected her in situations of physical threat."

"Yes, but an Egyptian pharaoh . . . ?"

Janet realised suddenly that she was tired. The meeting with Luke Webb had been interesting, even fascinating, but this conversation was beginning to go round in circles. She made a massive effort and said, "It's not so peculiar, especially now that you tell me about the kidnapping. Your son is a powerful man. He has very considerable wealth, authority, presumably political contacts. He has been accustomed to exercising that power all his life. Suddenly he's helpless, kidnapped. He's locked away somewhere. You haven't told me the details, but he may have been restrained, or threatened—"

"Both."

"Yes, I thought as much," Janet said. "This is a very serious assault for someone accustomed to a high degree of personal freedom. I keep telling you I'm no expert, but if this did cause a fragmentation, then the Egyptian persona does make sense of a sort. Luke told me this Nectanebo is some sort of magician. Only magic could possibly help Luke in the position he was in. Of course Luke doesn't believe in magic any more than you or I, but the unconscious is much more primitive."

"Are you aware he actually existed?" Harriet Webb asked.

"Who?"

"Nectanebo the Second. He ruled Egypt from 360 to 343 BC."

"I understand what you're telling me, Mrs. Webb," Janet said. "It must seem very strange that Luke's delusion involves an actual historical personality. But Luke may have read about Pharaoh Nectanebo at some point in his life. Forgotten about it consciously, but used the information to create the fantasy figure. It's fairly common."

Harriet stared at her for a long moment, then said, "You haven't asked how Luke got away from his kidnappers."

"I assumed he was ransomed or rescued."

"Neither," Harriet said. "The men were Islamist terrorists, religious fanatics of some sort. They were on the point of—" She hesitated. "They were on the point of killing Luke when one of them ran amok with an automatic weapon, shot his fellow conspirators, then turned the gun on himself and committed suicide."

"Good God!" Janet exclaimed.

"What would you say were the chances of that happening?"

"About as good as winning the lottery, I would think. Your son is a very lucky man."

"Lucky but ill?"

Janet prepared to wind the conversation to a close. "I don't want to raise false hopes, Mrs. Webb—I'm sure you're tired of hearing me say this isn't my speciality—but it seems to me that Luke's condition may well respond to treatment. This secondary personality has arisen in response to a very specific set of circumstances. Those circumstances are very unlikely to be repeated. I would imagine with patience and the right sort of therapy, it should be possible to reintegrate the two personalities. Once that happens, Luke will be perfectly normal again." She started to stand up.

"Sit down, Janet," Harriet Webb said firmly. "I can see I'm going to have to tell you the whole truth."

The Chronicles of
Nectanebo: Twelve

I n Nubia, I became slow and frail. My skin dried, wrinkled and cracked. My juices failed, my muscles withered, twining like old slack ropes around enfeebled bones. My teeth remained fine for longer than most but rotted eventually. In consequence, my diet changed, containing less of meat, which I could no longer chew, and more of gruel, more of pap, more of milk and dishes made from milk.

At that time, I often thought my life had turned an ironical circle, from babe to babe, from milk to milk. But my mind remained sharp, although many must have believed otherwise. Oddly, my powers decreased far less than I might have predicted, but perhaps it was experience and practice that compensated for the loss of energy. In any case, I seldom used them.

Seldom . . . yet what little use I did make of them was enough to enlarge my legend, and fortunately so, for it was my fearsome reputation, grown huge in impotent exile, that persuaded Artaxerxes, now Pharaoh and founder of a whole new dynasty, to permit my burial in Egypt.

It came about in this manner:

Within the first year of my exile, I befriended and was befriended by a Nubian prince named Khababasha. We had little in common save ambition, but I found him a sterling fellow. He was younger than I, a noble by birth, a fine sportsman and a great warrior.

When we first met, he was drunk and naked, besporting himself with a wench from my retinue. He did not recognise me, or was, perhaps, too drunk to care. In any case, he chose to attack me for the interruption.

His coordination was so impaired it is doubtful I was in any danger, but I used my powers to hold him. He found the experience distasteful and was sick on the floor.

Later it transpired he was part of an official delegation sent by the Nubian king to greet me. He had that superstitious interest in things Egyptian shared by so many of his countrymen and an inflated notion of the erotic skills of Egyptian women. Thus he had come ahead, in secret, to infiltrate my camp. He succeeded all too well, thanks to the cooperation of the women of my party, who found him, so one later confessed, adorable.

It was not an auspicious beginning, but once he sobered, our friendship grew. He was not a particularly tall man but very broad and muscular with enormous stamina and a ready wit. Unable to conceive that anyone could fail to share his special interests, he took me hawking and hunting for lion and once arranged a whole athletic contest in my honour. At first I endured him for his influence with the king, to whom he was distantly related. Later I came to appreciate him for himself.

Khababasha had a private army of four thousand men, well trained, reasonably equipped and highly disciplined. They were not a match for Egyptian troops in skill, and their numbers were minuscule when compared to the Persian hordes of Artaxerxes, but for years I nursed the fancy that they might become the nucleus of a force strong and skilled enough to retake my throne.

Khababasha had other ideas, although he humoured my whims to the extent of laying convoluted plans. These would, however, inevitably meet with some unexpected and quite insurmountable obstacle so that action had to be delayed. I came eventually to realise it was a game he was playing, but by then Artaxerxes had such a firm grip on my beloved Egypt that only a fool or a madman would have attacked without Greek or Spartan help, both of which, I now knew, were lost to me. Nonetheless, we continued to play the game, Khababasha and I, until old age mellowed my enthusiasm.

I might have drifted into peaceful senility had not Artaxerxes sent men into Nubia to kill me.

At first I thought he must have caught wind of the empty intrigues between Khababasha and myself, misunderstanding their real nature (as, indeed, I misunderstood it myself for so long). Later I learned it was my powers that frightened him or, rather, the exaggerated and distorted reports of my powers reaching him out of Nubia. In any case, unwilling to offend the Nubian king with a frontal attack, he dispatched eight men to accomplish my demise by stealth.

There can scarcely have been a greater fiasco in the history of humanity.

The first of his men was mauled by a lioness before setting foot in Nubia, and not even a wild beast but a pet, raised from a cub, in the menagerie of his mistress. The remaining seven continued into the land of my exile, where two promptly fell afoul of the sleeping sickness and died.

Although my whereabouts were far from secret, the party had some difficulty in locating me. One became enamoured of a native woman from whom he required directions: she took him in with hints of pleasurable comforts and poisoned him for the sake of his purse. The four remaining reached my villa but were seized by Khababasha's guards, who questioned them roughly, discovered the nature of their mission and put them to the sword.

That was the truth of it. But the stories that eventually filtered back to Artaxerxes credited me with having plucked the plan from his mind and visited the inept assassins with plagues and demons. In fact, I had not had the least idea they were there until it was all over.

Naturally, I was relieved to escape with skin intact, but that the attempt had been made at all disturbed me. Since I was not privy to the stories reaching Artaxerxes, it seemed to me reasonable that he might try again, and this time I might not prove so lucky. I was old then, but intimations of my own mortality remained unpalatable. I determined to divine the future, partly to guard against further assassins and partly to discover, once and for all, whether I might ever again be Pharaoh.

THIRTY-THREE

Janet pinched the bridge of her nose. The coffee was a help. The caffeine hit would probably leave her jangled in the morning, but for now it kept the worst of the sleepiness at bay. She looked up at Mrs. Webb. "What haven't you told me?"

"Quite a lot, actually," Harriet said. "Let's start with the kidnapping. This isn't general knowledge, but I had a private SWAT team set up to rescue him. They were actually in the building while the police were outside negotiating."

"Are you telling me the gunman who ran amok was one of your men?"

Harriet shook her head. "No, no, I'm not saying that at all. It happened exactly as I said. One of the terrorists killed his colleagues, then killed himself. Nothing to do with me. But it might have had something to do with Luke."

Janet frowned, then said carefully, "I'm not sure I understand you. How could it have had something to do with Luke? Do you mean he . . . caught the gun or something?"

Harriet was still shaking her head. "No, the terrorist, did it—the suicide—by shooting himself in the stomach. In the stomach, Janet. It was an automatic weapon. It cut a swathe across his body. Killed him all right. But doesn't that strike you as strange? You're a doctor. You must have had some experience in this area."

This time Janet shook her head. "Not with terrorists, believe me. But I take your point. I understand the thing is to put the gun in your mouth."

"Exactly!" Harriet exclaimed. "It's quick, it's certain, you probably don't feel a thing. Nobody opens up their stomach with a gun."

The coffee wasn't hacking it any more. Janet felt exhausted. "Mrs. Webb, I don't know where you're going with this."

"He used the gun as if it were a knife. Or a sword." She looked at Janet expectantly.

171

It still made no sense. Janet said nothing.

"You don't get it, do you?" Harriet said after a moment.

Janet was too tired to play guessing games. She closed her eyes briefly, then said, "Let's come back to that. What happened afterwards?"

"Afterwards?"

"When the men were dead. What happened?"

"It was messy. The place was surrounded by cops. They didn't know my people were inside. Far as they were concerned, the negotiations were going just fine. Then there was all this automatic fire. The NYPD had their own SWAT team on standby, just in case. They sent them in. Of course my boys were already inside, so they got to him first. Only they weren't supposed to be in there. They knew once the shooting started, the police were bound to hit fast and hard. They'd come in, see armed men with Luke and think they were the terrorists. Doesn't take Einstein to figure what would happen next."

"So what did they do?" Janet asked.

"Thing was, they couldn't just pull back either. They had to make sure Luke was okay. They also had to make sure when the cops did come in, they didn't come in guns blazing, maybe hurt Luke in the crossfire."

"So what did they do?" Janet asked again.

"Only one thing they could do. The leader was a guy called Philip Vandenberg—the leader of my boys, you know? Marine—ex-marine—very cool in a crisis. He thought the only thing was to snatch Luke, try to get him out before the cops hit. He'd come up from underneath, through the sewers. His plan was to take Luke back the same way, worry about what the cops had to say afterwards." She took a deep breath and released it explosively. "Thing was, Janet, Luke wouldn't let them take him."

"He fought them?"

"Not the way you're thinking. I talked to Vandenberg. He says he wanted to grab Luke but couldn't. Luke was just standing there, calm, not resisting. Vandenberg says he knew what he should do but just couldn't.

I believe him. I think Luke did something to Vandenberg, the same way he did something to the terrorist who started shooting."

"Did . . . something?"

"The police didn't go in with guns blazing, as it happened. Maybe Luke did something to them as well; I don't know. My people pulled back—Vandenberg said he felt compelled. The police didn't even know they were there. They found signs of their entry when they went over the building afterwards, but I suppose they put that down to the terrorists. Or maybe they put two and two together and didn't care—they couldn't trace anything back to me anyway. As it was, the police took him out and called me, then brought him over to Regis HQ. I had medics standing by, and first thing I did was have him examined. There wasn't a scratch on him. A rope burn on one wrist where they tied him: that was it. He was acting strangely, but I put that down to shock. So did the doctors. We asked him what had happened, but he wasn't making much sense."

Neither was Harriet Webb, in Janet's opinion. She made one more attempt to get things clearer. "What do you think happened?"

"Luke killed those terrorists," Harriet told her promptly. "Or, rather, Nectanebo killed them. I think Nectanebo also stopped Vandenberg from grabbing Luke. He did it with the power of his mind.."

Janet said patiently, "Mrs. Webb, the persona Luke refers to as Nectanebo is a construct. It's a fictional creation of his own unconscious. It doesn't have a mind outside Luke's own, let alone any mysterious power."

Harriet leaned forward in her chair and locked eyes. "Janet," she said flatly, "I still haven't told you everything."

Book Three: Harriet's Story

THIRTY-FOUR

You could see why the Egyptians were such keen astronomers—the night sky was something else. While she waited for Lucas, Harriet stared up into the velvet blackness. The constellations stood out with a clarity she'd never seen before she visited North Africa—Orion was particularly prominent. There was a crescent moon, but instead of hanging sideways, the moon had both horns upwards, and you could see a ghost of the full orb between them, like the headdress of Isis.

It was still hot. The sandstone massifs of the Valley of the Kings reflected stored heat like a brick oven. Even in T-shirt and shorts, the slightest exertion brought out a sweat. She hoped he wouldn't be too long delayed. What she had in mind would be a lot better for them both if she were still comparatively fresh.

For Harriet, the Valley of the Kings had been a disappointment. Before she came, she'd imagined the place to be a remote site somewhere in the desert, a sort of Shangri-La necropolis, where the ancient pharaohs crept away to die. In fact, the valley was just across the Nile from Karnak, as remote by felucca as a two-cent coach ride. Worse still, the authorities had opened it to tourists. Nepherites's tomb, where they were working, was roped off during the day, but even so, you got strangers wandering around. Most of them were fellow Americans, the women with blue hair, the men in blinding shirts and Bermuda shorts, both utterly unaware they might be interrupting important work with dumb questions about mummies. They probably thought they were talking to real archaeologists.

Sleeping quarters were some distance from the project site because of a theory the project leader Melville had had about the effect of cooking fumes on the plastics they were using. He'd insisted they pitch camp in a sheltered hollow behind the ticket kiosk that guarded the entrance to the valley. Harriet headed for the kiosk now. It was little more than a wooden shack beside a barrier, manned during the day by an ill-shaven

Arab with the worst squint she'd ever seen. At night it stood like the silhouette of a rotten tooth. Lucas was already there.

He started violently as Harriet tapped him on the shoulder. "Wow," she said, "you're nervy!"

"Just . . . you know . . ." He grinned self-consciously, then reached for her.

She pushed him away firmly. "Not here! Christ, we might as well be in Times Square!" She took his hand. "Come on."

"Where are we going?"

"Do you have condoms?" Harriet asked. "I was planning to use my cap, but something's eaten bits out of it. God, I hate this country!" It wasn't entirely true, but there were aspects of Egypt that certainly left a lot to be desired.

"Condoms?" Lucas echoed foolishly. "Well . . . yes, actually, I think I may—"

"You think? Don't you know? Not exactly flattering, Lucas."

"No. Yes. Of course. Sorry. Condoms. Yes. Yes, I do. Definitely."

"Thank God we've sorted that out," Harriet said. She grinned to herself. He was so English, so cute. But he needed really firm handling, or he was all over the place. "We're going to the tomb."

"Nepherites's tomb?" Lucas asked foolishly.

"Of course Nepherites's tomb! What did you think—Tutankhamen's? It's private. We won't be disturbed, and it doesn't have a mummy in it. What more do you want?"

"Sorry," Lucas said again.

Nepherites was a historical personage so obscure that she'd trawled two entire encyclopaedias without finding a single reference to him. Then she found a passing mention in a book on ancient history. The man was a pharaoh who'd lasted only four months before being overthrown by one of his generals in 380 BC.

His tomb was discovered in the Valley of the Kings in 1886. The grave goods had been stolen, the mummy was missing and the internal plastering was of an inferior quality, so most of it had crumbled away, taking the wall art with it. What remained was of little interest to anybody, which was why the Egyptian Department of Antiquities had agreed to the Melville experiment.

The experiment—or project, as Melville preferred to call it—involved the use of spray plastic to protect the wall art of ancient Egypt. It was something close to the heart of the Egyptian authorities, who were faced with a dilemma familiar to every poor country interested in preserving ancient sites. Preservation cost money and the most effective way to get it was from tourism. But tourists were themselves a threat to the sites. The moisture in their breath did more damage to wall paintings in a year than the dry climate of Egypt did in a century.

Time had already taken its toll on Egyptian art. The bright, stark, primary colours of the originals had faded with the millennia into the muted russets for which Egypt was now famous. Experts estimated that a really successful tourist programme—one that would attract the sort of numbers needed to boost the Egyptian economy—would probably destroy the more popular of the remaining paintings by the end of the century.

Project leader Melville offered a solution. A research scientist turned entrepreneur, he'd developed the tough, transparent plastic he believed could act as the barrier needed to preserve the art. But he'd had a problem selling the idea to the Egyptian authorities. They were concerned that the spray might damage the paintings. That it would not resist moisture and heat the way Melville claimed. That it would create an aesthetically unpleasing sheen. That—

Melville cut through the host of possible objections by offering to demonstrate. He asked for a wall painting anywhere in Egypt, subject to whatever conditions the Egyptians designated. He would fly in a team at his own expense, treat the painting without charge or obligation, then allow the Egyptian authorities to decide whether or not the treatment was a success. The Egyptians gave him Nepherites's tomb.

Harriet climbed over the low rope barrier that was supposed to protect the project from the public, and Lucas followed without letting go of her hand. They walked downhill together to where the tomb entrance was cut into the rock wall. It had a padlocked iron grille to keep out intruders, but Harriet had her own key—as had Lucas, come to that, but you couldn't trust him with important arrangements. She opened the gate, waited for him to come through, then closed and padlocked it behind them. They began to descend the long, shallow flight of wooden steps the Egyptians had put in to give tourist access.

Harriet had been surprised to discover the sheer size of these old tombs. Even minor nobility had massive rock-cut chambers to house their remains. An Arab guide, with nothing better to do, had told her just last week that the Egyptians had called their tombs "Houses of Eternity" and constructed them as if they were making homes to live in for the rest of time. Then he'd held his hand out for a tip. The Arabs wanted to be paid for everything, even useless information.

Near the entrance, the walls of the descending passage were devoid of hieroglyphs or murals except for one small area, about the size of a man's hand, where the plaster hadn't crumbled. But as they neared the bottom, other fragments presented themselves, and in the main chamber of the tomb, perhaps a quarter of one wall retained portions of the hieroglyphic prayers—although not all in one place or one piece.

There were signs of the day's work in the main chamber as well—backpacks, a plastic lunch box, water bottles and a small mountain of cleaning equipment. Melville's plastic spray gear hadn't been moved in yet. A prerequisite of the process was that the treated surfaces must be absolutely dust-free. That was why Melville had put together the team of student archaeologists—students because he was saving money, archaeologists because that reassured the Egyptian authorities—to which Lucas and Harriet belonged. They'd spent three weeks of their first paid job cleaning the inside of the tomb and would probably spend the next month doing the same thing. It had to be among the worst jobs in the country, in the same league as the Arab who stood at the door of the portable toilets, gracefully accepting tips from tourists who thought he was an official attendant.

Harriet had used her torch to show them the way down. Now she threw the light switch hanging precariously from loose wires at the bottom of the steps. Nothing happened. "Shit!" she muttered.

"The generator's not on," Lucas told her. He sounded nervous, as if she might think it was his fault.

"I got that," Harriet said. "Where does Brian keep the emergency lamps?"

"In the main equipment pack, I think," Lucas told her. He hesitated. "Look, do we actually need—?"

"I want to see you," Harriet said shortly. She went over to the piles of equipment, leaving him in darkness. After a moment, she found what she was looking for. "That's better," Harriet said. She began placing half a dozen battery lamps at strategic points around the chamber. She came over to stand in front of him and grinned. "You undress me, and I'll undress you," she said.

THIRTY-FIVE

It wasn't working out quite as she'd expected. She stared down at his semi-flaccid penis and wondered if maybe she'd come on too strong. A lot of men got funny if you took the initiative—even men like Lucas who wouldn't know how to take the initiative with a woman if you paid him. He licked his lips. "You don't imagine there's anything in those stories of Egyptian curses, do you?"

For a second she thought he was making a joke, then realized he was serious. "You're not worried about offending old Nepherites, are you? Jeez, Lucas, the whole team's been down here for weeks." *Not fucking each other, admittedly*, her mind added irreverently.

Lucas's erection drooped another notch.. "No. It's just . . . you know, in a tomb . . ."

"You're the most inarticulate man I've ever met," Harriet told him kindly. "Are you going to undress me before that thing drops off altogether?"

Dumbly he reached for her, and as his hands touched her breasts, his hydraulics began to work again.

THIRTY-SIX

The chamber featured a stone-flagged floor, about a third of which had turned to rubble. Where the plaster had fallen, the walls were rough-hewn from the bedrock of the valley, towering to a high, vaulted ceiling. There was a huge granite sarcophagus, mercifully empty, in the western quarter of the main chamber and two subsidiary chambers leading off of it. There was a Dunlopillo mattress on the floor.

"You'll have to inflate that," Harriet said. "There's a bicycle pump thing." She glanced at his member again, now fully erect. "I suppose I should have mentioned it before we got this far."

"No problem," Lucas told her. He knelt by the mattress, attached the bicycle pump thing and got to work. "How did the mattress get here?"

"I left it," Harriet said. "How do you think it got there?"

"But you weren't down today."

"I left it the last time I was down."

"You mean you knew we'd be doing this—we'd be down here tonight, days ago?"

"Well, us, or I could have brought some other stud." She caught his expression and added quickly, "Only kidding."

"You were very confident," he said a little petulantly. "I mean about me."

"Oh, come on, Lucas, put the plug in the goddamn thing!"

The mattress was a wonderful idea. They lay together in the semi-darkness, exploring one another's bodies in a lot more comfort than they'd have enjoyed in the tent. With her hand curled around his engorged penis, Harriet said, "I wonder what that tastes like?"

Lucas groaned. "I wouldn't try to find out," he told her. "At this point I'm likely to come."

She glanced at his face and grinned. "That's the whole idea."

"But wouldn't you . . . ? I mean, wouldn't you prefer, you know—I mean for your own . . . ?"

"Jesus, Lucas, at your age you should be able to come more than once a night!"

"Yes, I know, but—" He broke away from her suddenly.

"Hey, where are you going?"

"Get a condom," he said breathlessly, scrabbling in the pocket of his shorts. He stretched the rubber membrane over his penis and turned back to her. "Come on," he said, "let's do this properly!"

"Ooooh, dominance!" Harriet said and grinned. "Come on, Big Boy, show me who's the boss!"

He entered her like an express train, and her legs came up to encircle his waist. "Oh God," she whispered in his ear. "Oh God, I knew you'd be good—I just didn't think you'd be this good." She squealed like an injured rabbit, a long, trailing wail that sent him into a sudden frenzy.

They were approaching their climax when the earth moved.

The Chronicles of
Nectanebo: Thirteen

Divination is a curious pursuit, a compound of skills rather than a single ability. I had a talent for it. But talent or no, the art is practised only at serious risk to health and sanity. Nonetheless, Artaxerxes's attempt on my life persuaded me that inaction would be the greater risk.

Thus I entered my private chamber, locked the door and began the sacred ritual taught me by the priest Khonsu so many years before. I burned incense to Thoth, imbibed the herbal potion and pronounced the Words of Power that opened the gates of vision.

Those familiar with this art will know that prophetic utterances are most often a fragmented patchwork. My own were generally little different, but on this occasion I saw clearly, with no room for alternative interpretation. This was my vision:

I saw Artaxerxes murdered and Khababasha's men attack Egypt: with success. Momentarily I wondered if I saw only what I wished to see. Certainly I would have wished Artaxerxes dead: for his defeat of me, for his hubris in seizing Egypt, for my own safety—and for my ambition, which had dimmed with age but not died completely. With equal certainty, I would have wished Khababasha military success, as the first step on the road to our joint victory.

But for all this, the vision failed me in one vital respect: I saw Khababasha, and I was not at his side. I saw the man who ascended the golden steps to Pharaoh's throne, and it was not Nectanebo returned triumphant but Khababasha himself, although I knew, without knowing how I knew, that he would hold that seat of power for only three short years.

This then was my major vision. But with it came a fragment of more personal import. Khababasha, black face tear-stained, in all his pharaonic finery, walked with his retinue to visit a tomb. I beheld the tomb, and it was my tomb. Miracle of miracles, it was in Egypt.

I know now that the priestly doctrines concerning death are false, but I did not know it then. I believed in the importance of the tomb as fervently as I believed in the importance of the Saros floods to Egypt's crops. In my glory years as Pharaoh, I commissioned architects to design a monumental tomb, its entrance a fortress guarded by innumerable traps, its antechambers littered with vicious talismans of magical protection.

When the plans were drawn, I commissioned engineers and builders to begin work on the structure, which was prominently situated in the great necropolis of Luxor. At the same time, secretly, I had my most trusted servants begin a second tomb, no less ambitious, but infinitely better hidden, in the desert valley where so many of the ancient great of Egypt rested.

But work on both went slowly: the former because of interruptions, technical problems, changes of mind and, later, the exigencies of war; the latter because the need for secrecy meant progress must be slow. Neither was ever finished. Artaxerxes destroyed what had been built at Luxor, as he destroyed all monuments to the previous pharaoh. The secret tomb became home for burrowing animals and eventually filled with sand.

In exile, of course, there were always more pressing, if not more important, matters than the planning of another tomb. Besides, I had been Pharaoh, which made me—symbolically at least—the son of Ra. Outside Egypt, there was no fitting place for my corpse.

But as my ambition withered with age, so did the problem of my tomb. In retrospect, it occurs to me that I was engaged in subtle self-deception: I did not wish to face the fact that I had lost the Twin Kingdoms forever. Perhaps, too, I did not wish to face the fact that I was mortal. I have never truly believed that I will die, although like any sane man, I know I must. But then again, I never truly believed I would grow old, even when my back bent, my sight failed and palsy shook my wizened hands. Yet grow old I did, beyond the years of many men. But still I did nothing to assure the safe journey of my heart to the Hall of Judgement.

My vision changed all that. The fragment grew in my mind until it loomed in importance beyond the murder of Artaxerxes, beyond even the enthronement of my friend Khababasha. I grew obsessed with the thought of an Egyptian tomb and with the problem of providing what my destiny decreed. In the event, it proved simple.

I confided in Khababasha, and, practical soul that he was, he put the matter in hand at once. He persuaded his cousin the king to send emissaries to Artaxerxes simultaneously protesting at the dispatch of assassins (although this was old history by now) and pleading the boon of a royal burial in Egypt for my mummy to make amends.

The diplomatic equivalent of horse-trading immediately followed. I was required to renounce formally any claim I believed I might have to the Egyptian throne. In return, Artaxerxes offered not only a suitable site for a tomb (although it was neither in Luxor nor the sacred valley) but also to finance its building.

Khababasha presented the offer as generous, doubtless because he felt it would free him of the necessity of our ongoing invasion game, and I agreed. I now knew I would never return to Egypt in this life, so the tomb was all-important.

While I had certain understandable reservations at the time of signing the agreement, Artaxerxes proved a man of his word. In three months (far less time than my own architects had taken when I was Pharaoh) he forwarded me plans which left little to be desired, either in terms of religious necessity or honour for my rank. I intimated my satisfaction with a small gift of Nubian spices in a rosewood casket, and he put the building in hand.

I was not permitted to see the tomb completed, of course, but he granted leave for my representatives to inspect it. Their reports, which coincided closely with my vision, convinced me that my mummy would have a fitting resting place.

The tomb was my last great earthly concern, and when it was complete, I sank into a torpor of days in which nothing much happened and nothing much concerned me. I grew comfortable, and while I was not precisely happy, I was not unhappy either. Events, great and small, flowed at a distance from me.

In the fullness of time, heavy with the weight of years—and not a little discomforted by jaundice of the liver—I died.

Khababasha had long undertaken to have my corpse embalmed in the Egyptian manner and to escort it personally to its final resting place. I have no reason to believe he failed to keep his word, and I like to think it was this visit to Egypt which inspired him to raise an army against Artaxerxes in his later years.

THIRTY-SEVEN

Lucas convulsed inside her. The whole interior of the cavern was ringing like a gong. From somewhere behind him came a resounding crack. There was a rushing sound beyond the main chamber, a waterfall that became thunder. In the aftermath of his climax, he found himself trembling. Harriet was trembling. The world was trembling.

Then suddenly it stopped.

"Christ! What was that?"

In the brutal silence, Harriet began to giggle, then to laugh. Lying beneath him, she laughed as he withdrew from her, laughed as he carefully rolled to one side of her. "Earthquake!" she gasped breathlessly. "Earthquake! What timing! What fucking amazing timing!" She giggled helplessly, then the laughter seized her again.

"Earthquake?" Lucas echoed stupidly.

She pushed herself up on one elbow and somehow got control. "They're not all that common in Egypt, but you do get them. We just had one now. Unbelievable!" She smiled broadly at him and added, "So were you."

"Thanks," Lucas said. He began to peel the condom from his penis, then twisted it and tied the end. He glanced down with a curious mixture of fondness and disgust. "I don't suppose I can just throw this in the corner."

"Not unless you want everybody to know what we've been doing. The management respectfully requests that you take your litter home."

He tossed the condom onto the crumpled heap of his shorts. "I'll stick it in my pocket when we go and dispose of it later." He stretched out beside her, drawing her into the crook of his arm. "Do you really think we had an earthquake?"

Harriet snuggled up to him. "Mmm," she said. "What did you think it was?"

Lucas grinned up into the darkness above. "The heat of our passion."

"God, but you're a lot more articulate now that we've done it."

"That's me," Lucas said. "Shall I tell you my life story?"

"You're too young to have a life story. Tell it to me later, when you're middle-aged. And stop tweaking my nipple. It makes me incredibly randy."

"We could always have a second round . . . ?"

"What happened to men who just want to fall asleep afterwards?" Harriet asked. "Don't you want to fall asleep?"

"Do you?"

"Maybe for a little while. I like the way you're holding me."

"Then after?"

"After we wake up again?" Harriet burrowed. "We'll see."

The ground trembled. Lucas sat bolt upright. "Christ! What was that?"

"Aftershock," Harriet told him sleepily. "You can relax now. That's all; tonight's excitement's over." She reached up to pull him back down beside her.

But Lucas was staring at something behind them. From somewhere beyond the main chamber came a dull, reverberating thud. "Come on," he said in sudden alarm. He scrambled to his feet, tugging her arm.

The sleepiness fell away. "What's the problem?"

"I don't know," Lucas said.

Harriet caught sight of what he'd been staring at—a crack in the wall behind them that certainly hadn't been there when they lay down. The opening was wide enough for a small person to squeeze through and seemed deep as a fissure, although it was difficult to tell with so little light. "Good Lord!"

"Never mind that!" He grabbed her wrist and half dragged her into the main chamber. The emergency lamps were still bright.

In their light, they could see the exit passage was blocked by a rockfall.

THIRTY-EIGHT

"Christ!" exclaimed Lucas. "What do we do now?" There was sweat on his forehead, even though the temperature inside the tomb was relatively cool.

Harriet walked over to the rockfall and poked it with her toe.

"Careful!" Lucas said. He was so nervous he could scarcely stand still.

"I don't think any more would come down if I went at it with a steam roller," Harriet told him. "Fancy trying to dig our way out? There must be shovels down here somewhere."

"We could make things worse."

She'd liked him a lot better when he was all take-charge and dominant. "How the hell can we make things worse?" she asked impatiently. "We're trapped!" She looked around, searching for the shovels.

"It's a heck of a long entrance," Lucas said. "If it's all blocked, we'd need special equipment to shore up the ceiling if we tried to tunnel out."

"It's not all blocked," said Harriet impatiently. "We won't have to tunnel."

"You don't know that!"

Harriet looked around again. "What would you estimate the volume of air down here?"

"Volume of air? I don't know. What do you want to know that for?"

"That's the other option, " Harriet said. "If we don't dig our way out, we wait for somebody to do it for us."

"I'd rather wait," Lucas said promptly.

"I'm not sure I would," Harriet told him. "Depends how long it takes."

"They'll start straight away. We could be out in an hour."

"No they won't. Why would they? There's been an earthquake. They'll be up there picking up the pieces. Nobody's going to notice we're gone right away. Even when they do, there's no reason for them to suppose we're down here. They probably won't even know there's been a rockfall until they start work in the morning. At the very least, we'll spend the night here."

"I'd prefer that," Luke said quickly.

He might have a point. "Maybe I would too," Harriet told him thoughtfully. "On balance. I don't know if there's air getting in from anywhere, but if there isn't, we'll survive longer if we avoid heavy work, like digging." She grinned at him suddenly. "Or making love."

"Somehow the urge has left me." Lucas said sourly.

"Come on!" said Harriet. She grabbed his hand.

"Where are we going?"

"To investigate that crack. It might be another way out."

The crack was about five feet high and varied in width along the whole of its length. Harriet was holding one of the electric lanterns into it at arm's length, but since the lantern didn't function as a torch, she still couldn't see very well. "I think there might be a cave in there," she said. "I don't think it's very big."

"I can't make out anything," Lucas told her. "Try holding it higher. Or lower. I can't see through the glare."

"I'm going to try squeezing in," Harriet said suddenly. She turned and handed him the lantern. "You hold this and pass it through to me."

"Hey, wait a minute! What happens if you get stuck?"

"Don't be stupid—you could drive a tank through there. You could probably squeeze through yourself if you held your breath."

"It may get narrow further in. Honestly, Harriet, I don't think this is such a hot—"

"Oh come on, Lucas, you can't live your life like this. If I'd known you were such a wimp, I'd never have taken you for a lover."

"I'm not a wimp," Lucas said. "There's a difference between wimp and bloody foolhardy."

"God, I love the English. An American would never use a term like 'bloody foolhardy.'" She bent over and started to squeeze through the crack.

"Careful!"

"It's okay. Just a bit tight around the chest. Lucky I'm not wearing a . . . Shit!"

"What happened? What's wrong?"

"Sharp stone under my foot. Made me turn my ankle."

"Is it sprained?"

"God, no. I just like making a fuss. Actually, it's okay in here. There's only a couple of feet before it widens out. I think it is a cave. Can you pass me the lamp?" Her arm emerged, the fingers of her hand wiggling impatiently.

"How's the air? Does it taste fresh?" Lucas placed the lamp in her hand.

"Much the same as back there." She moved forward cautiously. "I don't think this is going to be a way ou—Jesus Christ!"

"What?" Lucas asked in sudden alarm. "What is it?" He put his face to the crack. "Come on, Harriet, what's in there?"

The silence dragged for several heartbeats before she said, "You have to come through, Lucas."

"What? What is it?"

"The opening's wider at the bottom. If you crouch down or crawl you'll be okay, even with your shoulders. Come on! You have to see this!"

"What is it?" Lucas insisted. But he dropped down and stuck his head into the crack. Then he crawled until he bumped into her legs.

"Sorry," Harriet said as she stood aside.

Lucas clambered to his feet. As he stood upright, he said, "Good Lord!"

The cavern was a good deal smaller than the one they'd just left, but definitely man-made. There was a stone sarcophagus, heavily inscribed with hieroglyphs, no more than ten feet away from them. Several small statuettes lay in pieces on the floor.

"I'm right, aren't I?" Harriet exclaimed excitedly. "It's a tomb! We've found another tomb!"

Lucas stared around. "You're right all right. You couldn't be more right!"

"Do you think it's a pharaoh? We've got to be the first! Do you think we've discovered a pharaoh's tomb? Jesus, Lucas, we'll be famous! We'll get our names into the history books!" She turned and threw her arms around him.

When, eventually, they disengaged, he took the lamp and moved forward, treading carefully around the fragmented statuettes. Harriet followed closely behind. There were several wall paintings, badly faded. One set showed the Judgement Halls of Osiris from the raising of the mummy by the jackal-headed Anubis to the weighing of the heart against a feather. Another depicted the Sekhet-Aaru, the Field of Reeds that was ancient Egypt's most primitive vision of the afterlife.

"Look at this!" Harriet called. She'd found something that looked like a broken wooden frame. "It's the perch for his ba, his bird-soul."

"I don't think we should be moving things," Lucas told her. "If this really is a new discovery, they'll want to photograph everything in situ."

"Oh fuck that!" Harriet said crossly. But he was right, and she set the frame down carefully where she'd found it.

There was a hieroglyph inscription on another segment of the wall but so faded she could make out only a character here and there. In almost all the rest of the cavern, the plaster had cracked, crumbled or fallen. Harriet turned her attention to the floor. The statuettes were of sandstone and soapstone, all but one of them broken. Where she could see heads, she recognised representations of Sekhmet, Bastis and Hathor, but the unbroken statuette was neither of a goddess nor a god. It was a small, almost crude, representation of a seated scribe. She moved to kneel beside the sarcophagus, peering at the inscriptions. "Can you bring the lamp over here?" she called. "I think I've found a cartouche."

Lucas walked across, frowning at his own thoughts.

"Hold the lamp down," Harriet ordered. "See—" She pointed.

Lucas knelt beside her.

"It is, isn't it?" she asked excitedly. Only pharaohs wrote their names inside a cartouche. If this was for real (and if they ever got out, the voice of caution whispered in her head), they could have found a pharaoh's tomb. It would be incredible. They could end up as famous as Carter and Carnarvon.

The incised hieroglyphs were far clearer than those fading on the walls. "It's a cartouche, all right," he told her.

"You can read hieroglyphs, can't you?"

"Up to a point."

"Me too." It wasn't strictly true. She knew bits of the hieroglyphic alphabet, but without reference books, her translation skills were close to zero. "Can you see what it says? I mean, can you read the name?"

Lucas held the lamp closer.

There were nine of the pictograph symbols inside the oval. The first was the wavy line that represented a river and stood for the letter N. This was followed by twin wheat sheaves, which she'd never seen before, although one wheat sheaf on its own signified an E. Then came a little drinking bowl that represented C or K.

After a moment, Lucas said, "Nectanebo. It's the cartouche of the Pharaoh Nectanebo."

Harriet felt a surge of disappointment. She'd been hoping for one of the Ramesseses. "Who's he?"

"I'm not sure," Lucas frowned. "I think he was one of the late ones, wasn't he?"

"The Ptolemies?"

"I think so. I'm not sure. The E uses the old form of the hieroglyph, but that might just be a formality."

"Do you think it's his tomb?"

"I think it could be," Lucas nodded. "We'd really need to decipher the rest of the inscription."

"Go on, then!" Harriet urged.

Lucas sighed. "Darling," he said, "I'm not really that much of an Egyptian scholar. It could take me weeks."

Harriet said, "What did you call me?"

Lucas glanced at her, then said sheepishly, "'Darling.'"

"Well, try to sound as if you meant it. I hate a man who uses terms of endearment when he's exasperated."

They split up again to examine the rest of the tomb.

"This looks like the entrance," Harriet called.

Lucas moved across. "That's odd," he said.

"What?"

"The seals aren't broken."

Harriet looked at him quickly. "That means we're the first to enter the tomb since he was buried, doesn't it?"

"Well, yes . . . except . . ."

"What?" snapped Harriet impatiently.

Lucas held the lamp and pointed with his free hand. "It's definitely still sealed. See? There and there. Unbroken. And this one's got a curse on grave robbers." His finger traced the hieroglyphs as he read them: "May they be as nothing, those who attack my Name, my Effigies, the Images of my Double, my Foundation. They will be deprived of their Name, of their Ka, of their Ba, of their Ku . . ."

"How come you can read that so easily when you can't tell me what it says on the sarcophagus until next week?"

"It's a more or less standard curse. Most of the tombs have it in one version or another. I just recognised it, that's all."

Harriet said, "But if the seals are intact, that means we've discovered an untouched pharaoh's tomb! We've discovered Nectanebo's tomb!"

Lucas hesitated. "Yes, but look around you."

"What am I supposed to be looking for?"

"Don't you remember what Carter said when he first looked into Tutankhamen's tomb? Somebody asked him what he saw, and he said, 'Wonderful things!' The tomb was packed with stuff."

"What's your point?" Harriet asked a little stiffly, although she thought she might be ahead of him.

"Well, just look," Lucas said helplessly. "What have we got here? A stone sarcophagus and a few little broken statues. The seals are intact, but this tomb's been robbed."

THIRTY-NINE

After a moment, Harriet said, "That means there's another way in. The way we got in wasn't there before the quake. If the robbers didn't come through the front door, there must be another way!"

They spent close to an hour searching for it, even systematically tapping the walls for any hint of secret doors, but there was nothing. When they'd finished, they sat down together, backs against a wall. "This is a mystery," Harriet said.

"Yes," Lucas agreed. He stared despondently into the gloom of the cavern.

Harriet scrambled to her feet abruptly. "Let's see if we can open the sarcophagus!"

"Hey, wait a minute—we can't do that!" Lucas scrambled after her.

"Why not?" Harriet asked. "Grave's been robbed. Doesn't much matter what we do now."

"Oh, come on, Harriet! You know that's not true. The robbery probably happened a thousand years ago. How they left the tomb is historical interest in itself. You know that."

"Oh, come on, Lucas!" Harriet mimicked. "You know you're being a pompous prick. If anybody tries to slap our wrist, we'll tell them we found it with the lid off."

"We won't be able to get that off anyway."

She was beginning to wonder if he was the most negative man she'd ever met. "You don't know that till we try," Harriet said. She gripped an edge of the lid. "Come on, I won't manage it on my own. We'll just push it to one side a little bit. Just enough to look in."

He obviously wanted to see inside himself, despite all his caution, for he took the other edge of the lid. To her surprise, it lifted easily. It seemed to be made from very light stone, possibly porous. Or perhaps it wasn't stone. The Egyptians had been very ingenious in some ways. They might have discovered a way of disguising wood or some other material as stone.

"Shit!" Lucas said. He looked at her. "Well, that was a waste of time."

Harriet glanced down. The sarcophagus was empty.

Lucas started to push the lid back.

"Hold on," Harriet said. She peered into the empty sarcophagus, frowning. There was something wrong here, although she couldn't quite figure out what. "Look, can we get this lid right off?"

"Why?" Lucas asked, but he gripped the lid again just the same.

They lifted the thing off and placed it carefully on the floor beside the sarcophagus. Harriet pulled herself up so she could get her head inside. "Can you give me some light in here?"

"Hang on—" In a moment, he was holding the light directly behind her head.

"Well, I'll be damned!" she said.

"What?"

Instead of answering, she heaved herself up and dropped inside. Lucas gave a strangled gasp but obviously decided it was pointless making any more protests. She crouched down and began to run her fingers along the bottom edge of the granite.

"What are you doing?" Lucas asked. "Harriet! I'm talking to you!"

"Well, I'll be damned!" Harriet said again. She glanced up at him over her shoulder. "This thing has a false bottom!"

"Are you sure?"

"I'm sure, all right. I just don't know how to get it open."

———— • ————

Janet said, "But you did get it open?" What Mrs. Webb was telling her was extraordinary. She had actually been instrumental in the discovery of Nectanebo's tomb. Perhaps that's where her son's obsession had started.

Harriet nodded. "Eventually. The two of us were in and out of the thing maybe a dozen times. Then we found a catch. It was disguised as an ornamental scroll. Amazing mechanism, utterly ingenious and still functioning after—what? Two thousand years? The stone rolled over on itself, and we just stood there gawking."

———————

"Clever!" Lucas whispered. "Clever! Clever! Clever!" He turned to Harriet. "You know what he did, this old Nectanebo character?"

Through the bottom of the sarcophagus, they could see a second chamber, hewn into the bedrock of the floor. It was about the size of a large walk-in wardrobe and contained a mummy case, a golden bird perch and several archer figurines. The mummy case looked intact.

"What did he do?" asked Harriet without taking her eyes away.

"He faked a robbed tomb! Can you believe it?"

"I believe it," Harriet said. She started to pull herself back up into the sarcophagus.

"What are you doing?"

"Going down to have a look. What do you think?"

For just the barest instant, Lucas looked as if he might object. Then he said, "I'm coming with you."

Close up, the structure was even more ingenious. The floor of the sarcophagus pivoted into an accommodating niche. Set to one side was a short flight of shallow stone steps giving easy access into the second chamber. The chamber itself was high enough to allow Lucas to stand upright, although with the two of them in there, it was beginning to get a little crowded.

"Did you ever see Tutankhamen's tomb?" Lucas asked.

Harriet shook her head. "No."

"It's disappointing. You read about all the treasure and all the fuss, but when you get there, it's actually quite small. Once they took the grave goods out, there's not much to see. But this is smaller, a lot smaller. I don't think there's ever been a find of a pharaoh's tomb so small."

"Why does that worry you?"

Lucas frowned. "Well, it doesn't worry me. I mean, not exactly worry. But, you know . . ."

"Sometimes I think you're the most inarticulate human being I've ever known."

"Well," Lucas told her with a pained expression, "they believed they were going to have to live in their tombs forever. Can you imagine any pharaoh wanting to live in here? It's smaller than a bed-sit."

"Maybe he thought it was more important to preserve his mummy."

"Yes," Lucas said uncertainly, "it must have been something like that." He hesitated. "Unless it isn't really Nectanebo's tomb."

"What about the cartouche?" Harriet asked.

"I'd need to translate the whole inscription to be sure of that. It might be just 'This is the tomb of poor old Joe Bloggs who died in the reign of Pharaoh Nectanebo.' They'd still use the cartouche for the name, but it wouldn't mean this was a pharaoh's tomb."

"Pessimistic wimp," Harriet muttered.

The mummy case was set a little off-centre in the chamber with the canoptic jars that held the entrails of the pharaoh—if it really was a pharaoh—lined up to one side. There were five archer figures in all, carved from wood and painted in what must once have been a very life-like fashion before the flaking started. Harriet held the lamp closer to the nearest one. "Notice anything?" she asked.

"There are only five," Lucas said. "That's very few guards for a pharaoh. Actually, it's very few guards even for a noble."

"They're all female," Harriet said.

"What?"

"The archers. They're all female. That's unusual isn't it?"

"Very," Lucas told her. "Are you sure?"

"Use your eyes, for God's sake! You should be able to recognise a woman—you've just seen me with my clothes off."

Lucas peered at the figurines one after the other as if there might be some doubt, then shook his head in bewilderment. "This has to be the oddest tomb ever."

"Question is," said Harriet, smiling suddenly, "do we have a quick peek at the mummy?"

"Hello?" called a distant voice, above them. "Is anybody in there?"

FORTY

"It was the cavalry, of course," Harriet said. "We were missed far sooner than I thought. Actually a character named Renfield saw Lucas going out to meet me and put two and two together. God knows how he guessed we'd be screwing in the tomb, but he did. He organised a search immediately after the quake, and, of course, they found the rockfall. Fortunately it wasn't half as bad as it looked from the inside, so they broke through in less than an hour. The voice we heard was Melville shouting through the first opening they made."

"Who was Melville?" Janet asked. A lot of her exhaustion had evaporated.

Harriet nodded. "Dr. Brian Melville. The man running the show. Name mean anything to you?"

"Should it?"

Harriet shrugged. "Maybe not. There was a lot of press publicity when he went to jail, but it was a long time ago. Anyway, he was our boss at the time—team leader. He directed the party that dug us out."

Janet was tempted to ask about the jailing but didn't want to divert Harriet, so she said, "But he wouldn't have known about the second tomb at that stage—he'd have thought you were trapped in, what was it—?"

"Nepherites's tomb. That's right. Once we heard his voice, we came up fast. They'd made an opening where the entrance passage was blocked." Harriet poured fresh coffee into her cup and offered the pot to Janet, who waved it away vaguely. "It wasn't big enough for us to squeeze through, but it let air in, and it allowed us to talk. We went back to Nepherites's tomb and told him we were all right."

"And told him about the second tomb, presumably."

"Not right away," Harriet said. "We . . . you know . . . well, we were young. We suspected we'd found a pharaoh's tomb. We wanted to keep things quiet until we'd sorted out what to do. I suppose we were afraid somebody would take it away from us."

"Had you?" Janet asked. "Found a pharaoh's tomb, I mean? Was it really Nectanebo's?"

"Yes," Harriet said. "It was Nectanebo's."

She remained quiet for so long that Janet prompted, "What happened?"

Harriet's expression was almost startled as she looked at her. "What happened? What happened was it turned into a mess. You wouldn't believe what a mess it turned into."

FORTY-ONE

"You did right not to shout about it," Dr. Melville told them. "The fewer people who know, the better."

"I'm not sure I understand the need for secrecy," Lucas muttered.

Melville smiled. He was a good-looking man who managed to appear well-groomed however hot it got. "I'm sure Harriet does," he said.

Harriet said nothing. She was still trying to adjust to the speed of events. Everyone now knew about their discovery of the supposedly robbed tomb, but apart from Lucas and herself, there were only two other people who knew about the secret chamber underneath the sarcophagus. One of them was Melville. The other was her father, who had already flown to Egypt and was due to join them at any moment.

"Drink while we're waiting?" Melville suggested. They were a hundred miles south of the Valley of the Kings, in the bar of the Great Cataract at Aswan. Melville was taking no chances with this meeting. He had been paranoid about absolute secrecy from the first.

"I'd like a beer," Lucas said. He was obviously overawed by the opulence of his surroundings—the Cataract was a big change from a communal tent—but determined to make the most of it.

"What about you, Harriet? Gin and tonic?"

But before she could answer, he was clambering to his feet, his PR smile pasted wider than ever. Harriet glanced over her shoulder. Her father was bearing down towards them. "Daddy!" she squealed and ran to throw herself into his arms.

"You have caught the sun," said Stanislav Regis, smiling.

Harriet kissed him. "Not surprising. It hasn't rained here for three thousand years."

Stanislav disengaged himself to shake hands with Dr. Melville. "Brian," he acknowledged, "it is good to see you again, even if you made me take such a long, uncomfortable flight. And the road journey down!

Ach—" He made an expressive gesture with his hands. "What a nightmare!"

"I think you may find it very worthwhile," Melville murmured quietly.

"I also think I might," Stanislav said. He turned to Lucas and extended his hand. "And this must be the young man who made so exciting a discovery with my daughter."

"Pleased to meet you, sir," Lucas said as they shook hands.

"I've booked us a suite," Melville said. "I thought it sensible to have somewhere we could speak privately."

"Yes, excellent," said Stanislav. "Please lead the way."

The suite was enormous. Melville obviously wasn't one to spare expense—especially when, Harriet suspected, he wouldn't be the one paying. A uniformed waiter brought drinks. Melville waited until he left before saying, "Stan, your daughter and her friend have made the discovery of the century! This could literally be more important than Tutankhamen."

"So you told me on the telephone," Stanislav said. He reached for the jug and poured himself a long glass of tamarind juice. He never touched alcohol while engaged in business or research. "Now I wish you to tell me the details."

Melville leaned forward. "I'll let these two tell you the details, but let me give you the broad picture first. The original find was luck. Harriet and Lucas were in Nepherites's tomb five nights ago when there was a smallish earthquake. This opened a rock fault that allowed them access to a hitherto undiscovered tomb."

Stanislav turned to Harriet and said soberly, "I suppose I should not ask what it was you were doing with a young man in Nepherites's tomb in the middle of the night."

"No, you shouldn't," Harriet grinned. Out of the corner of her eye, she noticed to her amusement that Lucas was blushing.

Stanislav turned back to Melville. "Please go on, Brian. This was a pharaoh's tomb, I understand?"

"Yes, that's now been confirmed. The texts on the sarcophagus show it's the tomb of the Pharaoh Nectanebo. He was the last native ruler of Egypt—"

"I know," Stanislav interrupted. "I looked him up."

Melville seemed momentarily taken aback. "I didn't think I'd mentioned the name."

Stanislav nodded. "Yes, you did."

"Well, anyway, you know all about him," Melville said. "The tomb gave every appearance of having been robbed. The sarcophagus was empty; there were no grave goods except for a few broken statuettes on the floor. Nothing else."

"No mummy," Stanislav said. It was as much a statement as a question.

"No," Melville confirmed. "Now, I have to tell you this find—the despoiled tomb—is known to the workmen on the site and will have to be reported to the Egyptian authorities."

"How soon?" Stanislav asked.

"Actually, it should have been reported by now. I estimate we can hold out for a few more days, possibly even a week, without getting into too much trouble. After that . . ." He shrugged expressively. "But, of course, the story may well get out before we make the formal report. There's no way of telling how long that will take—they may even know already."

Stanislav nodded. "I see." He sipped his juice.

There was something going on. Harriet knew her father well, and her whole instinct told her there was something between him and Melville she didn't know about. Her eyes flicked back to Melville as he started speaking again.

"What isn't known to anyone outside this room is that Harriet and Lucas made another discovery. There is a second, secret chamber underneath the first. This chamber had not been entered since the original burial until Harriet and Lucas did so. Actually, the upper chamber had also never been entered before Harriet and Lucas. It was cunningly constructed at the time it was built to give the impression of a despoiled tomb. But the point is, Stan, that the burial is intact."

"Including the mummy?" Stanislav asked.

"We have a mummy we believe to be"—he corrected himself—"we are certain is that of the Pharaoh Nectanebo."

"And what else?"

Melville licked his lips. "There are five life-sized wooden statues of female bowmen—bow-women, I suppose I'd better say—"

"Say 'archers,'" Harriet murmured.

"Thank you, yes—archers. The fact they're female is extremely unusual. In fact, I rather think they may be unique. Their archaeological value is immense. There is also a small casket Harriet and Lucas didn't notice when they entered this chamber initially. It contains coinage—gold coinage—of the Nectanebo era. These coins are in excellent condition, quite excellent. Scarcely any wear at all. Mint condition, you might say. Their value is literally incalculable."

"How many?"

"Coins? Just short of five hundred—four hundred and ninety-seven. Nectanebo's little hoard to pay his way in the afterlife."

"Anything else? You told me this second chamber was small."

"Comparatively speaking. But you're right—far smaller than the usual Egyptian tomb, far smaller than the chamber above. And there was nothing else Harriet and Lucas overlooked. Just the statues and the coffer and the mummy case in the secret chamber. But when we opened the mummy case—" He hesitated. "Do you know the details of the Tutankhamen find?"

"As a layman," Stanislav shrugged. Not for the first time, Harriet noticed how very still he held himself. It was his way of hiding what went on in his mind.

"There were coffins within coffins," Melville said. "Like Russian dolls. Nectanebo's case was like that. There were three cases inside the outer case, before you came to the actual remains. In every case, there were at least three craftworks in pure gold. One of them had five. Chalice . . . ritual dagger . . . statuettes . . . drinking bowl . . . There was a golden death mask covering Nectanebo's face. These things are absolutely priceless, and every one is portable."

Stanislav said, "Before we come to that, what can you tell me about the mummy?"

Melville had begun to sweat, and he reached out for his own drink, a gin and tonic with a slice of lime. Like Harriet's, it had no ice. Only native Egyptians could take ice in their drink. It was made from Nile water and gave visitors the trots. He drank about half the contents of his glass before setting it down with a look of satisfaction. He sucked his bottom lip. "There are actually two mummies—"

"Two?" Stanislav glared at him. "You did not tell me this."

"I thought the less I said over the phone the better. One of the mummies is a woman. My guess is Nectanebo was buried with his wife. His chief wife, probably, since he's likely to have had more than one. Or a favourite wife."

"It is a large coincidence that she died at the same time, is it not? If the tomb was intact, as you say, she could not have been buried later."

"Well, she could," Melville said. "I mean it's possible, assuming she knew about the secret chamber. She could have had herself interred with him and the seals replaced. But, no, I agree. I think that's stretching things. It's much more likely that he had her murdered."

"Do you really think so?" Lucas asked. It was the first time he'd spoken since they'd come up to the suite.

Melville glanced at him in surprise. "It happened. The pharaoh had to have guards and servants in the afterlife."

"I thought they made statues, like the archers," Lucas said.

"Yes, they did," Melville told him impatiently. "But any guard or servant is as good as any other. A wife's different. My guess is Nectanebo wanted this specific woman with him."

Obviously tiring of the exchange, Stanislav cut in. "What is the condition of the mummies?"

"Not good," Melville said. "The woman is rather better than Nectanebo. It's peculiar—she seems to have had the better embalming techniques, which isn't at all what you'd expect, given that he was a pharaoh. Not that it made all that much difference: they're both . . ." He shrugged. "Maybe it was something to do with temperature, or maybe there was an invasion of groundwater at some time, although frankly there's no sign of that. But whatever the reason, both bodies are in a poor state of preservation. You're really talking more about a collection of body parts than actual bodies."

Stanislav nodded. "I see." Curiously, he did not look particularly displeased. He said to Melville, "You have a proposition for me?"

There was a sudden tension in the room. Melville actually glanced towards the door, presumably to be sure it was tightly closed. He said, "Stan, if we report these finds to the Egyptian Department of Antiquities, we'll get a pat on the head and an oily thank-you. At best, they'll release a few thousand pounds Egyptian as a token of their appreciation. The artifacts will disappear for a few years, then turn up as an obscure exhibit in Cairo Museum. But on the open market, the collector's market, they're worth millions—millions! And as I mentioned, everything's portable. Apart from the death mask, they're easily portable."

"You are suggesting we smuggle them out of the country?"

"I'm suggesting I smuggle them out of the country. There would be no risk to you or your daughter. Or this young man here," he added as an afterthought. "I would take the risk of bringing them out of the country. I would be responsible for finding a buyer—or buyers, more likely. We would split the proceeds. Half for your daughter and yourself, a third for me and the remainder as a gift to Lucas to ensure his silence—you could set up a sheep farm in Australia, Lucas."

"Here, wait a minute—" Lucas bristled, but Stanislav waved a hand to silence him.

"What about the mummified remains?" Stanislav asked.

Melville blinked. "What about them?"

"Would not they be valuable?"

Frowning, Melville said, "Well, valuable in the sense that they're obviously historically important, but you won't find a buyer. I mean, a respectable museum would never touch them, and private collectors don't go in for that sort of thing—too grisly."

"Nonetheless, were I to require that these body parts also be smuggled from Egypt, would you do it?"

Bewildered, Melville said, "Yes, yes, of course. Whatever you want."

"I want that you should bring the mummified remains, both bodies in whatever condition, out of Egypt and into the United States. I shall make available such funding as you may need to ensure this is done successfully and secretly. To encourage you to do the job properly, I shall waive my share of the proceeds of the sale of the artifacts in your favour. In return, I shall take possession of the mummified remains. Would such an arrangement be satisfactory to you?"

Melville looked as if someone had just reminded him today was Christmas. "Perfectly," he said. "Yes, perfectly. Perfectly satisfactory."

"In that case," Stanislav said, "I agree."

Harriet stared at him openmouthed. She'd just watched her father become a grave robber.

FORTY-TWO

"It was quite a shock for me," Harriet said.

"I can understand that," Janet told her. "We all tend to idolise our parents. It's painful when they fail to live up to expectations. Did you make any protest at the time?"

"Not as much as I should have," Harriet said. "If it had just been Melville . . ." She shrugged. "But I've always hesitated to take on my father."

"I understand that too," Janet murmured. Her own father was long dead, but even now, as an adult, the idea of going head-to-head with her mother was almost unthinkable.

"Anyway, it was presented as one of those 'everybody wins' deals. We looted the secret room, closed the floor of the sarcophagus, then officially reported the find of the upper chamber. The Egyptians got Nectanebo's tomb, or so they thought. Melville got more money than he'd have made with his damn plastic, Lucas and I got a cut, Dad got his mummies. The argument was that, without us, the Egyptians would never have found the things anyway."

"Why did your father want the mummies?" Janet asked curiously.

"That's getting ahead of the story. Let me tell you what happened," Harriet said.

"Okay."

"We had a lot of discussion—a lot. Even if I didn't protest much, Lucas did. But eventually, between them, Dad and Melville bullied him into it. We all had a hand in the actual looting of the tomb. It was real horror movie stuff—dead of night, looking over your shoulder, terrified somebody might stumble on us accidentally. You get the picture. The bodies were the worst. Melville wasn't joking when he said they were poorly preserved. They started to fall apart as soon as we tried to move them. Bits literally fell off. It was ghastly. I tried to persuade my father to leave them—I couldn't imagine they'd be worth anything to him, but he wouldn't hear of it. Anyway, we got them out and crated. It was the worst night of my life."

"But you weren't caught?"

"No. If I weren't squeamish, I'd have said it went smooth as silk. It actually went very fast. The bodies were the only problem. The artifacts were small, and there weren't that many of them. We only took the gold. The archers were too big—did I mention they were life-size? Melville would never have gotten them out of the country—it would have been like trying to smuggle five bodies on top of the two mummies he was already committed to. Once we had everything out and hidden, it was all up to Melville. Dad flew home. He wanted me to come with him, but I stayed over a few more days, mainly to be with Lucas."

"You'd formed an affection?"

"That and the fact that I didn't really trust him to keep his mouth shut. I wasn't much worried about Melville, but I didn't want my father implicated."

"Did he? Keep his mouth shut?"

"He was a lamb. Melville shut down the project three or four days later, paid everybody off. By that time, of course, he'd made whatever arrangements he was making to get the things out of the country. Lucas flew back to England, and I never saw him again. I found out later Dad had given him an advance on his cut—a hundred thousand dollars, about fifty-five thousand pounds: a small fortune in those days. He used it to emigrate to Australia. He really did start a sheep farm."

"I think I will have some more of that coffee after all," Janet said. After Harriet poured, she asked, "So Melville got the artifacts out?"

Harriet shook his head. "No, he didn't. This was 1973. We couldn't have picked a worse year if we'd tried."

"Why's that?"

"The Yom Kippur War," Harriet said.

The Chronicles of Nectanebo: Fourteen

"Of all the arts of combat, this is the most important," Lipta once told me. "This, hear, Pharaoh, for it is more important than all you have learned from Rena or all you will ever learn from her. Power resides not in the muscle, or the reflex, or even in the brain, but in the flow."

"Flow, Abbess?" I was stretched naked in a chamber of the Elephantine Convent while she, decently concealed within the abba, pretended she required a cane to aid her faltering steps.

She moved beside me and bent so that her mouth was close to my ear. "Flow, Nectanebo. Flow!" she hissed. "The energies of your body may be accumulated and directed."

"Directed, Abbess?" I asked innocently, and grinned.

She pulled back, those feral eyes glinting. "Must you echo everything I say, fool? You are aware of the channels, however imperfect your perception. You must feel the flow. It is impossible not to."

"Quite," I said. Then, fearful of driving her into real anger, I added, "I have known the flow. It is a cyclical thing, having certain peaks and valleys throughout the night and day."

"Good," she muttered, mollified. "Good. You notice. That is good. Now learn. Your mind, with the proper concentration, may accumulate the energy in a given spot, may release it to another, even project it outwards, although that is an advanced matter which will be beyond you for many years—and may be beyond you forever." I sought to say something, but she waved her cane at me in warning. "Listen and learn. By means of this discipline, you may direct your vital energies into your hand, into your arm, into your head—where you will. And in so doing, may increase strength tenfold."

So had I been taught, laid naked before the crone. So did I learn the means by which the mind may direct subtle energies throughout the body to protect as armour protects, to dull pain, to strengthen. Lipta sometimes walked from me, sometimes towards me, sometimes bending close, sometimes shrieking from afar like a gigantic crow. But always intriguing, always enticing, always binding my interest to her in a thousand ways.

And when it was done, that lesson, she crouched near me, and I arose, seized by an unexpected impulse, and kissed her full on the lips. This she permitted without demur or hindrance or, indeed, response, and when I was finished, said only, "Clothe yourself, Pharaoh: you are indecently exposed."

FORTY-THREE

"Melville made his attempt to leave the country on the sixth of October," Harriet said. "That was the day Egypt and Syria got fed up waiting for Israel to return the territory it took in the Six-Day War and launched a surprise attack. Syria struck into the Golan Heights. Egypt sent its troops across the Sinai. The soldiers who stumbled on Melville were convinced he was an Israeli spy. It was touch and go whether they would shoot him on the spot. The only reason they didn't was they were afraid gunfire might alert the Israelis—he was far closer to the border than he thought. Anyway, they held him in military custody until the war was well underway, then took him back to Cairo. At some stage, they got around to searching the Land Rover and found his little horde of Nectanebo's artifacts. He was charged with looting and given a twenty-eight-year sentence. It was harsh even for an Islamic court, but with a war on and Egypt losing, tempers were a little short."

"How did you find out about this?" Janet asked.

"Read it in the paper. It was our first indication anything had gone wrong." Harriet smiled wanly. "Later I visited him in jail. But that was two and a half years after he was put away and the war was history. He refused to tell the Egyptians where he got the artifacts or to implicate any of the rest of us. To this day, no one else knows about the second chamber in Nectanebo's tomb unless poor Lucas has mentioned it to his sheep."

"And now you've told me," Janet said.

"I think you'd have found out before long," Harriet said enigmatically.

"What happened to Melville?"

Harriet took a deep breath and released it with a sigh. "He's dead. He served fifteen of the twenty-eight years. Egyptian jails are no fun. He got TB, and they missed it until it was too late to treat effectively. My father was pushing diplomatic buttons and laying down a lot of bribes to try to get him out, and eventually when he was ill enough they let him go. He died three months later in one of our sanatoriums in New Jersey. He was a crook, of course. But he didn't deserve what happened to him."

Janet chewed her bottom lip. Despite the coffee, she felt utterly exhausted. She fought the tiredness down and said, "So your father never got his mummies?"

"Ah," Harriet said, "in fact he did. But you look bushed. What say you get a good night's sleep and I finish the story over breakfast?"

FORTY-FOUR

She was in an ancient city with paved roadways and towering buildings. The avenue down which she walked was guarded by twin rows of ram-head sphinxes. Her mother was walking beside her.

"It took you a long time to get here," Emma Winters said.

"I didn't know where to find you," Janet told her. "I'm not even sure where I am."

"Oh, you're sure all right," her mother told her in that annoying tone of utter certainty. "It's just that you haven't realised who you are."

"That's psychobabble, Mother!" Janet retorted. "I'm not one of your patients."

Luke Webb was standing at the end of the avenue. He was dressed only in a folded kilt and wore a cobra headdress so that he looked like an Egyptian pharaoh. He held out his arms to her. "It took you a long time to get here," he said.

"I didn't know where to find you," Janet told him.

He began to remove her clothes. She was wearing the silk blouse and trouser suit she'd bought in London, the one that made her feel special, but her underclothes were brief and tarty. He tore them from her so that she stood naked. She felt wet fire between her legs.

"I love you," Luke Webb whispered. The kilt was gone, and he was naked but for the cobra headdress. His erection was monstrous, far larger than that of any normal man. Janet wondered if she could accommodate it.

"Shall I help you, darling?" asked her mother. Emma encircled Luke's engorged penis with both hands and guided it towards Janet's open vagina.

Janet shut her eyes and wakened. She had trained herself to remember her dreams as an aid to self-knowledge. The technique was to go over the dream consciously the moment she was awake, and she did this now. She visualised the city and her mother, replayed in her mind the conversation and the sexual encounter with Luke. Then, from habit, she began the analysis.

The Egyptian setting was interesting but probably not important—she'd obviously drawn the symbolism directly from her earlier encounter with Luke Webb. His obsession with the Pharaoh Nectanebo, combined with his mother's story of how she and her lover had found the tomb, provided vivid imagery—the sort the unconscious always found useful when it wanted to attract your attention.

The appearance of her mother might be more relevant. Janet was aware she had problems with her mother. Emma was a strong character, both opinionated and dominant. The fact that they had both followed similar careers, Janet as a clinical psychologist, Emma as a psychoanalyst, sometimes made the problems more acute. But when Emma appeared in her dreams, she didn't always—or even usually—represent the living breathing woman back in Britain. She represented the mother archetype in the depths of Janet's mind and as such was the original pattern on which Janet had based her own femininity.

In her personal development, Janet obviously had goals, but not all of them were conscious. *You took a long time to get here*, this embodiment of her femininity had said. Which meant, *You took a long time to reach this goal*. What goal?

Janet moved cautiously in the bed. She didn't want to make any major change in her position since to do so often fragmented the memory of the dream. The goal had to be internal, the person she hoped to become. "It's just that you haven't realised who you are," Mother had said in the dream, this time in the role of an authority figure. Janet had responded by accusing her of psychobabble, but this almost certainly reflected her own repressed anger towards her mother, because it wasn't psychobabble, just a statement of fact.

The dream figure of Luke Webb had also told her it had taken her a long time to reach wherever she had reached. The question was, what did Luke represent? She was familiar enough with Emma as a symbol, but Luke was new to her life. She'd only met him yesterday, and it was unusual to find someone so new featuring in a dream. He had obviously made a very strong impression. Why?

"I didn't know where to find you." This was what she'd said to him. Exactly what she'd said to her mother. Why?

Janet was aware she was sexually aroused. Her vagina felt so moist she was tempted to masturbate. The remainder of the dream was overtly sexual. Was this a question of what you see is what you get? Was she attracted to Luke Webb?

Of course she was attracted to Luke Webb. She'd known that the instant she'd set eyes on him. Nor was it particularly surprising. By any objective measure, he was an attractive man, the sort of man she'd have tried to get to know better in other circumstances. There could be nothing between them now, of course. Luke was suffering from a serious psychosis, but even if he improved or recovered, the fact she'd been called in as his therapist made any personal relationship impossible. And unwise, even if it had been possible. Not that that made any difference to the unconscious, which was quite prepared to recognise the reality that she found Luke Webb sexy as sin.

It occurred to Janet that it had been a long time since she'd had a man in her bed. A very long time. Sod's Law that the first one she found attractive was unavailable.

Or was that purposeful? Was that part of her pattern in avoiding intimacy? Did she carefully decide that only an unavailable man would attract her? What had her mother said the last time they'd met? "Janet, you don't have a sex life"? Something like that. It was true enough. Was that because she didn't really want one?

Still pondering the problem, Janet slid back into the dream.

"You're missing it," her mother said. "You were always far too convoluted when you tried your hand at dream interpretation. That's why you'd never make an analyst."

Surprised and surprisingly amused, Janet said, "You're not trying to tell me how to analyse this dream are you, Mother? We're not awake now, you know. This is like the dream analysing itself."

"No, it's not!" said Emma flatly.

But Janet wasn't listening. She'd just realised what she herself had said. *We're not awake now, you know.* She knew that she was dreaming! The dream had gone lucid!

Janet had long been fascinated by the phenomenon of lucid dreaming, because while lucid dreaming was no less real, no less vivid than ordinary dreaming, it did have one important difference. In lucid dreams, the dreamer took control.

Which meant she too could take control!

Janet looked around for Nectanebo and found him smiling at her in the flawless body of Luke Webb. She reached down to rip away his apron and felt her heart leap at the sight of his magnificent erection.

"I want you," she said hoarsely. Even though it was only a dream and ethical considerations no longer applied, she was surprised, even shocked, at the urgency of her own arousal. Nevertheless, she gripped his member fiercely. "I want you," she repeated. "I want you inside me!"

"Not until you take your mask off," Nectanebo said.

The Chronicles of
Nectanebo: Fifteen

I t was long my custom—before the infirmities of old age forbade it—to
rise before dawn and deliver unto Ra at his rising the glorious hymn
of Qenna, which begins: "Homage to thee, O Ra, when thou risest, O
Temu, in thy risings of beauty."

The oration complete, I would then walk for a time in my gardens,
or by the Nile, or the lakeside, or, more often, the desert, contemplating
beauty where I found it. This ritual calmed me, I had long discovered,
and prepared me for the rigors of the day.

In Nubia as in Egypt, the desert lured me like a lover, for always in
Egypt I was called by the wastelands. Of all who knew me and knew of
it, only Lipta, the Gegum abbess, understood. She spoke of messages
carried on the desert winds, of spaces vast enough for men to find their
souls, of whispers in the night revealing secrets lost, of blazing days when
only strength and knowledge can ensure survival.

But there was a wildness in Lipta no less than in me, a reptile strength
and many ancient secrets. Not merely men but Gegum witch-nuns found
their souls in rolling wasteland.

On one such walk through desert wastes, a premonition came to
me. The premonition was a vision of an ancient hand that reached out
to me. I did not understand it, though I knew the hand was Gegum. But
it prepared me, as nothing else could have done, for what was to befall,
so that when the time came, I recognised the need and did not hesitate
to take the necessary action.

In the second year of my exile in Nubia, I received a summons to
return to Egypt and made immediate arrangements to depart.

The development disturbed my friend Prince Khababasha, who
deduced an attempt to regain my throne and concluded that the likeli-

hood of my survival—let alone any possibility of success—was minimal. Nor was he reassured by my silence, for I told him nothing beyond the bare fact of my departure.

We had to some extent already begun our long game of invasion planning at this time, and while my preparations did not include the raising of an army, it was perhaps inevitable that his suspicions be aroused. As gently as I could, I declined his increasingly determined offers of assistance (aimed, of course, at discovering my plans), for I knew he was prompted only by friendship. But while I sought to allay his fears concerning my intent, I would not, for all his urging, tell him more.

It was, of course, impossible to hold everything a secret. The women of Khababasha's household learned, doubtless from the women of mine, that I planned to travel with no more than three companions, a valet and two men-at-arms. If anything, this information disturbed Khababasha more profoundly than his fear that I might head an army. For, locked as he was within a single caravan of thought, he suspected I must plan to murder Artaxerxes. Although I did nothing to foster this delusion, I did little to rid him of it, either. But then I had my own concerns, and Khababasha's curiosity ranked low amongst them.

On the matter of my actual departure, I lied to him, fearing interference. He believed my intent was to leave Nubia on a date determined by the next new moon. In fact, I left almost at once, in darkness. At the borders of my former kingdom, the women of the Gegum met me. The witches had their favoured roads and ways of concealment not granted to lesser mortals, so that we moved through the land like ghosts, unsuspected by the Persian pretender, undetected by his legions throughout Egypt.

I beheld many changes in my kingdom—and sorrowed at them. I was full of questions for my Gegum retinue, they being the first of my sisters I had seen since my departure, and I was anxious for news of politics. But they told me little. By contrast, my own observations told me much. I saw the sullen people of a land subdued, far-reaching changes in the social structure, interference with the lawful practice of religion, a diminution of native trade and Persians everywhere, arrogance personified.

There were fewer changes in the Sinai arrowhead. With little in this demon-ridden land to attract the Persians, it was as if the rape had never taken place. Nomad tribes pursued their whims as they had done for generations, leading foul, restricted lives of small importance and great hardship. The Hebrew god of thunder still muttered darkly on his mountaintop. And the eternal Gegum schemed and plotted in their granite convent.

No snow this time but biting cold and a hard journey. I sighed in gratitude to unnamed gods the day we reached the brooding keep.

My men were spirited from me. Alone with the sisters, I experienced a profound change in my welcome. On the first occasion, I had been feted as Pharaoh: warmed, bathed, perfumed, fed and serviced like a stag in rut—all (as I now realise) aimed towards manipulation and control. On this, my second visit, no longer Pharaoh, no longer of importance in the eyes of the outside world, I was greeted like a lover, with gifts of tender affection and an instinctive recognition of my needs. But there was no formality, no pretence of awe, no innuendo, no games designed to set my mind as others wished it set. I prepared my own bath and that of a sister, Jaennah, who was among the escort of the journey, and we enjoyed a profound intimacy, without, however, making love. I felt, as I had not felt before, responsibility for myself and for my fate. I was like one who, having wandered far afield, had now come home.

I wished to see her at once, but the sisters dissuaded me, insisting that I rest first, assuring me that she would await me on the morrow and required nothing of me now, so soon after so rigorous a journey. There was substantial wisdom in their words, for when I saw her on the morrow I was shocked and, in my exhaustion of the previous day, might well have shown it.

She received me in her private chamber, the first and only occasion I had entered it. I had expected a Spartan room, but it was not. On the instant, my eyes absorbed the interests of a lifetime, a jumble of scrolls, of tomes, of tablets (some seeming ancient beyond reckoning), of alchemical equipment, of exotic weaponry, of plants and herbs. Aye, and of items like the mummified hand and the grotesque waxen image, which spoke of her darker side.

And among it all, the spider at the centre of her web, propped by cushions in the vastness of a great bed, Lipta, Gegum Abbess. She could have weighed no more than sixty pounds. Her skin, translucent, stretched like yellowed parchment across the skeletal structure of her withered frame. She had shrunken. Devoid of the abba (for she now wore a simple white night garment) she seemed no larger than a child. I was reminded, horribly, of the tiny, naked, leather corpse of the first abbess propped in its corner of the catacombs, staring blindly into the eternal moment. But for all this, the wolf-like menace had not completely left her eyes.

"Abbess," I said formally from the doorway.

The death's-head turned towards me. "Is that you, Nectanebo?" Her voice was like the rustle of dried leaves.

"It is I, Lipta." I felt my Gegum companion take her silent leave, and the door of the chamber closed quietly behind me.

An emaciated hand rose up to beckon. "Come closer, Nectanebo. I cannot see you there." I moved quickly to her side and knelt.

"I am here, Mother." Impulsively I took her hand. But she withdrew it almost at once and, though the term I had used was no more than a courtesy within the order, said, "'Mother,' is it? When was I mother to you, Nectanebo?"

For an instant I thought the old hand might flick out to touch me with genital intimacy, but in the event it did not. I declined the challenge and the game, saying only, "You look well, Lipta."

The thin lips drew back in what might have been a smile of pleasure . . . or amusement. "Do you think so, Nectanebo? Do you really think so?" I nodded, silently. The smile vanished. "Then you are a fool, Pharaoh. Or blind. I have never looked worse. It is the result of dying."

I began to mouth some futile reassurance, as people do in such circumstances, but she sighed and lay back and stared at the inlaid slabs of the ceiling and eventually waved me into silence. "I am dying, Nectanebo!" she said sharply, her voice no longer the sound of rustling leaves. "I would not have asked you to come here if I were not dying: I have a great many better things to do."

I swallowed a smile of my own and said, "I am here, Abbess."

"Dutifully," Lipta scowled. She relaxed again against her pillows, allowing her eyelids to droop, as if the exchange had exhausted her. "Tell me of your life in exile."

I shrugged. "I am comfortable. But I am not Pharaoh."

"No, not Pharaoh, but perhaps—" She stopped, hesitant, then went on, obviously travelling a different road. "Nubia: is the country ripe for a convent?"

I stared at her. Was she truly asking my opinion on the establishment of a Gegum order in Nubia? Or was she simply ensuring I should never suspect one secretly existed there already? In any case, the only truthful answer I could give was that I did not know. How could I determine what conditions were necessary for the establishment of Gegum in a country?

If she was disappointed in my answer, she did not show it. Indeed, I had the impression that her attention wandered, as if age had at long last taken its toll of that fine mind. "And you, Nectanebo," she said, her voice again perceptibly weaker. "Are you in good health? Are you well? Do you miss your sisters?"

Cautiously I nodded, more suspicious of this line of questioning than if she had offered me wine from a jar marked POISON. I took a deep breath. "I want to thank you, Lipta, for what you did—" I had, of course, long since conveyed my appreciation of the help given in spiriting me out of Egypt, but this was the first opportunity to express thanks face-to-face.

She waved it away, before even the sentence was complete. "No need for gratitude between such as you and I," she told me sharply, and I felt the truth of her words and the intimacy they conveyed.

We sat in silence for a time then. Eventually, her voice having dropped to a whisper, she said, "Have I truly aided you, Nectanebo?"

"I should not have escaped Egypt without your help," I told her stoutly, thinking she referred to my earlier words.

But the death's-head slowly shook from side to side, as if this was only part of what she meant. "But in other ways, Nectanebo. Have I not aided you in other ways, more personal?"

"You have, Lipta," I assured her, meaning my words, but wondering the while where the convolutions of her inner logic took her.

She turned towards me with the air of one who has come to a decision. "I wish a boon of you, Nectanebo," she said firmly. "I wish to be buried in your tomb."

My jaw dropped. At the time, I had no tomb. Work on my monument at Luxor had been abandoned on my flight and the structure later destroyed by Artaxerxes. And the days in which Khababasha negotiated for my tomb in Egypt still lay far into the future. But in my surprise at her words, none of this impinged on me, so that I only asked foolishly, "But where then shall I be buried?"

"Not instead of you!" Lipta snapped. "Alongside of you."

"Alongside of me?"

"Are you deaf as well as stupid, Nectanebo? Must you echo every word like a macaw? Alongside you! Alongside you! I wish to lie with you in death!"

"Lie with—?" I began, then halted dumbfounded as the weight of her words eventually caused the collapse of my disbelief. I stared at this shrunken creature on the bed, this wasted vessel which still somehow held a soul so large it filled my life. Quietly, I said, "You shall lie with me in death, Lipta, if that is your wish."

"Your word on it, Nectanebo? Your word? This is important for my vision, for our resurrection."

"Abbess, I have not now a tomb, but when it is constructed, there shall be a twin sarcophagus for you: my word on it."

Then there occurred that which I was to remember to the end of my life and beyond. The wizened husk of Lipta pushed away the bedclothes, swung feet onto the floor and stood. I jumped to my feet and reached instinctively to steady her, but she brushed my hand away and reached for me in a lover's embrace, kissing me with passion on the mouth.

I held her then, fragile as an insect's wing, fearful that the frail old body might snap like sun-dried twigs should I draw it too closely to me. And in that moment, I saw beyond the delicate, translucent veil of matter, beyond the world of seeming and appearance, beyond the death's-head and the husk, and knew that I loved her, knew that I had always loved her.

FORTY-FIVE

J anet awoke to a curious buzzing sound. It took her a few sleepy moments to realise it was the phone beside her bed.

"Don Wright," the voice said cheerfully. "Did I wake you?"

She glanced at the bedside clock. Its digital readout showed it was almost nine o'clock. "No," she lied, fighting to put a little force into her voice, "not at all."

"Good," he said cheerfully. "Mrs. Webb presents her compliments and was wondering if you'd like to join her for breakfast in the botanical gardens. You haven't eaten already, have you?" he added as an anxious afterthought.

"No," Janet said again, truthfully this time. "Where are the botanical gardens?"

"I'll send someone round to pick you up. Fifteen minutes okay?"

"Make it half an hour," Janet said. It would give her time to shower.

The botanical gardens were spectacular, an immense dome with covered tunnels that seemed to stretch forever. Her driver, a much more taciturn young man than Joachim, her earlier driver, keyed in a security code at the entrance and led her to a small pavilion where Harriet was already at an outdoor table laid for breakfast.

"Sleep well?" she asked as Janet approached.

"Very. You?"

Harriet shrugged. "Off and on. It's my usual pattern these days. They tell me it's an overactive mind, but I think I'm a bit too young for sleeping pills, so I put up with it. Orange juice?"

"Thanks," Janet said as she sat down. Beyond the pavilion was a veritable jungle of exotic plants stretching as far as the eye could see. Although she was no expert, one immense drooping purple flower looked suspiciously like something she'd admired once in South Africa. The temperature in the dome was just as high as outside, but the air felt fresher somehow. "What is this place?"

"You know the station's devoted to the development of arid-environment food crops—the secret project everybody knows about in town?"

Janet smiled lightly. "Yes."

"This facility is our development stock. You probably got the impression of one dome when you came in, but in fact there are seven. The link tunnels have air locks so each dome can maintain its own controlled environment ideal for the particular vegetation. We grow more stuff in the tunnels themselves. There are plants from all over the world here, literally from every continent. We play around with all sorts of factors to see if we can persuade them to grow better. Have you noticed how fresh it feels in here despite the heat?"

"I did, as a matter of fact."

"That's because the air is charged with negative ions. We do it electrically here. In nature, they're generated by running water and thunderstorms. For some reason, they make people feel better—that's why it's so nice to picnic by a waterfall and why you always feel such a sense of relief after a storm. But they aid plant growth as well, which is the real point. I usually breakfast here when I'm visiting—it's like getting a shot of vitamins."

Janet finished her juice and reached for the coffeepot. "The Regis Foundation seems to be involved in some far-out research," she remarked pleasantly.

"You haven't heard the half of it," Harriet smiled.

Harriet worked her way through a breakfast of bacon, egg, sausage, mushroom and tomato. Janet, watching her with a mixture of revulsion and alarm, settled for rolls with her coffee.

On the third refill, Janet said, "I was thinking about what you told me last night, Mrs. Webb—"

"I think you'd better call me Harriet. I've a feeling we might end up being friends."

Janet looked at her, struck by the same feeling. She smiled. "Okay, Harriet. Anyway, I was thinking about what you told me last night, and there's obviously some sort of connection between Luke's psychological state and your discovery of Nectanebo's tomb. Of course Luke wasn't born when that happened, but I was wondering if you made much of the discovery while he was growing up, talked to him about it, showed a high degree of interest, that sort of thing?"

"There's a connection, all right," Harriet said. "I'm not sure I'd call it psychological—at least not the way I think you mean it. But, listen, you need to hear the end of the story I was telling you last night. There's not much more to tell—I sent you to bed because I wanted you fresh to discuss the implications."

"Okay," Janet said again. "You were about to tell me what happened to the mummified remains."

"You know I mentioned that Brian Melville was a crook?"

Janet nodded. "Yes."

"He swore to me in jail he'd intended to play it straight with us on the deal with Nectanebo's artifacts, but I've never believed that. My father's only real interest was in Nectanebo's mummy—"

"I didn't quite understand that," Janet interrupted.

"You will in a minute," Harriet said. "The important point is that Melville undertook to smuggle the remains out of Egypt as part of the deal. It was the only important part so far as my father was concerned. He gave Melville a lot of money so he could do it, a blank check, really: whatever Melville wanted, he got. Except the only thing that seriously interested Melville was the gold. He made real plans to get that out of the country. I know he failed, but that was just bad luck. The idea of getting the artifacts into Israel was sound: he had papers, buyers lined up, everything. The mummies meant nothing to him. They weren't even intact—I told you the state of preservation was poor. They were really only a collection of badly mummified body parts. Melville figured he had enough problems. He decided not to bother with the mummies."

"He left them behind?" Despite herself, Janet felt vaguely shocked.

Harriet shrugged. "I reckon Melville decided to sell the artifacts and disappear, keep the money for himself. Nectanebo's remains were of no interest—he said himself there would be no chance of finding a buyer."

"So what did he do? Just leave them? Destroy them? What?"

"He crated them and sent them to my father by the Egyptian equivalent of Federal Express. He described them on the documentation as 'commercial samples.'"

"You're not serious!" Janet said.

"I think he had some idea that if Dad had his precious mummies, he mightn't make too much of a fuss about the rest of the deal. Dad was the only one who worried Melville, of course, because of his money. Lucas and I were just a couple of kids."

"But wait a minute," Janet broke in. "He can't seriously have expected to send mummies out of Egypt by commercial carrier?"

"I don't suppose he did, really," Harriet said. "I think he just decided to take a long shot. If it came off, great. If it didn't, he lost nothing—he had the valuables, the gold. He must have known how slim the chances were of the consignment's getting through. Have you had any experience of Egyptian bureaucracy?"

Janet shook her head. "No."

"It's a nightmare. They check everything. Papers, contents, everything. That's why you can never get anything done in Egypt. They're all too busy pushing paper around. 'Commercial samples'? He hadn't a prayer! But it got through."

"The shipment? The whole shipment?"

"Crazy, isn't it? Melville dreams up a whole elaborate plan about taking the stuff out via Israel, and he ends up in jail. He virtually posts the remains, and they get through intact. If he'd played it straight and risked packing the gold with them, he'd probably still be alive today, enjoying a prosperous retirement in his old age."

"But Nectanebo's mummy actually reached the United States?"

"Inside five days—can you believe it? I think the war must have been causing problems in the civil service. Anyway, they didn't check. Just stamped the crates and let them through."

"So where's the mummy now?"

"In storage in a hermetically sealed cabinet at one of our facilities in Detroit. I don't have to tell you, very few people know about it."

"But Luke does?"

Harriet dabbed her mouth delicately with a linen napkin and sighed deeply. "Janet, I know you're still looking for a psychological explanation for Luke's condition. Did he develop a childhood interest in the mummy? Is he compensating because his mother took too much of an interest in a dead pharaoh? That sort of thing—right?"

"Something like that," Janet said.

Harriet held her gaze. "Janet, Luke doesn't have an interest in Nectanebo. Luke *is* Nectanebo."

"I appreciate Luke believes himself to be, in a sense, the dead pharaoh, or at least possessed by the—"

"Shut up, Janet," Harriet said without rancour. "Luke doesn't believe he's Nectanebo—he *is* Nectanebo. My father had the pharaoh cloned."

FORTY-SIX

The silence dragged on for an eternity. Eventually, Janet said foolishly, "Cloned?"

"Do you know anything about cloning?" Harriet asked her.

"I know it's illegal. For humans, at any rate."

"It wasn't when we did it. The legislation wasn't in place then."

"I didn't know the technology was in place then, either," Janet said.

Harriet pushed back her chair. "Come on, let's take a walk. You can admire our wonderful gardens while I tell you all about it."

As they walked, Harriet talked.

The official story was that the first successful cloning was carried out in Scotland in 1997—Dolly the sheep. Dolly was a clone of her mother, grown from cells taken from her milk. Born successfully and grew up healthy. When the scientists made the announcement, there was panic in certain quarters. The press whipped up scare stories about armies of cloned soldiers and humans cloned so doctors could harvest their organs for transplant.

The scaremongering led to legislation. The American president at the time was Bill Clinton, who approached the problem cautiously. He didn't ban cloning research outright, but he ringed it round with caveats where the research might involve humans. The more recent, tighter legislation introduced in many countries closed off funding for clone research. Practical problems started showing up as well. Early attempts at commercial animal cloning ran into the brick wall of giantism.

Even Dolly was a problem to her mother at the time of birth: she was a large lamb. The scientists who delivered her scarcely noted the fact. They simply assumed her mother had been a large lamb too. But subsequent attempts at cloning—in sheep, in mice, rats, dogs and, in one ambitious attempt, even a horse—all resulted in the same problem. The cloned offspring were too large. In most cases, they were too large for natural birth and had to be delivered by Caesarean section. Many, unlike Dolly, failed to survive.

"I'm not sure I know how cloning actually works," Janet said.

"The principle's straightforward," Harriet told her. "At the cellular level, your body's holistic. Any cell from any part contains the DNA necessary to replicate the whole. The trick is to take a body cell and persuade it to behave like a reproductive cell—to split and keep growing until it turns into an embryo. We can do that now through genetic engineering."

It seemed the Regis Foundation had been able to pull off the trick far earlier than anybody else. Harriet's father, Stanislav Regis, had been fascinated by the theory of cloning and poured more money into its research than almost any other aspect of his far-flung scientific empire. But with a fine-honed instinct for self-preservation, he had kept the research secret.

"If the press ever get hold of it," he once told Harriet in an impressive anticipation of what eventually happened, "they will turn it into Frankenstein. This will panic the politicians, and they will introduce so much red tape it will be impossible to carry out proper research anymore."

By the mid-seventies, Foundation scientists had not only cloned animals—including a chimpanzee and an orangutan—but had solved the problem of giantism. Regis clones were viable, almost routine. Stanislav Regis began pushing his team hard to take the next logical step.

"He wanted them to clone a human being?" Janet asked.

"That's exactly what he wanted," Harriet said. "But typical of my father, he didn't want to clone just anybody. He was fascinated by the idea of bringing back the dead to life."

Janet stared at her. "Are you telling me what I think you're telling me? He wanted to use cells taken from a corpse? Would that work?"

"Nobody knew," Harriet said.

Despite herself, Janet smiled. "No wonder he thought the press would call it Frankenstein technology."

Harriet smiled back. "It was worse than you think. This wasn't just a question of harvesting a few cells an hour or two after somebody has passed away. My father believed it might be possible to bring back the ancient dead."

At the time, Stanislav had been thinking about the bog burials of Scandinavia, but later it occurred to him that the Egyptians, with their extraordinary mummification techniques, might have preserved enough of the cellular structure to allow cloning to take place.

He discussed the possibility with the head of his scientific team, who suggested an experiment. They arranged for the purchase of a mummified cat. A year later, the man walked into Stanislav's office carrying a basket tied with blue ribbon. Inside was a kitten.

"A kitten?"

Harriet nodded. "It lived eight years, then got knocked down by a car."

After a long moment, Janet said, "And then he tried it with cells from Nectanebo's mummified body parts?" She had a crazy desire to giggle. It was B-movie science fiction.

"Yes," Harriet said soberly.

After another long moment, Janet said, "You'll have to forgive me. I really know absolutely nothing about cloning. The cells . . . when you persuade them to begin the reproductive process . . . you grow the embryo how? In some sort of test tube?"

Harriet said, "You grow it in a womb."

FORTY-SEVEN

At the time, Harriet had a modest apartment on New York's east side. It was less than she could afford, but she was in revolt against the Regis opulence, and the place was a political statement as much as somewhere to live. It irritated her enormously that her father didn't seem to mind.

One evening when she invited him for dinner, he arrived promptly on the stroke of seven, shook the snow from his hat and kissed her fondly. She noticed he'd left his bodyguards behind, although they were no further away than the limo outside.

It was several weeks since they'd seen each other, and she heard herself say, "You're looking a bit pale, Daddy—are you feeling all right?" She tried to bite her tongue as soon as she'd said it. She'd made a New Year's resolution to stop mothering him.

But Stanislav failed to notice. "It is the cold," he said. "It pinches the cheeks." He handed her a bottle wrapped, for some reason, in silver foil. "This is to save us from that dreadful supermarket wine you buy. I know it makes a point about something or other, but, frankly, I'm too old to care. Is red all right? You were not planning to feed me fish?"

Harriet shook her head. All his life her father had been a red meat man. Lately his doctors had been worried about his cholesterol levels and suggested he eat more chicken, but he'd ignored them.

"What are you cooking? This weather calls for T-bone."

"Spaghetti Bolognese," Harriet told him shortly. "But I've made you a bread pudding for dessert."

"How exotic," Stanislav remarked. But she knew he was neither disappointed nor displeased. He enjoyed Italian food and bread pudding, made the Latvian way with too much sugar and an abundance of cinnamon; it had been a favourite from childhood.

The wine, when she unwrapped it, proved to be a reserve Margaux, which wouldn't have been her first choice with spaghetti but was probably far more drinkable than her first choice would have been. She pulled the cork and set it on the radiator to warm, making sure he didn't see what she was doing. Then she went back to the stove to check the Bolognese.

The door to the kitchen was open so he could talk to her from his favourite perch in her only easy chair.

"Are you still going out with that peculiar young man?" he asked.

"Which peculiar young man?" Harriet dipped a wooden spoon and tasted. "Frederick? Or do you still think it's Gareth?"

"How should I know?" her father shrugged. "They all look like Hitler Youth. I'm amazed you can tell one from the other. Which was the one with the nervous knee and the sports car?"

"That was Gareth. I stopped seeing him months ago."

"Who is this Frederick person? Do you have a serious relationship?"

"I doubt it," Harriet said. "I finished with him last night."

"Ah," said her father. For some reason, even though he obviously couldn't remember his single meeting with Frederick, she had the feeling he was pleased.

He returned to the theme as he finished his spaghetti, mopping the sauce from his plate with a round of garlic bread. "Have you ever considered settling down with any of these Hitler Jungen?"

"No," Harriet said.

"You are not getting any younger."

"Nobody is," Harriet told him, grinning.

"Do not you like them, any of them?"

"Not especially."

"You sleep with them." It was neither a question nor an accusation, just a statement.

"That's not the same thing," Harriet told him.

"Have you no dreams of beginning a family? I thought all women dreamed of having children."

Harriet elected to take the question seriously. "Yes, I do want children. Or a child. I'm not sure how many—I think I'll make up my mind about that when I've had the first one. But my problem is, I don't want a permanent man in my life, and that seems to go with the territory if you're planning a family."

"I have a proposition for you," Stanislav said.

FORTY-EIGHT

They had come full circle back to the pavilion. Janet said, "Would you mind terribly if I sat down?" She sat and looked up at Harriet. "Are you saying your father asked you to . . . ?"

Harriet looked down at her, waiting.

". . . asked you to carry something . . . grown from a two-thousand-year-old mummy?"

"You make it sound like mould," Harriet said. She shrugged lightly. "It was entirely logical. My father needed a healthy womb, but even more than that, he needed a woman he could trust. Can you imagine the opportunities for blackmail in that sort of situation? Once you start to think of it, I was an obvious choice."

"And what did you say?"

"You know what I said." Harriet pulled out a chair for herself. The breakfast things had been tidied away, but there was a bowl of fruit on the table now, and she helped herself to a plum. "Actually, I didn't even hesitate. Remember how young I was. I was heavily into do-your-own-thing and revolt against authority. This was the seventies, for God's sake! Women were striking out. Here was a chance to have a child out of wedlock, without any interference from a man, without any involvement from a man, a child who would be absolutely unique, the very first of its kind in the whole history of humanity—"

"And a rare chance to put your father in your power," Janet murmured thoughtfully.

"Perceptive!" Harriet grinned. "I have to say in my own defense that I didn't think of that at the time, but I'm sure it was a factor. You put all that together, and do you really think I would hesitate?"

"Was there any risk?"

"No more than with a normal pregnancy, so my father assured me."

"What about the giantism?"

"We'd solved that—I told you."

There was silence, then Janet murmured, "I don't know what to say."

Harriet said, "It was a model pregnancy. I had the best specialists in the world, of course, but to tell the truth, they weren't needed. Labour lasted less than two hours, and he popped out grinning." She smiled. "He had lovely eyes."

After a moment, Janet said, "I'm stunned by all this." As an afterthought, she added, "I don't know what you want me to do."

Harriet said, "I want you to go with him to Egypt."

Book Four: Destiny

The Chronicles of
Nectanebo: Sixteen

My resurrection was much different than what I had expected. Where was the golden barge of Ra? Where was the jackal-headed Anubis? Where the stately, copper-skinned Osiris who would place my heart upon the scales? I had been taught that I would meet these beings after death, yet I did not. Nor did I fly to join the circumpolar stars.

This is not to dismiss the tenets of religion or deny the wisdom of the priests. The magical arts of divination, khemeia and herbal healing lore, while greatly exaggerated by the general populace, were real enough. But in the matter of death and the afterlife, the priests erred greatly.

I do not think our Egyptian sages were alone in their mistakes. In the days of my glory, because such matters interested me, I spoke of life, death and the afterlife with wise men from many distant lands. Most agreed that individuals (at least great and powerful individuals like a pharaoh) survived the fact of physical demise, although outside of Egypt, Anubis declined to guide the soul and Osiris naturally refused to judge it.

In truth, many races had only the most rudimentary ideas about what the afterlife might be like. The Hebrews talked about a listless underworld without colour or form where weak and mighty alike endured a shadowy existence. Even the Romans, so sensible in many matters, seemed confused about what happened after death. They too had an underworld, but in true Roman fashion, there was nothing shadowy about it. There were even rumours one could go there and come back, although I never met anyone who actually did so.

I might go on at length about the various stories I heard from various peoples, some in outright contradiction of the others, none bearing any resemblance whatsoever to Egyptian doctrine, and all presented to me as truth. But it is enough to say that none forewarned me of the post-mortem experience that did, in fact, become my lot.

One came closer than the rest: a sloe-eyed Hindu who told me of a process called reincarnation, widely accepted by his countrymen. But I did not reincarnate, except in the most pedantic sense. There was no passage through the portal of a womb—animal, avian, insectile or human. I died, yet I endured. There were flickerings, like dreams, passing glimpses of a world bewildering and strange, old memories returned, then suddenly full consciousness. That was the essence of it and the mystery.

My first, near-overwhelming sensation was of my revitalised body with its lean, firm musculature, its lush growth of dark hair, its strength and its vitality.

I cannot begin to express what the possession of such a body meant to me. In youth (by which I mean that span of life before my forty-fifth year), I had always taken the efficient working of my body for granted: a law of nature, almost, like the rising of the sun. Nothing threatened me.

With middle age, this attitude began to change. I would awake to find my back pained for no great reason, or that a finger joint had swollen or a small buzzing developed in one ear. These problems were never serious, never crippling, but they recurred, and sometimes they remained as discomforts that became permanent aspects of my life.

At about this time, my hair began to grey and thin, my stamina lessen (only slightly, so very slightly, but progressively). My senses were less sharp, so that food no longer tasted quite so fine unless spiced with piquant sauce. Because these changes were gradual, they were accepted without thought, creating a totality that emerged virtually unnoticed. There is no mystery about what was happening. I was, without realising it, leaving youth behind.

Old age—for I lived a long time—was much worse. There is no joy in growing old. The bladder weakens, so that more and more energy is expended on self-control. The bowel does not function—or functions far too well. Food loses almost all of its former appeal, for the stomach no longer accepts the piquant sauces without complaint. One moves slowly and grows clumsy. There is always pain somewhere: in the hip, in the back, in the knee, in the fingers. A good day is when it lessens, not when it disappears, for it no longer disappears.

I lived so long that I came to forget how a fully functioning, pain-free body once felt. The wizened, wasted, feeble, trembling, smelly corpse that eventually succumbed to jaundice became, in my mind, all I was and all I had ever been. Thus the experience of my resurrection was like a thunderclap.

I poked and prodded and pinched myself like a child or one whose wits are addled. I blinked and giggled and smiled and stretched—oh, how I stretched, luxuriating in the sensation of movement without pain. But it is the nature of man that he becomes accustomed quickly even to a miracle, so that my attention was eventually directed outwards into my environment.

And therein I discovered I was in deadly danger.

FORTY-NINE

"I wish my father were still alive," Harriet said. "He could discuss this with you far better than I can."

They had returned to Janet's villa, but Harriet was in the kitchen making more coffee for them both. Janet, seated on a stool by the breakfast bar, was content to let her. She was feeling overwhelmed. But beneath the churning confusion was a star point of pure excitement. No psychologist in history had ever had an opportunity like this.

"I expect I'd just have irritated him. I can't get my mind around it at all."

"I don't blame you," Harriet said kindly. "I've lived with this for thirty years, and it still scares me silly sometimes. I mean the sheer . . . magnitude of what we did. My father always had an arrogant streak. He probably knew what he was doing. But I walked into it like some kid dancing through the daisies. I had my head so far up my ass it was coming out my mouth. All I could think of was I could have a baby without a father. It never occurred to me that Luke's father was some old Egyptian who's been dead for two thousand years. God, it's such a relief to talk freely to somebody about this!"

"Yes, I expect it is," Janet said.

Harriet poured two cups of coffee and sat down beside Janet. They looked like two friends planning a shopping spree, or possibly even a mother and daughter who'd gotten together to find out why the daughter hasn't married yet. But then Janet spoke again, and the illusion shattered. "What about his early life?"

"You mean growing up? As a child?"

"Yes."

Harriet glanced into the middle distance and released a deep breath. "He was normal. What can I tell you? He was a perfectly normal baby, colic, woke up in the night, cried when he was teething. He was a perfectly normal little kid—"

"You brought him up—?" Janet hesitated, frowning, wondering how to put what she wanted to say.

Harriet helped her out. "My father and I agreed he was to have exactly the sort of upbringing he'd have had if he'd been my natural child. Little League, high school, college if he was smart enough. Give him a baseball mitt for his birthday, all-American upbringing, probably spoil him a little, bearing in mind his family was obscenely rich."

"You didn't tell him he was . . . ?"

"Cloned? Good God, no!"

"Don't you think you should have?" Janet ventured.

"Don't be stupid," Harriet said.

Janet let it go. "He never showed any . . . how shall I put this . . . ?"

"Let's agree you can ask anything you want, as plainly as you want. If you're going to help Luke, you need to have the information. I'm not going to take offence, and if I do, that's my problem, okay?"

"Okay," Janet agreed. "I was wondering if he showed any signs of oddness when he was a child, any indication that he wasn't, you know, just your average youngster."

"He was studious," Harriet said. "Even from an early age he was a bit of a nerd. But that's personality, isn't it? I mean there are lots of American kids who are nerds. I expect you have them in Great Britain."

Janet smiled slightly. "I was thinking more of anything that would have made you stop short and wonder if it came from his being cloned or his being Egyptian or his . . . you know . . ."

"Nothing. Not really. You probably didn't even notice, but his skin has a very slight reddish cast, but that could have come from Native American blood somewhere in his background if he'd been my natural child. The same goes for his eyes."

"Anything in his psychology . . . ?"

"Not until now," Harriet said.

Janet took a long drink from her cup, then set it down decisively. "Let's talk about now," she said.

Harriet said, "The change was recent—just a few months. Before that, he was a serious young man who worked to help his grandfather—" She stopped, smiled. "We always referred to Stanislav as his grandfather. Luke loved him, and it was mutual. The only bone of contention was the Foundation. Luke was a whiz as an executive, and as my father got older, he took on more and more. Stanislav liked that—it freed him up to irritate his research scientists. It was quite clear that Luke should take over the Foundation when Stanislav died. Especially since I didn't have the slightest interest. But my father was wary about leaving it to him."

"Because of . . . ?"

Harriet nodded. "I don't think my father ever really trusted Luke. Maybe he was afraid of something happening. I don't know. The thing was, for years his will was made out in my favour, leaving me control of the Foundation, and sometime before his death, a year, two years, more—I'm not sure—he had the lawyers insert a clause forbidding me to hand it over to Luke."

"Would you have?"

"Yes. My father knew me very well in that respect. I've never had any interest in the Foundation. I always thought running it would be a millstone."

"Is it?"

"By and large. There are a few compensations, but I'd break that clause like a shot if my lawyers could find a way to do it. At least, I would have if Luke were still . . . you know, Luke. As it is, I've left the day-by-day running of the Foundation to him. He might as well own it."

"You'd better tell me what exactly happened. When he changed."

"I don't know what exactly happened!" Harriet snapped. "Oh, I'm sorry. There's not much I can tell you. I think Luke started to have flash-backs—fragments of memory, little glimpses of his . . . well, of his life in Egypt."

"How is that possible?" Janet asked. "Memories are stored in the brain. The brain he had before he died. You can't restore that by cloning."

"Christ, I only wish I knew," said Harriet.

The Chronicles of
Nectanebo: Seventeen

Of all the mysteries that attended my resurrection, this was the
strangest: Nectanebo risen was no longer Nectanebo alone.

As I came to consciousness, I realised that my mind was shared. I
had the familiar awareness of my self, my thoughts, my memories and
emotions, but there was something else besides. Any introspective man
will find that the kernel of his soul stands within a sort of inner space,
sometimes floating in darkness, sometimes illuminated by the transient
structures of imagination. But apart from artifacts of his own creation,
he is alone therein—or at least such has always been my experience.

But now another stood beside me.

He was male and carried in his spirit the attitudes of power. He was
complete in himself. I did not see but, rather, sensed him, yet I had no
doubt of his reality. He was a stranger to me, as alien in his thoughts and
knowledge as a scarab beetle.

At first I thought him a demon or some other denizen of the nether-
world. The Gegum had long taught me the mind is not a closed system,
whatever the ignorant believe. It allows for intrusions. These arise most
often in dreams when natural defenses are relaxed but may occur at any
time in visions, impressions, intuitions or similar pressures from beyond.
The gods, of course, have power to walk within men's minds whensoever
they choose but choose seldom since the cramped confines are inimical
to them. But lesser beings, accustomed only to foul hells, will sometimes
seek to take permanent possession of a man's inner domain.

Unless by invitation—and there have always been those who will
sell space in their souls in return for demonic favours—such possession
is possible only when the defenses are weakened through illness or infir-
mity or by means of magical attack. Was I now possessed? Certainly I

had passed but lately through the portal of death. Could there be any greater weakening of the natural defenses than that?

But then I looked closer and realised this creature was no demon. While the mental disciplines developed by the Gegum enabled me to shield my thoughts from him, he was in no way able to hide himself from me. With a simple effort, I became aware of his memories, his current thoughts, his immediate concerns. Above all, I knew the smell of his fear, which all but devoured him at this time.

For a while I was simply puzzled, then gradually the truth dawned. He was not something that possessed my mind, but, rather, I was something that possessed his. He was the soul who had grown with this body, who had matured in the experience of this world. I was the interloper.

With the realisation came a moral dilemma as bizarre as it was unexpected. Should I abandon the body I had somehow invaded? I knew not how, short of destroying the body itself, which seemed a paradox of such dimensions I doubted even the Gegum could have stomached it. Should I then share? I was not such a fool as to believe the palace of the flesh could long endure two masters, for when do the desires of two people always and ever coincide? In multiplicity lies madness.

Thus it seemed to me that I had little option but to destroy the spirit that held this body, as I once destroyed Tachos when he held the throne of Egypt . Only in this way could I claim it for my own.

FIFTY

They spent the morning together, then had a buffet lunch in a private room at one of the facility's two restaurants.

"Given what you've told me," Janet said, "I'm surprised your son isn't in more trouble than he is."

"What's that mean?" Harriet asked her.

"Try to imagine what it must be like to grow up as a normal boy, grow into a man, then suddenly have that flooding of memories."

"We may learn more about that before long," Harriet said.

Something in her tone or her body language alerted Janet immediately. "What haven't you told me?"

The Chronicles of Nectanebo: Eighteen

He was a creature of mind-stuff, real as my own thoughts, distinct from me, yet sharing my soul. His name, I divined, was Luke Webb. Thus I reached out with my mind and began to disassemble the very elements of his being.

I am Nectanebo. I was Pharaoh in Egypt, priestly trained and Gegum nurtured with a lifetime of experience in the mystic arts. The boy was no match for me. He collapsed beneath my attack with no more than a token resistance. I felt his consciousness dim.

But as I did so, a chilling realisation dawned. As the consciousness of Luke Webb waned, I experienced a profound change in my own perceptions. While the world of my resurrection presented itself to my awakened senses as vividly as it had done before, I found I could no longer understand it. Even the cramped confines of my chamber presented me with a multitude of mysteries. Structures became unfamiliar, artifacts a bewilderment. I could no longer understand the language of my guards.

As this unwelcome phenomenon increased, I came to realise I had somehow been using Luke Webb's consciousness to make sense of my new environment. The realm of my resurrection was his world, not mine. Without his experience and knowledge, I was as helpless in it as a newborn babe.

At once I ceased my attack. For a moment it seemed I was too late, for the consciousness of Luke Webb continued to diminish. But then he rallied, although I felt the fear of me that welled up in his soul. I placed him in a mental cage to prevent his interfering with my plans, then fed him a little of my own essence to calm him. He responded at once, and I was rewarded with a return to my former level of understanding.

It was only just in time. My guards came for me then. I knew at once they meant to kill me.

FIFTY-ONE

The formal meeting took place in Harriet's office later in the day. Don Wright escorted Janet there but left after a few pleasantries. With Harriet in the office was the young man Bernstein whom Janet had met, briefly, the day before. Luke Webb was not present.

"Bernstein's my lawyer as well as my lover," Harriet said without preamble. "I want him here to formalise any agreement we may work out between us. But that's all he'll do. We're doing the negotiating."

"I see," said Janet, who saw nothing of the sort. She wondered if Bernstein knew the whole story of Luke Webb or whether they would have to tiptoe round its more delicate aspects.

"Bernstein knows all about Luke," Harriet said as if reading her mind. "I only threw him out yesterday so he wouldn't cramp your style: I thought you'd have problems enough taking it all in without having to cope with an audience."

Janet glanced at Bernstein, who smiled. He looked young enough to be Luke's brother.

"I have to tell you that while he knows everything, he doesn't necessarily believe everything," Harriet added. "But that doesn't stop him being a good lawyer, which is all I need from him today. I don't give a damn if he thinks you're deluded and I'm nuts."

"I'd never dream of thinking either," Bernstein said pleasantly. "I'm not sure I'd dare."

"Specifically," Harriet said, "Bernstein knows Luke is a clone, so we don't have to pussyfoot. I'd suggest we pretend he isn't here until we need him."

"Story of my life," Bernstein grinned. He looked over at Harriet, and Janet realised suddenly that he adored her. It was probably just as well. Harriet was trusting him with an awful lot of dangerous information.

267

But then again, Harriet had trusted Janet with the same information. She obviously made up her own mind about whom she could trust.

"Janet," Harriet said, "I'd like to cut to the chase. What's your feeling on the offer I made you this morning?"

Janet blinked. "I wasn't aware you'd made me one. Or are you referring to my working for the Regis Foundation?"

Harriet said. "I wasn't talking about you working for Regis—at least, I was, but obviously not the sort of deal that was presented to get you over here. You didn't know what was involved then. You do now. Let me spell it out. Luke wants to go back to Egypt. I don't know if this is a good thing or a bad thing." She hesitated. "Do you?"

Caught off guard, Janet sat and looked at her. Then she said, "I don't know either. It might help with the integration process. On the other hand, Egypt today is nothing like the Egypt he remembers. He might find the changes . . . disturbing."

"Yes, that's what I thought. On the other hand, it might help him adjust."

"Possibly," Janet said. She took a deep breath. "Harriet, what do you propose to do with Luke?"

Harriet glanced away. "I'm not sure I follow you."

"You created this clone," Janet said bluntly. "It's a clone of an Egyptian pharaoh that was brought up as a modern American, and now, suddenly, it's recovered its memories of Egypt. What are you going to do with it?"

"First of all," Harriet said, "if you ever refer to my son again as 'it,' you are going to find out why I scare the pants off Don Wright and the rest of the boys."

"I'm sorry," Janet said at once. "That was stupid of me. And thoughtless. I just wanted to bring home the situation as I see it, but I do apologise. Nonetheless, my question still stands."

"Well," Harriet said, "let me put it this way. First, I didn't clone Nectanebo. My father did that. I only facilitated the procedure with the loan of a womb—probably for all the wrong motives. But you know something? Carrying him got me kind of involved." She leaned forward. "I went into labour with that child. I gave birth to him. You can't do that and still think of him as an experiment. Tell you the truth, I've always had trouble thinking of him as an Egyptian. All the time he was growing up, none of that mattered. Luke was my son. It's only become a problem now that he's recovered his memories—something we never dreamed could happen. But to answer your question, I'm not going to do anything with him, Janet. Luke, or Nectanebo, is my flesh and blood—or might as well be. The only thing I plan to do is help him make his way in the world. That's what this meeting's all about."

"Are you saying you're going to let him make his own decisions?"

"You don't get it, do you?" Harriet shook her head. "Luke may be the strangest human being on the face of the planet, but he's still a human being. Getting cloned doesn't change that. What's his legal status, Bernstein?"

Bernstein shrugged. "God knows what would happen if the news ever got out—they might rush through all sorts of legislation. But as things stand at the moment, the law doesn't recognise a clone in any way whatsoever, not in this country, not in any other I know of. He came out of a womb like the rest of us. There's nothing on the statute books to say he's legally any different from the rest of us. He's over eighteen. He's got the vote. He's a consenting adult. If there were a war on, they could probably draft him." The easy smile came back again. "He's also rich. That tends to confer a special status in this country."

In Britain, too, Janet thought. Only the poor went mad. The middle class became neurotic, and the aristocracy were eccentric.

Harriet said, "Are you hearing this? Even if I wanted to, I couldn't tell him what to do."

Bernstein coughed. "One delicate point. Is Luke any longer legally responsible for his own actions? In short, is he nutty as a fruitcake?"

Harriet turned to Janet and said, "That's your department, Doctor. Is my boy insane?"

269

Janet looked from one to the other, feeling suddenly trapped. She took a deep breath. "When I saw Luke, I thought he was. Insanity's a very imprecise term, and I don't like using it, but I certainly thought he was mentally ill. I told you as much, Harriet."

"And now?"

"And now," Janet said, "after what you've told me . . ." She thought about it. "I have absolutely nothing to help me make a diagnosis. I've no idea what's normal for a clone. I don't know if it's normal for Luke to have recovered his original memories. I don't know if it's normal for him to manifest his original personality. Nobody does. From what you've told me, he's a world first. This is virgin territory from beginning to end. In a hundred years' time we'll find out what's normal by comparing the experiences and responses of other clones and noting a statistical consensus—if there are any other clones in the next hundred years. For now, the only thing I have to go on is how he appears to be functioning in the real world."

"How does he appear to be functioning, Janet?" Harriet pressed her. "In your professional opinion?"

Janet knew what she was supposed to say, what Harriet wanted her to say. She looked Harriet in the eye and said it: "He appears to be functioning well, given the circumstances."

Harriet glanced at Bernstein, then said, "Thank you. I appreciate your honesty."

But Janet had no intention of letting her off the hook that easily. "There is one problem . . . the business with Dr. Schaeffer. Luke attacked him violently."

"Luke attacked him," Harriet admitted. "I never said he attacked him violently."

"You said he nearly killed him. That's violent enough for me."

Harriet said patiently, "Dr. Schaeffer had a heart condition. A fairly serious one by all accounts. Luke wasn't aware of it. The situation as I understand it was that Luke got upset and wanted to end the interview.

Schaeffer refused. Luke tried to walk away, and Schaeffer made the mistake of trying to restrain him physically. Luke pushed him, Schaeffer stumbled, struck his hip against a desk and had a heart attack. You can hardly turn an incident like that into a federal case, can you?" She leaned forward. "Janet, Dr. Schaeffer didn't even sue."

Janet found she was breathing heavily, which was a bad sign. "You can get as sophisticated about this as you like, but the bottom line is you have a son who now believes himself to be an Egyptian pharaoh—"

"To have been an Egyptian pharaoh," Harriet said. "There's a difference. Especially when it was true."

"All right, to have been an Egyptian pharaoh," Janet allowed. Then immediately corrected herself. "No, dammit, he believes he still is! Maybe not a pharaoh, but he's aware of the Nectanebo personality. In fact, he claims the Nectanebo personality is dominant. Or the Nectanebo personality claims it's dominant—Jesus, you can see the problems we're in just talking about it! What I'm trying to say is, it doesn't matter that what he believes is true; it doesn't matter that he really was—in a sense, really is—Nectanebo. Just how well do you think anybody could function in modern America believing he is King of Egypt? Can't you see this? It's like believing you're Napoleon, only worse!"

"He's still Luke," Harriet said. "He still has all of Luke's memories and experience to call on. When I talk to him, I can still see Luke in him. It's not like some horror movie where they revive the mummy and it doesn't know how to work a light switch."

Janet sighed. "All right. You said you had a proposition for me, Harriet. What is it?"

Harriet licked her lips. "Luke wants to go to Egypt. He wants to visit places he knew. He wants to do some research, study surviving texts. He wants you to go with him. My proposition is simple. You can name your own terms. The Foundation will pay whatever you want." She looked long and hard at Janet. "What do you say?"

It was more or less what Janet had been expecting. But if she went to Egypt with Luke Webb, it was only a matter of time before she slept with him. That frightened her. "I'm sorry," she told Harriet. "I'm afraid the answer's no."

Harriet said, "Can I ask you why?"

"I'd prefer not to go into my reasons," Janet said.

"You know he needs you, don't you?"

Janet glanced away. "That's flattering but hardly true. To be honest, I can't think why you called on me in the first place."

"Your expertise in the area of amnesia," Bernstein said quietly. "Recovering lost memories and helping patients integrate the experience."

Janet turned to him. "Yes, I certainly do have experience. It might even be considered relevant, although I'm not at all sure about that now. But I'm not the world's leading expert, not even remotely approaching the world's leading expert. Schaeffer was more in that league, not me. The Regis Foundation can well afford the best. I appreciate you mightn't want a huge medical or psychiatric team because of security, but you sure as hell could have done a lot better than me."

"This isn't about your expertise, Janet," Harriet said soothingly. "I want you to go to Egypt because Luke wants you to go to Egypt. Or Nectanebo wants you to go to Egypt, if you prefer. Not just a doctor or a psychologist or somebody to hold his hand—you. He's specific and insistent."

Janet wondered why. She'd suspected her sexual attraction to Luke Webb might be mutual but was wary of her instinct. Given the ferocity of her own response, the conclusion was all too likely to be wishful thinking. The possibility that it might not be wishful thinking aroused her still further . . . and cemented her resolve. If he desired her, there was no possibility whatsoever of keeping their relationship on a professional plane.

"I appreciate that Luke's wishes must carry weight with you," she told Harriet, "but you must realise that for me there is no emotional attachment—" What a lie! "—so I'm afraid the answer must remain no."

She steeled herself for a lengthy argument, but Harriet only glanced at Bernstein, then pushed a button on her desk intercom. "Can you come in, please?" she said quietly. To Janet, she said, "There's someone here who might change your mind."

Janet turned as the door opened behind her. Her eyes widened. "Good God, Mother—what are you doing here?"

The Chronicles of
Nectanebo: Nineteen

I knew from the mind of Luke Webb that the creatures who came for me believed themselves to be Egyptian, but they lacked the distinctive eye-fold of my race, as—less surprisingly—they lacked the elongation of the skull that marks the Egyptian nobility and, in particular, the royal family. (I had already noted that the body I now occupied had both, coincidentally no doubt, but welcome for all that.) They seemed, if anything, to be Semitic. Skin and eye colour, the structure of their features all pointed to such origins, although I would not have taken them for Hebrews.

I knew not where I was at this time, but if these men were Egyptians, whatever their racial origins, then Egypt itself still existed. The thought excited me, excitement confused me and, in my confusion, I offered no resistance. It was a mistake of near-fatal proportions. Rena, my Gegum Combat Mistress, taught me the value of ferocity, for it is the ferocity of the leopard that permits this relatively small beast to kill a man. But genuine ferocity must be called upon at once to meet a threat. This I did not do, distracted as I was. Thus I allowed them to take me, docile as a cow, and walked with them, slack-jawed and marvelling at the strangeness around me.

These men carried neither sword nor spear but, rather, devices which the mind of Luke Webb informed me were weapons of another kind, although at that point the principle behind them utterly eluded me. As we walked, I saw around me devices of a different sort, the workings of which even Webb did not comprehend, except in the most general way. Thus, I grew more confused and, in my confusion, more passive still.

We reached a chamber, my guards and I, in which stood two men. One bore the unmistakable air of authority that marks a prince or military general. The other, a man of brutal features and dead eyes, I knew at once for the creature who will kill without question and torture for sport: the type was common enough in Egypt although not, curiously, in Nubia. Even then, I failed to recognise the depths of my danger. It was as if my mind had somehow distanced itself from my immediate reality, so that while a part of me was well aware they meant to kill me, another part, the greater part, remained fascinated by the strangeness of it all.

The man with dead eyes—I took him for a Turk—said something in a language neither I nor Luke Webb understood. Those who had brought me to the chamber began then to remove my clothing.

Soon I was naked. In this state, I was taken to a table and laid down thereon supine. It is a measure of my confusion that I failed to struggle, even when two men seized my ankles and two others seized my wrists. Then the prince—if prince he was—spoke for the first time to the Turk. They were two words only—"Flay him!"—but words I fully understood, which is to say the mind of Luke Webb linked to my mind understood them.

I decided for the first time since my resurrection that I must take action to preserve my newly granted life.

It was simply done, for these were simple minds. I seized the soul of one guard and required him to slaughter his fellows. This he did with great efficiency, for the weapon he held was far more powerful than any lance or bow. Then I required him to kill himself.

There was much blood, for he naturally used the weapon as one might use a sword, for self-evisceration. It was the smell that persuaded me I truly lived again.

FIFTY-TWO

The facility had a small park for the recreation of employees. Janet and her mother were there now at Emma Winters's insistence. "We'll never get weather like this at home, darling—I certainly intend to enjoy it." They sat together on a bench near a small ornamental fountain.

"I can't remember when I was so surprised to see anyone," Janet said.

Emma smiled at her fondly. "Good to know I still have the capacity to surprise. A few months in a wheelchair and you begin to wonder if you'll ever be effective in the world again. Can't say I recommend it."

"You're looking astonishingly well," Janet told her honestly. After the initial shock, she had found herself delighted to see her mother but a little wary and very much confused. She still had no idea how Emma had gotten here or, more importantly, why.

"The remission continues," Emma shrugged lightly. "In some ways it's the most cruel aspect of the disease. You know you're not cured, but your body feels so well a part of you believes you must be. If it goes on long enough, you forget you've ever been ill. You certainly forget you still are—the infinite capacity of the human mind to repress unpleasant truths. When the remission ends, it's devastating. I remember the last time."

For some reason, Janet felt guilty. A reason she hadn't had the courage to analyse. The day was fast coming when she would have to look squarely at their relationship, examine the dynamics that had crept in since her father died. But not yet. She felt like that saint—was it Anthony?—who'd prayed to God, "Lord make me chaste but not just yet." Everybody wanted one more night. "Enjoy it while it lasts," she told her mother with forced cheerfulness.

"That's the sort of advice I give my patients," Emma said dryly.

"Must be good, then," Janet told her. She decided it was time to get to the point. "Mother, what are you doing here?"

"Getting set to stop you from making a mistake, I should think. I gather you've told Harriet Webb you won't take her son on as a patient?"

"I've told her I won't go to Egypt with him, if that's what you mean." How much did her mother know about all this? What had she been told? Harriet must have arranged to bring her here—but why?

"Much the same thing, isn't it?"

"I suppose it is," Janet admitted. "Mother, how much do you know about . . . Luke Webb?"

"Everything," Emma said. She waited a moment, then added, "Please take it I know everything. Luke is a clone. The cells were taken from an Egyptian mummy. His original memories have revived. That was the real ace in the hole, wasn't it? Or do I mean fly in the ointment? The real surprise in a whole litany of surprises. It sounds so much like science fiction, doesn't it? Or comedy. When I was a girl, there was an old black-and-white movie called *Abbot and Costello Meet the Mummy*. Abbot and Costello were American comedians, darling, like Laurel and Hardy only not so well known. It was all slapstick. The mummy kept lumbering out of crypts and cupboards and chasing them. You almost expect that sort of thing with Luke, don't you?"

"You obviously haven't met him," Janet told her.

"Oh, but I have! It was the first thing they arranged after I got here. Dishy little number, isn't he? I'm amazed you can even think of refusing a trip to Egypt with a man like that."

How did she do it? Janet wondered. Her mother had an unerring instinct for spotting men Janet found attractive—especially men Janet didn't want to admit to finding attractive. Usually they were married, but Emma obviously hadn't let the bizarre reality of Luke-cum-Nectanebo cloud her judgement. "We're not talking about a holiday romance," she said prissily.

"What are we talking about, Janet?" Emma asked her, suddenly serious. "How you've declined the career opportunity of a lifetime?"

In a less serious situation, Janet would have walked straight into the discussion, tried to justify her decision, accepted the battering of her mother's arguments and, in all probability, eventually given in. But this was too important, too close to the emotional bone for her to let the familiar pattern repeat. "Mother," she said firmly, "before we go into that, I would very much like to know what you are doing here. The last time I saw you was in your clinic in London. You were looking forward to a remission, but there was no suggestion you might be going globe-trotting, certainly not following me to the States."

"I didn't follow you, darling," Emma protested. "At least not directly. If you must know, I'm here at Harriet Webb's invitation. Nothing more exciting than that. She paid my ticket—it's the first time I've flown first class without an upgrade." She smiled disarmingly.

Janet declined to fall for it. "I'd like to know why Harriet invited you."

"I expect she wanted my help in preventing you from making a huge mistake. And you would be making a huge mistake if you don't take on this—"

"Mother," Janet cut in, "Harriet didn't know my decision about Luke until half a minute before she called you into the office. Unless the Regis Foundation has invented some sort of Beam-Me-Up-Scotty, that means she must have flown you over and introduced you to Luke before I decided not to go to Egypt with him. Fuck it, Mother, you must have been here before she even asked me!"

"There's no need for sarcasm," Emma said. "Or objectionable language either, come to that. Perhaps Harriet knows you better than you think. Perhaps she realised you were likely to say no."

"Harriet doesn't know me at all," Janet said. "We only just met yesterday. And most of the time since I've been here she's been briefing me about Luke." Did Harriet ever sleep? She'd obviously spent time briefing Emma as well. And that was one more person who knew about the cloning now. Christ, Harriet had to be desperate to persuade her.

"Well, whatever," Emma said dismissively. "That's not important. The important thing is what you're going to do. That's why I'm here. To advise you. As your mother."

It came out so smugly that Janet actually smiled. Then wondered if it had been phrased that way as a manipulation. Her mother was nothing if not subtle. She was perfectly capable of presenting herself as foolish to persuade someone to lower their guard. Janet's smile vanished. "I'm not sure I need any more advice. I've heard all the arguments."

"You've heard all the arguments from Harriet and that nice young man Bernstein—does he dye his hair, do you think? He's got a most peculiar colouring. They'll have offered you obscene amounts of money and presented the whole thing as a career move, financially based. I doubt if Harriet will have tried to push the fame and prestige button—she's too concerned to keep the whole cloning thing quiet to let you publish. But I suspect she may have told you poor Luke needs you, sweet helpless little thing that he is."

Janet felt her eyes widen. "You're right," she said reluctantly. "That was more or less the conversation."

"It's all nonsense, you know," her mother said. "Or, rather, it's not all nonsense. Money's important, and these people are desperate enough to make you rich. And even if you can't publish now, you'll be able to publish eventually, and that will arguably make you the most famous psychologist in the history of humanity, assuming you don't make a mess of the actual work. But none of that's important. They're hiding the real motivation."

A tiny voice deep inside her warned Janet this was her mother at her most dangerous. There was a hidden trap, and though Janet couldn't see it, she had to be so very, very careful. The obvious question, the question that positively cried out to be asked, was, What's the real motivation? Perhaps if Janet didn't ask it, she could avoid the trap.

But before she had time to react, she heard her mother asking, "What I can't understand is why you said no in the first place. Unless this is one of your ridiculous sexual reactions?"

How did she do it? Bloody, bloody, bloody woman!

"It *is* one of your ridiculous sexual reactions!" her mother said triumphantly. "I can see it in your face! My dear, what's happening to you? You haven't turned this into one of those interminable inner moral dialogues, have you?"

"Mother—" Janet began, without having the least idea what she was going to say.

"You find him sexually attractive. Don't you?"

Janet felt one wall of her reserve collapse. "Yes. Yes, I do."

"I thought so," Emma said. "Can't say I blame you—he positively oozes sex appeal. But what's the problem?"

"You know what's the problem!" Janet snapped. "This man is supposed to be a patient!"

"And you think shrinks—sorry, clinical psychologists—never sleep with their patients? My dear," she added archly, "think of Jung. Sometimes it's the only thing that does them any good."

With a sudden, welling suspicion, Janet said, "Mother, you haven't—?"

"Of course I have. How do you think Robin and I got together after your father died?"

"Robin was your patient? I never knew that."

"Well, obviously one doesn't put it on the BBC. These things happen, but you can usually keep them under control if you've a mind to."

Janet let go of the rest of her barriers. "I don't think I could keep this one under control."

"Ahhhh," Emma said knowingly.

There was silence, a professional silence that was meant to encourage Janet to talk. She recognised it for what it was but broke it anyway. "This isn't just some businessman I fancy. He's a clone. He's . . . I don't want to say this, but he's a freak. He's one of a kind. He's unpredictable. He thinks he's an Egyptian pharaoh. Dammit, he *is* an Egyptian pharaoh. Or was. Or something."

"And you've always had a problem with your sexuality," Emma added kindly.

"I've not always had a problem with my sexuality!" Janet snapped. "I don't know why you say that. You always say that, and I don't know why!"

"Perhaps because I'm not the one who's in denial."

This was her mother at her very worst, a total, utter nightmare. Janet pushed down her rising fury and forced calm into her voice. "Look, think about it. I mean, really think about it. Think what we're talking about. Think how bizarre this situation really is. In my position, if you were in my position, would you enter into a sexual relationship with Luke Webb?"

"It would depend whether I thought the rewards outweighed the disadvantages," Emma said easily.

"What rewards?" Janet demanded. "Go on, tell me the rewards!"

"Well, you might get some genuine sexual gratification for a change," Emma suggested. "Instead of these safe, colourless little men you've fiddled round with in the past."

Janet stared at her, stunned. "My . . . my men friends haven't been safe, or colourless or—"

"Yes they have," Emma broke in. "And even then there have been precious few of them. You have to face up to this, darling. God knows how I managed to produce a daughter with this problem, but you really aren't at all happy with your own sexuality."

Janet made a gargantuan effort not to strangle her. "Let's just forget my sexual gratification for a moment," she said tightly, "and tell me what other advantages you see for me in this situation?"

"Well, everything we've just been talking about. The money. The eventual prestige. The fascination of an absolutely unique study. But there's another aspect I think you may have overlooked, even though I know it's a huge motivation for Harriet and must become a huge motivation for you, eventually. For us all. I don't want to sound grandiose, but for the whole of humanity really."

"What?" Janet demanded.

"Resurrection," said her mother.

Janet waited. When Emma made no move to explain, she asked, "What are you talking about, Mother?"

"You still don't see it? This is what I was trying to tell you earlier. Harriet's real motivation. Or at least her hidden motivation—she has a lot of other reasons for wanting to keep Luke happy and sane, of course. The point is, Luke isn't simply a successful clone. He's a clone who remembers his past life. In a sense, the Regis people didn't just clone his body—they cloned his personality as well. They didn't expect to, of course, but that's what happened. What we have here is a literal resurrection. If Luke can stay mentally stable—or, rather, if Nectanebo can stay stable, can function effectively in the cloned body—and assuming cloning revives the original memories and persona each time it's carried out . . . well, darling, it means humanity has at long last beaten death."

"Beaten death?" Janet echoed. She found she could not take her eyes off her mother.

"That's why Harriet wants you to go with him to Egypt. Luke . . . Nectanebo apparently wants this. Harriet will give him anything he wants, anything he needs. She is utterly, absolutely desperate to make sure he doesn't fall apart. There's not been much sign of it so far, but this is too important. She wants to be certain."

"Beaten death?" Janet said again.

"Well, think of it," her mother said. "If you died tomorrow and we had you cloned, in thirty years you'd be alive and well and living on Planet Earth again. From your subjective viewpoint, it would be like taking a long sleep and a little jump into the future. You're not an ancient Egyptian, of course, so you wouldn't have two thousand years of catching up to do. And even the few years you did have to catch up on would be filled in from the memories of the secondary personality you would absorb when your primary personality became active again. It's virtually another step in human evolution. If you keep cloning the same individual, you're not just talking about resurrection—potentially you're talking immortality."

"This . . . this is . . . Harriet . . . you think Harriet has been thinking on these lines?"

"I'm sure of it. Once she's certain the Nectanebo persona is stable, she plans to clone her father."

"Her father?" Janet seemed to be doing nothing but echo words, but her mind was reeling.

"Yes, of course. She loved Stanislav. She hopes to give him life again."

"Would anybody want that?" Janet asked. "Would anybody really want that sort of . . . immortality?"

"I certainly would," her mother said. "It's what Harriet promised me if I can persuade you to go to Egypt with Nectanebo."

Janet felt the trap spring shut. It was the ultimate in emotional blackmail. Did she believe it? She could find no flaw in Emma's logic. But if she really did believe it, how could she refuse her mother immortality?

Book Five: Revenge

FIFTY-THREE

The *Empress* was not an old boat, but it might have come straight out of Agatha Christie's *Death on the Nile*. The designers had gone to a great deal of trouble to give it a luxurious, almost decadent, fin de siècle look, right down to the cheerfully rotund, impish nudes that hung on the walls of the cabin corridors. It even had a smokestack and paddle wheel despite the fact that it ran on diesel-driven screws like any self-respecting modern cruiser.

Janet boarded her at Aswan, just south of the dam, escorted by an Egyptian soldier—who seemed a schoolboy despite his Kalashnikov and bandoleer—and two cheerful porters who sweated under the weight of her luggage. Luke was already on board, having flown in the night before. She reminded herself he was travelling under the name of Pearson Arnold—a security precaution—and marvelled again at the ease with which he had acquired the necessary papers.

A tall, bespectacled young man, wearing a tie despite the heat, was waiting for her at the head of the gangplank to shake her hand.

"Dr. Winters," he said in heavily accented English, "so pleased you could join us. I am Adrian Pikaar. It will be my pleasure to ensure you and Mr. Arnold find everything to your complete satisfaction during our voyage."

They walked together into a carpeted reception area. Two uniformed staff nodded at her nervously from behind a small counter. "With the moustache is Abdul," Pikaar said. "If there is anything you need, you must speak with him if I am not present. The other is Emile."

Janet nodded back at them. Since she had landed in Aswan she had not seen a single woman, not at the airport, not in the limo that picked her up, not even in the town, although she suspected that was probably a coincidence. It was beginning to look as if she was the only female on the boat as well.

Pikaar was saying something. "I'm sorry?" she said, turning to him.

"There is a Royal Suite which would naturally have been offered to Mr. Arnold or, should he not wish it, to yourself, but you must forgive me that it was and is currently under refurbishment. Thus, it is not possible for you to live in it. But you have been allocated the very finest of our luxury cabins, which I hope will be suitable. Mr. Arnold has already approved his. Please follow me."

The cabin was pleasant, although the air conditioning was a little noisy. It housed twin beds, a dressing table, a telephone and, strangely, a television set. There was a marbled shower room en suite with a large, old-fashioned loo installed. Opposite the door were French windows opening onto a small private balcony.

"It is pleasant to sit out, especially when we are cruising," Pikaar told her, "but please take care not to be bitten by mosquitoes." He gestured towards the dressing table. "In the drawer is a map of the boat so you may find your way around, but please, until you are accustomed, simply lift the phone, and a member of the staff will come to be your guide. You may watch television today if you wish, although the programmes are in Arabic and not very good. Once we are underway, the set does not work. If there is anything you wish, please use the phone. It will be our pleasure to provide it. Now I leave you to freshen up. Mr. Arnold has asked me to present his compliments and invite you to join him for dinner when you have rested. It will be served on the main sundeck at seven o'clock if that is acceptable to you."

"Thank you," Janet said. "Please tell Mr. Arnold I look forward to seeing him then."

As Pikaar closed the door behind him, she wondered if it was true. In the three weeks since she'd agreed to accompany Luke Webb into Egypt, she'd seen nothing of him, nothing of his mother, nothing of her own infuriating mother. She hadn't even remained in America but had instead returned to London, having been instructed to "put her affairs in order." The legal phrase was Bernstein's, and it reminded her irresistibly of the sort of thing that was said about suicides and terminal cancer victims. Just one more tiny factor that made her feel as if she were stepping off a cliff.

Except now that she was here, now that she was actually in Egypt, she didn't feel as though she was stepping off a cliff anymore. She felt excited.

She walked across to the window and looked out. The scene was far from edifying—the concrete structures of the wharf carried the eye up to mean, prefabricated buildings that looked eerily like a 1950s British primary school. But at least the view would change once they were underway. She was looking forward to that.

As she let the net curtain fall back into place, there was a knock on the door. When Janet opened it, two very black and very smiling stewards bustled in with her cases.

"Bonjour, Madame," one greeted her cheerfully. "Vous désirez quelquechose?"

Janet blinked. "Do you speak English?"

"Of course," the steward said.

"I too," put in his companion. "You are extremely pretty."

Janet smiled despite herself. "Thank you," she murmured, wondering if he really knew what he had said.

"There is something you would like us to do? May we unpack for you? This is what happens in the great houses of England, is it not?"

Janet had not the slightest idea what happened in the great houses of England. But the idea was appealing, and she almost told them to go ahead until the thought of what these young men might make of her underwear gave her pause. She'd bought silk for the trip, pretending to herself that it would be cool. "I think perhaps just a drink," she said.

Apparently it took both of them to bring the drink, some sort of exotic ice-cold fruit juice that was both sweet and tart at the same time. As they left, it suddenly occurred to her that the *Empress* still had its full complement of staff. Thus, Luke and she were being taken care of by the same number of stewards and crew who normally looked after eighty. No wonder they were falling over themselves to be helpful.

She locked the cabin door, removed her blouse and skirt and lay down on the bed to cool off. Later she planned on a long shower, but for the moment she was too tired to bother. The flight from Gatwick had taken only a little over five hours, but for some reason it had exhausted her.

Listening to the gentle hum and rattle of the air-conditioning, Janet fell asleep.

FIFTY-FOUR

In the darkness, she felt around the smooth, concave surface that enclosed her and knew the time had almost come to emerge into the light. But that, for all its rightness and inevitability, required effort. She began to peck away at her shell.

As she worked, she thought about the Pharaoh Nectanebo, now one of the immortals. How ironical it was that he had not flown to the circumpolar stars, for while he might then have shone forever, she would never have seen him again, except at a distance, and perhaps not then, for she had never been much of an astronomer. But he remained on Earth and would live forever, the first God-King to do so.

He was a strange one, Nectanebo, with his ambition and his magic. Yet eternal life on Earth was the least of his achievements. Was he not the first male to be accepted by the sisters? No, he was not, she thought, as she remembered Akhenaten. But he was the first to be accepted fully. To be loved.

Did she love him? She certainly lusted after him, but was that quite the same thing, even for a doctor?

The shell cracked, and a shaft of daylight filtered through. This enabled her environment to expand. She examined her body with its reptilian skin, and developed the understanding that she was a serpent— but very pretty. She stretched and pushed some more so that the shell disintegrated with the noise and dust and rubble of a building collapsing.

Janet stepped free and found she was in Africa. Not North Africa which housed the glittering edifice of Egypt—how stupid of Nectanebo to capitulate to that Persian barbarian!—but the primitive dark of equatorial Africa with its huts of mud and straw, its disease-ridden jungles, its creeping things, its biting things, its sister snakes.

It would require all of her skills to escape the darkness, Janet thought. She felt tired, she felt ancient.

"My dear, how nice to meet you here," her mother told her.

Her instinct was to argue with her mother, but she didn't have the courage. All the same, she had to leave—and soon. The sun was going out.

She stretched pterodactyl wings and felt the feathers grow. She was a winged serpent. Was this what was really meant by evolution? A few seconds later, now transformed into a pure white dove, Janet beat her wings and flew.

FIFTY-FIVE

Janet woke to gentle movement and the soft background sound of engines. She felt cold, a little confused. Above her the air-conditioning system still hummed and wheezed. Then, with a feeling of excitement, she realised they were underway.

She swung her feet onto the floor and moved quickly to the window. The barren concrete of the dock had disappeared. She was looking across a broad expanse of water to a distant desert shore.

At once she was seized by a feeling of déjà vu so overpowering she was forced to grip the window handle for support. Although she had never been to Egypt before, she felt utterly at home. The desert had a beauty that sang to her. The water had a stillness that called to her. The sunshine was like honey.

She went outside onto the balcony, unmindful of the fact she hadn't dressed. Out of reach of the air-conditioning, the heat enfolded her like a blanket. She felt full, whole, primal, drinking great draughts of air and fantasising that she ran across the surface of the water, ran across the desert, free as a gazelle. She felt herself grow briefly to the proportions of a giant. She felt herself as Nectanebo must feel, powerful, beyond the reach of danger, and immortal.

The sun was low on the horizon. As she became aware of it, she began to wonder about the time. She went back into her cabin and picked up her watch from the bedside locker. Three minutes to six—just over an hour to get ready. She felt her stomach tighten like a teenager on a first date.

As she showered, Janet tried to collect her thoughts. She'd done a great deal of work on herself since she'd left the States, and one of her conclusions was that her mother might be right. Perhaps she really was afraid of her own sexuality. Certainly when she looked back on past relationships, they formed a pattern of a sort. Most of the men were intelligent, reliable and just plain dull. All of them were interested in sex, but not very. Her affairs were characterised by sympathy, warmth and understanding but seldom marred by passion. Two of them had involved no sex at all, and one of those had lasted almost three years!

Side by side with this pattern was another, even more pronounced. There had been men who attracted her sexually, men who turned her on with a glance and left her fantasising about breathless penetration. But none was available. She remembered four altogether. Two were married, one was en route to New Zealand and the fourth was a Roman Catholic priest. If she was honest with herself, their unavailability was no coincidence. Quite obviously she only allowed herself to become aroused when there was no opportunity to follow through.

Even Nectanebo had fitted into this pattern. Her arousal when she first saw him was far beyond anything she'd experienced before. But it was arousal that had occurred within the context of the doctor-patient relationship. At the time, she'd suspected he was mentally ill. In those circumstances, there could be no possibility whatsoever of consummating her passion . . . one reason, presumably, why she had allowed it to consume her so completely.

She could still remember the panic she felt when that excuse dissolved. Whatever else he might be, Nectanebo was not mad. And in his sanity he had to be one of the most fascinating men she would ever meet. Yet the thought of giving in to her attraction—she still looked on it as "giving in"—filled her with fear. Without her mother's brutal words, she knew Nectanebo would have joined the New Zealand emigrant and the priest.

As she started to get dressed, Janet noticed something that had not occurred to her before, even during her three weeks of introspection. She had begun to think of him entirely as Nectanebo now and not Luke Webb. Although not quite certain how or when that had happened, let alone why, she suspected it might be significant.

She found herself sitting at the dressing table applying makeup, something she rarely did even for the most formal occasions. She was paying particular attention to her eyes when it occurred to her she might be trying to duplicate the look she'd seen in so many Egyptian murals. The insight amused her so much that she laughed aloud . . . and immediately relaxed. Where had all the tension come from anyway? They didn't have to end up in bed, and if they did, was that the end of the world?

She was feeling positively cheerful by the time she headed for the sundeck.

FIFTY-SIX

She saw him seated at the table and knew at once that something had changed. He looked older, although not in any obvious way. The table was set under an awning and surrounded by large, guttering, citrus candles to keep away the insects that would gather at dusk. Fully a dozen stewards, including the two who had offered to help her unpack, were ranged like soldiers at a discreet distance along the rail. Because of the angle he did not see her right away, and she took the opportunity to study him.

Perhaps it was the clothes. He was wearing dark slacks, a white shirt and cravat, and some sort of lightweight smoking jacket, leisure formal wear that suited the ambience of the boat—if not the heat—but was a far cry from what she might have expected from a fashionable American like Luke Webb. Except, she reminded herself, this was not a fashionable American but an ancient Egyptian. She felt herself smile. What would an ancient Egyptian wear to dinner?

He turned as she approached, stood up to wait for her. Once again she felt the extraordinary sexual impact of the man, although now—thankfully—it was not so out of control as if had been before. She extended her hand coolly. He took it; then, to her utter astonishment, bowed and kissed it. Where on earth had he learned such a Continental gesture? It was wholly out of character for the American aspect of his persona, and she couldn't imagine that hand-kissing had been prevalent in Nectanebo's Egypt.

Those extraordinary Oriental eyes held her own as he said, "Thank you for coming."

"A girl has to eat," Janet told him lightly.

"I meant for coming to Egypt," Nectanebo said. "I am aware my request raised conflict in your soul, and I am grateful. Allow me to present our guest."

It was only then that she realised the white-haired Arab with him was not a servant.

FIFTY-SEVEN

"God, but I'm tired!" Harriet exclaimed and threw herself untidily onto the couch. "Tired, tired, tired, tired, weary! Must be getting old."

"You mean you're not up for a night of passion?" Bernstein asked impishly. They were together in Harriet's get-away cabin for the first time since Luke Webb's kidnap, and Bernstein was poking cautiously at the sullen stove. It responded with intermittent bursts of bilious smoke.

"Not without gin," Harriet told him. She shut her eyes. "Leave that fucking thing and come and hold me. I'm frightened."

He left the stove at once and came to sit beside her. She clung to him like a child. "I've been having bad dreams. Shit, I've been having nightmares."

"Luke?"

"Sure, Luke. What else? Except he's not Luke anymore, is he? He's some sort of walking mummy. Nectanebo! Christ! We're living in a Stephen King novel. I never thought this would happen. I never thought it could happen." Despite her exhaustion, she was starting to run off at the mouth but couldn't stop herself. "Men never know this, but you carry a child for nine months and he's yours. No matter what, he's yours! God, he was such a beautiful baby. Those lovely eyes. He had lovely eyes even then. Looking up at me, you know? I remember thinking they were such wise little eyes, as if he knew so much. Jesus, can you imagine? This thing came out of my body and grinned at me, and I wasn't even prepared to admit I was looking at an eighty-seven-year-old man."

"You weren't," Bernstein said softly, but she didn't even seem to hear him.

"But he wasn't an eighty-seven-year-old man, Bernstein. He was a lovely little baby. He was my Luke. And now I've lost him. That's why

I'm having nightmares." She drew even closer, trembling slightly. "Tell me I haven't lost him, Bernstein . . ."

Bernstein chewed his lip. Eventually he asked, "Isn't there anything left of Luke in him?"

"Of course there is. I still see bits of Luke. His smile. That funny way of holding his head. The voice is the same, although he uses it differently now. But it's a different man." She pulled away from him abruptly. "I'd never have done it if I'd known. Not even for Stanislav."

"Never have carried him?"

"I wanted a baby, Bernstein. That was the truth of it. Twenty-whatever and feeling broody. Not that I'd have admitted it. The trouble is, they don't stay babies. They grow up into great big hulking brutes like you. And then they change."

"How do you feel about him now that he's changed?" Bernstein asked.

"How? The same as I've always felt. He worries me. He frightens me. But I still love him. I know it doesn't make any sense. He's not my son anymore, but he's still my son. I look at him, and he's still the child I reared even if . . . even if . . ." She sniffed. "I've ordered another fucking stove."

For a beat he blanked at the switch, then said, "Pity. That one makes me feel manly."

"You didn't really come out here for a night of passion, did you?"

"Not entirely."

"So what's the problem?"

"You sure you want to deal with it now? It'll keep till morning."

"No, I want to deal with it now. I want to get all the shit out of the way, and then I want to drink some gin and feel you inside me, and after that I want to sleep like a baby. Sock it to me, Bernstein. There are no problems you could possibly have discovered that will make me feel any worse than I do already."

"Don't bank on it," said Bernstein. "I've found Nectanebo's diary."

The Chronicles of Nectanebo: Twenty

The days following my resurrection were fraught with dangers. Nor was I best equipped to deal with them. It is clear I should have fixed my mind on maintaining the illusion I was still Luke Webb, learning who I could trust and who I could not, dealing with the minutiae of my immediate environment. But this I found near impossible, fascinated as I was by the broader world. For I was resurrected amidst paradox and marvels.

The marvels were visible all around me. This was a nation that had created wonders such as carriages that required no horse, machines to view events at a distance, devices to speak with those neither present nor close by, gigantic metal birds carrying travellers within their stomachs. These and much more.

The first paradox arose when I searched the mind of Luke Webb for knowledge of these marvels. At once I discovered that while he knew their names and how to use them, he remained for the most part ignorant of the means by which they functioned. It became clear that, just as in Egypt, knowledge was the possession of a privileged few, an initiate priesthood of scientists who communicated secrets to their own kind only. But in Egypt, the fruits of this knowledge were confined to the priesthood while here in this nation of my resurrection, they seemed to be shared by all, even those wholly incapable of understanding them.

The second paradox ran deeper. The nation, I quickly discovered, had neither court nor pharaoh but was based on a peculiar corruption of Greek ideas. These always struck me as wholly ridiculous, but the Greeks at least had sufficient sense to limit their government to men of substance while actual rule, by and large, remained in the hands of the nobility. But here, in the land of my resurrection, every man has a say in who shall rule, irrespective of his social status, intelligence, wealth, property or contribution to society. Incredibly, so has every woman—a development that would have pleased the Gegum hugely.

Even more strange to relate, those who rule have no hereditary position, hence, no training in the art of command. Nor are they required to show experience in government. Indeed, they are not even required to have a talent for it. All that is asked is that they curry favour with the rabble. In theory, the country of my resurrection might be administered by a college of personable lunatics—as seems to be the case to some extent.

There is, of course, a supreme ruler, somewhat equivalent to Pharaoh in Egypt, but even he requires no breeding, ability or talent and is debarred from passing his office and the fruits of his experience to his son or any other of his choice. His rule is as absolute as was my own. Which is to say that to maintain it, he must manipulate certain bodies of men as I had to manipulate the priesthood and the army, and he may retain the throne for no more than eight years, conditional on his winning two popularity contests.

But beyond the political structure lies another, at once more subtle and more obvious, although so unaccustomed was I to something of this sort that I failed for a time to comprehend it. In Egypt, as in all other countries at the time of my glory, power resided mainly in force of arms, hereditary position or, as was the case with the Gegum sisterhood, animal cunning. Less often, a man—or woman—might gain power through magical practice or religious observance, compelling or beseeching favours from the gods. Wealth, in the form of goods, chattels and copious possessions, followed the acquisition of power but never occasioned it.

Here, in the land of my resurrection, wealth has a different face and function. It is apparent that wealth alone is sufficient to ensure status in this nation, something conferred only by breeding or position in my own. There is, indeed, a largely unacknowledged hierarchy based on nothing more substantial than possessions. Those within the higher echelons of this hierarchy find it possible—should they so desire—to trade a portion of their possessions for political or, less often, military power.

There is, too, an exercise of power which was quite unknown in the days of my glory and yet is clearly widespread in the world of my resurrection. This is the power of corporation. There exist in the nation endless groupings of people whose lives are dedicated to the acquisition of wealth by trade. Traders there were in the days of my glory and family groups among them, owning their retinues of slaves and servants, but I speak here of something other: companies of traders, some of enormous size, some indeed so large they might be nations in their own right, some so gigantic that their influence and substance stretches across several countries so that they might reasonably be considered empires. Nothing resembling this was known at the time I seized the throne of Egypt, nor at the time I abandoned it to the encroaching Persians. Within these companies, power is wielded in the old way, in a hierarchical structure where heredity will often play its traditional appointed part.

These houses of trade, along with their sister houses of administration, are accorded a status and importance in the land of my resurrection unlike anything known to the world I left. They constitute kingdoms within the kingdom.

I meditated much on these vast houses of trade, not least because it seemed I owned one.

FIFTY-EIGHT

Harriet stared at him silently for a long time. "Nectanebo's . . . diary?"

"Luke's . . . well, whoever . . . he's been keeping a sort of diary record—he calls it the Chronicles of Nectanebo—ever since he recovered the memories."

"And you have it?"

"I've made a copy."

"I don't suppose I can ask you how you found it," Harriet remarked sourly.

Bernstein shrugged. "No reason why you shouldn't: I did nothing illegal, as far as I'm aware. The papers were in a safe-deposit box. He used the same bank as the Foundation—one of the banks, branch closest to . . . well, you know."

"Yes, I do know," Harriet snapped impatiently. "Get on with it."

"I'm attorney to the Foundation, as you're aware. You appointed me yourself, you may recall—"

"Jesus, Bernstein, are you incapable of coming to the point without meandering?"

Bernstein smiled. "Sorry. It's the legal training. I needed some documents—Regis documents—that were also on deposit. The bank gave me the key to the wrong box."

"They did what?" Harriet exploded.

"I know, I know," Bernstein said.

"I hope we've changed banks."

"I'm afraid it's one of ours. But I did have the teller fired."

"Glad to hear it," Harriet said. "Now tell me how you happened, legally of course, to use this wrong key?"

"The two boxes were close together. The teller pointed out the wrong one—or the right one for the key, if you follow me. So I opened it."

"You must have known right away it was the wrong box."

"Yes."

"But you read the papers anyway?"

"Yes."

"Why?"

Bernstein sighed. "Come on, Harriet."

She had moved so they were no longer touching, no longer even close. "Okay, stupid question. You knew what they were? I mean, you knew what you were reading?"

"The first page was headed 'Chronicles of Nectanebo.' It caught my attention at once."

"This wasn't some sort of a book? I mean, a real diary?"

"Loose papers," Bernstein said. "Quite a lot of them, actually. They were handwritten, and you generate bulk that way. I suppose that's why he locked them away instead of taking them with him to Egypt. There were also scans of medical documents recording Nectanebo's... what should I call it?.. creation? I assume he used his identity as Luke to get the originals from the foundation research team. If he understood them, I'm afraid he now knows he was cloned. But the important thing is the diary."

Harriet said, "I can see why you would glance at the first sheet or two, enough to satisfy yourself you'd opened the wrong box. But you're a lawyer, Bernstein. You must have known you were invading privacy or some damn thing by reading the rest."

"Actually I think I could defend myself in court, but only on a technicality. I doubt I could justify making copies."

"Why did you make copies?"

"Because the content of the documents is important. Some of them are actually crucial."

"Crucial to what?" Harriet asked.

Bernstein shrugged. "The Foundation, I suppose. You. Me. The world."

"This is sounding very, very ominous."

"Yes, well, I'm afraid you may be right. Has . . . Nectanebo told you anything about his former life?"

"His life in Egypt? He's told me some things, sure." She shrugged. "I mean, I knew the broad outline right from the beginning. From research. But he's told me other stuff, personal . . . you know."

"About the murders?"

There was a long, long silence. Then Harriet said, "He killed somebody?"

"I'm afraid the term is 'murder,' even within the legal context of his own time. Several people, including a baby and his best friend."

"We're talking about ancient Egypt!" Harriet said. "Wars . . . assassinations—"

"A baby and his best friend," Bernstein repeated gently.

After a moment, Harriet said, "This was all of two thousand three hundred years ago."

"But Nectanebo is with us now."

"What are you trying to say?" Harriet demanded angrily. "That we put him on trial for something he did before Christ was born?"

Bernstein smiled. "I wouldn't bank on a conviction. I don't want to harm your son, Harriet. I'm just making the point that he's turned into something—someone—who's proved himself to be dangerous. Extremely dangerous." The smile had died, and he looked at her soberly. "I would have to say a ruthless killer."

"You think he's likely to kill somebody now? Here in America?" Harriet asked incredulously.

"I think he's capable of it. Why not?"

"Because there's no reason, for one thing," Harriet told him. "He's not fighting the Israelites or whoever—"

"Persians," Bernstein filled in quietly.

"All right, Persians. He's not fighting anybody now."

"He wasn't fighting anybody when he killed his best friend. He was seizing the Egyptian throne."

"Well, he's not doing that now, is he?" Harriet demanded.

"Ah," Bernstein said.

"You know something? That's a habit of yours I really hate. I mean, I really hate it. You say 'Ah.' Just 'Ah,' in that smug voice. The big put-down, and don't tell me you don't mean it as a put-down, because you do. It's one of your damn legal tricks. I'm going to get a drink. You want one?" Without waiting for an answer, she stamped off into the kitchen.

"I didn't mean it as a put-down," Bernstein called after her. "And since you're in there, I'd appreciate a small scotch, rocks, no water."

She came out of the kitchen carrying two glasses and handed him his scotch without a word. Then she sat down again, keeping a maximum distance between them, but at least on the same couch. She was drinking something colourless with lots of ice in a tall glass. He suspected it was gin.

"You don't think Luke's going to kill somebody now, do you?" she asked fiercely. "Here in America?"

He noticed it was Luke now, not Nectanebo. He said, "No, not here in America—" She started to say, "Well, then—" as he added, "I think he's going to kill somebody in Egypt."

FIFTY-NINE

The papers were spread out untidily across the table, but she noticed the pages were numbered neatly at each bottom right-hand corner. The precision was not the only thing unlike the Luke she knew. There was also a change in his handwriting.

Bernstein was gathering up a series of pages. "This is where he starts talking about his 'birthright'—"

"The Regis Foundation?"

"This is Nectanebo we're talking about, not Luke," Bernstein said patiently. "His birthright is Egypt."

Harriet looked at him blankly.

"He wants to seize the throne of Egypt," Bernstein told her.

"There is no throne of Egypt," Harriet said. Then light dawned. "Oh, my God . . ."

Bernstein sat silent. After a moment, she said, "This is crazy."

"Only from our perspective," Bernstein said. "It must make perfect sense from his."

"But he has to realise Egypt's changed. He has to."

"I expect he does. He's nothing if not intelligent. The point is, he may not have realised how much. How well do you imagine you'd cope if you were seized by the scruff of the neck and set down in a strange country two thousand years in the future? That's what's happened to him, more or less. Imagine you started thinking about New York. You'd know it must have changed, of course. You might think it had gotten bigger, better, with all sorts of fancy architecture and new systems. But you wouldn't necessarily think of it in ruins, half buried under sand."

"Until I actually saw it . . . ," Harriet said hollowly. Then she rallied, took a deep pull of her drink. "He knew what Egypt was like before he left."

"Did you tell him?"

"No," she said reluctantly.

"Neither did I," said Bernstein. "What makes you think anybody else did?"

Harriet drank more gin. "Jesus, Bernstein, I just assumed he knew."

"I know," Bernstein said. "So did I. I suppose everybody else did, too—except there isn't anybody else. Apart from Janet Winters, who's gone with him, I suppose. There isn't anybody else who talked to him and knew they weren't talking to Luke Webb. If you're talking to Luke Webb, you assume he knows ancient Egypt died with the Romans."

Harriet sat up suddenly. "He has access to Luke's memories!" she said eagerly. "Of course he knows Egypt's long gone!"

"He has access to Luke's memories insofar as he makes use of them," Bernstein said.

"What's that mean?"

"It's like having an encyclopaedia. All the information's in there, but you don't know anything until you look it up. If Nectanebo didn't think to look up ancient Egypt, he wouldn't know what happened to it. But, in fact, we can safely assume he didn't access Luke's memories on this point. The diary record makes it quite clear he's gone to Egypt in the hope of taking up where he left off."

"Jesus!" Harriet exclaimed tiredly. "What a shock when he gets there. You're worried about what it will do to him when he finds out?"

"Not entirely," Bernstein said. He caught her expression and added hurriedly, "I'm concerned, certainly. The difficulties in adjustment will be considerable. But I think our more immediate worries may be this—" He pushed a slim sheaf of the handwritten papers towards her.

Harriet took them reluctantly. In the neat handwriting that was not Luke Webb's, they were headed *The Chronicles of Nectanebo Twenty-One.*

The Chronicles of Nectanebo: Twenty-One

The end of innocence gives me little pleasure. The death of little Kanekht by my hand revolted me so that I was filled with self-loathing for long afterwards. But that is not to say I regretted my act, although I regretted the necessity of it. When I came to my glory, I realised the value of what I had done. Mercy may be the prerogative of a wronged pharaoh, but woe betide him if he extend it. It is vital that a man's enemies learn he is never to be trifled with; otherwise, they feel they may strike again with impunity. He who seeks to harm Pharaoh must be sought out and punished, whatever the cost, as a lesson to others. This I have always believed. This, when able, I have always done.

I was not, of course, always able. After the ludicrous assassination attempt mounted by the Persian usurper, I merely sank into a Nubian dotage. But then I was free of interest from those who would harm me, for it was obvious to all I was a threat to none. I grew old and frail, increasingly forgetful and stupid, so that the world deigned only to pass me by. I was not worth the energy it required to heft a sword or draw a bow. I came to believe all threats had withered away, save only that which threatens all men in the twilight of their years. How ironical then, that the first experience of my resurrection was an attempt to kill me.

At the time, of course, I sought only to escape from the immediacy of the threat and succeeded as I have already recorded. But I did not die a fool, and I was not reborn one, so that having dispatched those soldiers who had sought to harm me, I was moved to consider who it was who had ordered them against me. Using those friends and advisers I discovered in the memory of Luke Webb, I found eventually what I sought. The creature by whose authority I had been placed under threat was named Hasan al-Hakim, self-styled "Hawk of the Desert." Remarkable to tell, he was a citizen of Egypt.

Once this information reached me, I began plans for my return. I was determined, in any case, to reclaim my birthright, but it was important first to deal with him who had threatened my existence. Thus, acting through intermediaries (who assumed they were dealing with Luke Webb), I sent to him a message in which I revealed my plan to visit Egypt and offered, should he wish to meet me, a substantial donation to his cause. In the communication, I presented myself as one Pearson T. Arnold, a liberal philanthropist with Islamist sympathies.

It was suggested to me—by one of the intermediaries who knew not with whom he dealt—that I was naive to believe this creature would risk meeting with an unknown American. But the objection lacked understanding of human nature. The Gegum taught me that men are perennially blinded by their own lusts and tend to believe what they wish to believe, no more, no less.

The creature Hasan al-Hakim bore me no personal ill will, whatever his feelings towards my supposed country. To him, Americans were no more than pieces to be manipulated in some great game of which Hasan al-Hakim saw himself as the ultimate master. Such a mindset is dangerous. The overlord who takes the overview and sends his minions to spill the blood can all too easily believe himself invulnerable. I counted upon this when I made my proposal. I further assumed the creature lusted after money, as all men seem to lust after money in this age, and offered him such quantities of the useless trash that he must lose his common sense. I believed that, bound by lust and the illusion of invulnerability, thinking me his inferior in cunning, believing me to be no more than a foreigner of great wealth but little worldly experience, he would agree to meet with me.

This was my reasoning. I know not whether it was sound, but I know this:

For whatever reason, Hasan al-Hakim has agreed to meet with me on my return to Egypt. When he does, I shall ensure he dies.

SIXTY

"Pleased to meet you, Mr. al-Hakim," Janet said. She made to extend her hand but found that Nectanebo had taken her arm, smoothly preventing the familiar social gesture.

"Hasan al-Hakim is a great religious leader in this country," Nectanebo said. "His faith precludes him from direct physical contact with women. Is that not so, Mr. al-Hakim?"

The white-haired Arab bowed slightly and smiled a smile that did not reach his eyes. "It is nothing personal, Dr. Winters," he said in flawless English. "A matter of custom, no more."

"Of course," Janet murmured, wondering what Nectanebo was doing entertaining an Imam.

"Mr. al-Hakim was just taking his leave, in any case," Nectanebo told her quietly. He, too, smiled, and, like al-Hakim, the smile did not reach his eyes. "I should not wish you to think you were driving him away."

Janet knew at once that something was wrong but had no idea what. She watched as al-Hakim bowed again, this time respectfully, towards Nectanebo. "I wish to thank you, Mr. Arnold, and apologise for our earlier . . . misunderstanding."

Nectanebo said nothing, simply watched as the older man walked away. Janet noted that before he left the deck, he was flanked by two armed men, clearly bodyguards. What on earth was going on?

"Won't you sit down?" Nectanebo asked.

She made to do so and discovered a steward had materialised behind her to push in her chair. He favoured her with a brilliant smile when she sat down and turned to thank him.

"Nubian," Nectanebo said as the steward withdrew. "I look at them and see Khababasha. They are the most beautiful race in the world. Little changed—oh, their clothing, but nothing else. These men could be the

313

Nubians I knew. I prefer them greatly over the people who call themselves Egyptians now."

"What was that business with the Imam?" Janet asked him. She'd decided directness was the best policy with Nectanebo. It had certainly served her well enough so far.

He shrugged. "Nothing of importance. He is not actually an Imam. At least, I believe not. He seems to have formed his own religion, or something similar. He thinks of himself as a follower of Mohammed, but he is unlike others who do so." He hesitated. "I fear I do not fully understand the religion of Mohammed. There is little detail of Islam in the mind of Luke Webb, and the Prophet was born some eight hundred years after I died."

She could feel the strangeness in him, the strangeness of their situation. She was chatting to a creature out of history, a creature who saw the world differently from any other. A thought struck her, and she asked curiously, "Are you finding it difficult to adjust?"

"Adjust?"

"To the changes."

He glanced to his right, out across the broad expanse of the lake. "You know they drowned Nubia?"

Janet looked at him and waited.

"I learned this only when I came here. Possibly it was in Luke Webb's mind, but I did not access it. The building of the Aswan High Dam caused the Nile to flood and drown much of the country. This Lake Nasser was the result. All artificial. The villa that I made my refuge is somewhere deep beneath these waters."

More likely somewhere deep beneath the sands beneath these waters, Janet thought. This was the incredible, mind-bending thing. He was speaking, from personal experience, of something two thousand and more years ago.

His mood changed abruptly, and he smiled. "I have taken the liberty to specify the meal that will be served to you as well as myself. I hope this is acceptable to you?"

"I like a masterful man," Janet said, and instantly regretted it. The spirit that occupied this body was the spirit of a pharaoh. Flirtatiousness was wholly inappropriate. But what, she wondered, was appropriate?

He gave no appreciable reaction. "You have noticed the change in me," he said. "I saw that in your eyes."

Relieved at the change of subject, Janet said, "I did notice. I'm not sure what it is."

"It is ageing," Nectanebo said. "Since we met, I have become steadily more and more myself." He smiled delightfully and unexpectedly. "You would refer to it, I think, as the increasing dominance of the Nectanebo persona. Perhaps that is what it is. But to me it feels as if I were becoming more what I always was. I retain Luke's memories and his abilities, of course, but the influence of his personality is waning. With each new day I am more Nectanebo. This has caused the ageing."

"I'm not sure I understand you," Janet said.

"I was an old man when I died in Nubia. A very old man. I had the experience of eighty-seven years. In this life, I have lived a further thirty. Whatever you believe you see before you, I am in spirit one hundred and seventeen years. I believe this influences the body in subtle ways. My hair has not turned white, and my muscle tone is firm, yet certain . . . signals? Would you say signals? . . . are sent out. People sense a maturity. I have noticed a difference in the way others treat me from the way I was treated when I was only Luke Webb. This is not a reaction to power, for Luke had great political and financial power, but it is certainly a reaction to some change in me. I knew you sensed it too."

They were interrupted by a stream of waiters carrying their hors d'oeuvres and wine.

The food was wonderful. As she ate a wholly unfamiliar fish grilled to perfection, Janet asked without premeditation, "Why did you come to Egypt?"

"To reclaim my throne," Nectanebo said.

Janet blinked. "I'm sorry?"

To her astonishment, he laughed. "After one hundred and seventeen years of life, I somehow managed to retain my innocence. I came to Egypt to reclaim my throne."

"But . . . ," Janet began, then realised she had no idea how to continue.

Nectanebo continued for her. "But there is no throne to reclaim? The last king in Egypt was a fat, oversexed clown who was overthrown in 1952? No king, no throne . . ." He smiled ruefully. ". . . no Egypt. I know this now. I have seen it with my own eyes—the ruined cities, the decaying monuments. But I did not know this before I came."

"No one told you?"

"No one thought to."

"Luke's memories—"

"I did not access them. I came believing Egypt—my Egypt—still lived. Why not? In the days of my glory, my civilisation had endured two thousand years. Was I foolish to believe it would endure two thousand more?"

Quite suddenly, she saw it all from his perspective and felt her heart reach out to him. "No, not foolish, Nectanebo. I'm sorry. I'm so sorry."

He stared at her in surprise. "For what?"

"For not realising. For not preparing you. I'm supposed to be your doctor."

A small smile played around his lips. "Even a physician cannot heal reality."

"Can you bear it?"

"The loss?" He shrugged lightly. "All things pass away. Khababasha, Khonsu . . . even Egypt, it seems. I have learned that I was the last Egyptian king, although the Greeks carried on our customs for a time."

One of the crewmen appeared, a Nubian by his complexion, dressed in a livery so formal and unsuitable that it actually included white gloves. "The boat is ready, sir," he said to Nectanebo in heavily accented English.

Nectanebo stood up. "Will you come with me? I want to show you something."

SIXTY-ONE

One of the European crewmen helped her into the longboat. Nectanebo climbed in gracefully beside her. The *Empress* herself had anchored close by an island. As they sat, another of the crewmen jerked an outboard motor into life, and the longboat headed towards it.

"Where are we going?" Janet asked.

"I have been told that when this lake was created, the rulers of the country believed it important to preserve the ruins of the past. Artifacts, even whole buildings, were moved to high ground, which became islands when the waters rose. Is this not so?"

"I believe so," Janet said. "The most famous was Abu Simbel—Ramses's Nubian temple."

"Ah yes," Nectanebo said. "The showy and tasteless have always had universal appeal. There is something on this island I wish you to see—not so large but interesting in its own way."

As her perspective changed with the motion of the boat, Janet became aware of a building—or, rather, the remains of a building—rising from the eastern side of the island. It was obviously a temple. It grew larger as they approached and dominated the immediate environment when they beached.

One of the Nubians helped her from the boat, smiling and murmuring something obscure about wetting her pretty feet. Even Janet realised he was flirting with her. She stood on the sand and watched as Nectanebo climbed out. He was wearing a white linen suit with an open-necked white shirt, but suddenly, in her mind, she saw him as he must once have been, dressed in the fold-over kilt of ancient Egypt, sandals on his feet, his torso bare. The image stirred her profoundly and not just sexually, although the sexual element loomed large. She felt herself flush.

To cover her confusion, she turned towards the temple ruin and pretended to inspect it. An Arab in a dirty dhoti was hurrying towards them, grinning broadly with rotting teeth. She suspected he came with the temple, an official or self-appointed guide eking out a living in this remote spot by demanding baksheesh from tourists who wanted to take his photograph against the background of an ancient portal. Every monument in Egypt seemed to have several representatives of the type. In the big tourist centres north of Aswan, they swarmed like locusts.

Two of the Nubians tried to head him off, but he outflanked them easily and headed for Janet like a homing pigeon, his hand outstretched.

"Missie English, yes," he said. "English money, yes?"

She wondered what had marked her as English. "I'm afraid I don't have any English money," she said carefully. It was true enough. She'd changed sterling for dollars when she went to the States and dollars for pounds when she reached Egypt. Her purse bulged with the low-value Egyptian notes now, currency so tattered and filthy that she cringed to handle it.

The man shook his head vigorously, still grinning manically. "No, no, English pound. English pound. You English. Spending English pound. Give me Egyptian."

She looked at him blankly, then saw the chubby silver coin in his outstretched hand—an English pound.

"You spend?" he said. "Give . . . me . . . Egyptian."

Suddenly she realised what he wanted. Somebody, some tourist, had tipped him with a British coin. He wanted to exchange it for Egyptian cash, which he could actually spend, leaving her with a pound she could use when she got home. She broke into a smile and started to fumble for her purse, then stopped.

The Arab was backing away from her, eyes wide, grin gone.

"Yes, it's okay," Janet said. "I can exchange you some Egyptian—"

But the man was in retreat now, stumbling in his haste to get away. He looked terrified. Janet felt Nectanebo approach from behind to stand by her side. Together they watched the Arab run until he disappeared behind a group of rocks to the right of the temple ruin.

"What was all that about?" Janet asked.

Nectanebo shrugged impassively. "Perhaps he saw me on a mural."

She glanced at him but could not decide whether he was serious.

They walked together towards the temple, crew members trailing them discreetly. For the first time, she felt herself wondering about bodyguards. Luke Webb had been routinely guarded—she knew this from Harriet—but she had seen no sign of armed men on the boat, except those who had joined their visitor. Perhaps some of the Nubians or others in the crew carried weapons, but if so, they were well hidden.

As they reached the building, Janet asked almost nervously, "Do you remember it?"

He shook his head. "It's Ptolemaic. That is the term, I think. It was built nearly four hundred years after my death."

Once again she felt the strangeness. It was so difficult to adjust to the reality of the situation. She found herself wondering how he must be feeling. Her level of necessary adjustment was minuscule compared with his.

She had assumed they would be visiting the temple, but he walked her past it, and they strolled together in the high heat of the Egyptian sun across a stretch of barren sand. Their route kept them in sight of the water so that it felt a little like walking on a Mediterranean seashore. Seized by a childish impulse, she kicked a stone.

"That is perhaps not such a good idea," Nectanebo remarked softly.

"What isn't?"

"Turning over stones. I think there are still scorpions."

"Yes, there are, I think. Do they live under stones?"

"In the days of my glory they did."

He used the phrase quite often, without irony or any attempt at self-depreciation. The days of his glory . . . He had once been Pharaoh in Egypt, the most powerful human being on the planet, worshipped as a god, surrounded by grandeur and wealth. How had he done it? How had he managed to adjust?

"Who are you?" Nectanebo asked.

At least she thought that's what he asked. She glanced up at him and frowned, squinting against the sun. "I'm sorry?"

They were out of earshot of the others. "Who are you?" he repeated.

"You know who I am," Janet said.

"But not who you were." He stared at her intensely.

"I'm afraid I don't understand you."

He continued staring. Behind them, the crew had halted at a distance, well out of earshot.

"They have not told you?"

"Told me what? Who haven't told me?"

The stare was making her distinctly uncomfortable, but suddenly he shrugged and looked away. "It is nothing."

When it grew obvious he was going to say no more, she asked to cover her confusion, "What was it you wanted to show me? I thought it was the temple ruins."

"No," he said, "not the temple."

He walked off then, almost rudely. She watched for a moment. There was a fine sheen of moisture on his forehead, but otherwise he seemed impervious to the heat. Then she followed him, hurrying a little to catch up. Together they approached the broken remnant of a larger-than-life-size statue toppled so that it lay on one side partly covered by the sand near the lakeshore. The trunk was broken off at the waist, with the legs missing altogether. There was a deep crack in the neck, but the head had not yet separated, so that the massive face stared sightlessly out across Lake Nasser. She was reminded irresistibly of Shelley's poem "Ozymandias."

Nectanebo stopped. She caught up and stood beside him, looking down at the statue.

"This is what you wanted to show me?" she asked eventually.

"Can you see the resemblance?"

Janet felt as if a clawed hand had clutched her heart. "This is you?"

SIXTY-TWO

Later, on the boat, when the sun went down and a waiter served them chilled chardonnay, she asked him softly, almost timidly, "Do you think you are immortal?"

"I have always believed so."

She had been thinking of the cloning procedure, how if a clone was recloned when he died, the process of life might be extended indefinitely. But the idea of indefinite life was no stranger to Nectanebo. He was heir to the mystical traditions of millennia. He had always believed he would live forever, as the companion of Ra, as a circumpolar star, as a soul judged just by Osiris. His present resurrection was no more strange than any of these.

All the same, she needed his opinion. "Nectanebo," she said quietly, the first time she had ever used his Egyptian name aloud, "do you believe the memories of the original personality will always arise if the body is cloned?"

He looked at her strangely, then said, "Such memories must arise. It is a matter of the souls. Eventually you will remember."

"And this process could continue indefinitely? If, for example, you were cloned again."

This time there was no hesitation. "The priests have always taught that where the body is preserved the souls will live. We mummified our dead, but this is better." He waved away an over-attentive steward. "The problem with immortality may be madness. Have I told you I was Gegum trained?"

"Gegum?"

He was looking at her again with that strange intensity, but eventually he looked away. "No matter," he said. "A body of women dedicated to—" He hesitated, as if searching for the correct word. As if searching Luke Webb's memories for the correct word. "—I think today you would say 'yoga,' the mental disciplines of yoga. This is not quite correct, but approximate. Their methods strengthen the mind. Even so, I found the transition difficult. I awoke in a world that was alien to me, with all of my belief systems shattered and the ghost of a young man inside my head. The process of adjustment and integration was both painful and extremely frightening. It occurs to me that without the Gegum insights I might not have managed it."

"Do you believe I can help you with this adjustment?"

"No."

Just that and nothing more. She wanted him to explain, more urgently, to tell her why he wished her here in Egypt if not in her professional capacity. But again her nerve failed, and instead she only said, "I'm interested in your life. Harriet only gave me the broad outline. You're remembered in our histories, of course, but not in any great detail—I looked you up. There was no mention of the Gegum, for example. Is that the word you used? Gegum?" For some reason, it resonated in her mind.

"They were always secretive," said Nectanebo.

SIXTY-THREE

The *Empress* docked beneath the towering portals of the Abu Simbel temple. Janet recognised it from countless photographs. As crewmen scurried to put down a gangplank, she was joined at the railing by the manager, Pikaar.

"We are fortunate in the timing," he said without preamble. "All through the morning they fly in tourists. There is a constant drone of engines overhead, and in the temple itself you stand shoulder to shoulder with Japanese and Germans and listen to the tour guides trying to shout each other down. It is a nightmare."

"Sounds it," Janet agreed.

"But, you see, when we come in the afternoon, the heat becomes too much for them, so the flights stop and the temples are empty. Only the caretakers. At sunset it is pleasantly cool—well, comparatively. The temples remain empty. It is the best time to see them, in my opinion."

"Mr. W— Mr. Arnold plans to see them, does he?" Janet asked. For the past two days she had become a lotus-eater, cruising the immense lake, taking the sun, cooling off in the little pool on the boat's upper deck and dining each evening, by royal command, with the resurrection of an Egyptian pharaoh. They talked easily now but only of philosophy and history and generalities. He avoided any explanation of the voyage or discussion of where they might be going next. She had no idea at all of what he did during the day. She never saw him on the sundeck or in any of the lounges. She had only learned they were to visit Abu Simbel from the manager of the restaurant where she ate splendid, solitary lunches.

"Oh, but of course!" the manager exclaimed. "This is the whole reason for our visit!"

She doubted it but said nothing as he took his leave.

She took a shower because of the heat and was lying naked on her bed in her cabin when there was a knock at the door. She pulled on her dressing gown and went to answer it.

"It is time," Nectanebo said.

Something stirred in her so deeply and profoundly that she stepped back in sudden alarm. He was naked to the waist, wearing sandals and shorts and with an Arab turban round his head. Stupidly, she could only say, "My hair's wet."

"They have placed the gangplank. Join me in the reception area in ten minutes. The sun will dry your hair." He turned and walked away along the cabin corridor.

What to wear? What to wear? She found herself, incredibly, in a panic as she pulled on shorts and a shirt, then, despite the lack of time, changed them for a denim skirt and short-sleeved blouse. She ran to the reception area, where he was waiting.

He glanced across at her, then reached out and took her hand. He did not look at her as he led her down the gangplank. Three crewmen—Egyptians rather than Nubians—were seated on the rocks to her right sharing a water pipe. They would be smoking tobacco soaked in molasses, according to a guidebook she'd read recently.

The pathway wound steeply upwards, cut by stones. She needed to be careful not to stumble, yet her feet moved with unaccustomed grace. Nectanebo strode a step ahead of her, still grasping her hand, almost pulling her along. She could see the movement of the muscles of his back.

They topped the rise. The path wound briefly to a broad expanse of level space covered in chippings and pebbles, a modern courtyard. Beyond it loomed the great rock temples.

"Ramses built them," Nectanebo said. "He was revered in my day as a conqueror, but the Gegum loathed him. They said he used the sacred knowledge for self-aggrandisement. There is no greater sin—as the witches well knew, being so familiar with it themselves."

They had reached the courtyard now. Four gigantic statues of Ramses flanked the entrance. The head of one had fallen off and lay all of a piece on the ground. Shelley's words again entered Janet's mind: "On the sand, half sunk, a shattered visage lies, whose frown, and wrinkled lip, and sneer of cold command tell that its sculptor well those passions read . . ."

"I remember certain secret teachings," Nectanebo said. "The sacred nature of volume, which represents the extent of spirit trapped in matter . . . the proportions that elevate the soul . . . This is how I created my temples at Luxor and at Philae. They dwarfed no one, for they resonated rightness." He glanced at her but did not break his stride. "They moved this whole complex—I had not realised until you told me. When Nubia was flooded, they worked to move these temples stone by stone. Such irony! They should have let them drown!"

They were walking between the massive flanking statues. The original temples had been cut into solid rock just a few hundred yards away, a site now under water. "See?" Nectanebo exclaimed as they walked through the massive entrance door. "See how the sacred was profaned?"

In the dim light she could see the colonnades of pillars in the vast, rectangular hall of the pronaos. Each was hewn into the likeness of Osiris, but Osiris with the features of Ramses. Although the place was vast, she felt suddenly claustrophobic. "I think I need fresh air," she told him.

To her surprise, he did not offer to accompany her, merely released her hand and stood to one side. Janet walked out of the hall back into the sunlight. The sudden glare made her feel a little faint, and she walked away from the entrance towards the bench near the Queen's Temple. Egypt seemed so . . . familiar, as if she too had once lived here. It was a fanciful thought but one that had occurred to her before. She sat and swallowed deep breaths until the dizziness subsided, then turned slightly to stare out across the lake.

There was a British newspaper beside her, a copy of the *Guardian* left behind by the last batch of tourists. Had it not been folded open to an inside page, she might never have seen the story. The item warranted no more than a double-column heading. The few terse paragraphs beneath told how the body of an Egyptian cult leader named Hasan al-Hakim had been found floating in the waters of Lake Nasser.

Janet stared at the paper, wondering why the name seemed so familiar.

SIXTY-FOUR

Bernstein said, "There's something else."

Harriet stared at him mutely. She felt tired, jangled and bad-tempered, wishing she'd never agreed to come back to the cabin, wishing this hadn't turned into a crisis meeting, wishing most of all there was not something else.

"You didn't tell me about the second clone."

The Chronicles of
Nectanebo: Twenty-Two

I t has become clear that much of my resurrection remains a mystery even to those who facilitated it. My body was regrown, seeded from flesh preserved by the skill of my embalmers. It is here that the Heliopolis priesthood was correct, for they taught that the preservation of the mummy was vital to the afterlife.

But where did my souls reside before this body was regrown? Where were my ba and my ka and my ib? My memory serves me little in this mystery. My experience was death in the heat of Nubia, followed, without pause, by resurrection, fully formed. I have learned that more than two thousand four hundred years have passed since my distant death. Where, then, was I throughout this stretch of time?

From childhood, I was taught that after death my spirit would be met by Anubis and conducted to the Judgement Halls, wherein Horus would weigh my heart, my ib, against a feather. Is it possible I underwent this judgement . . . and forgot it, as one forgets a dream? These are profound questions and have come to concern me greatly. I long to discuss them with she who has resurrected with me.

That she is Lipta I am certain. I have studied her closely while we were in Egypt, and I can see the woman in the girl. The basic structure of the bone is Lipta's face. Janet Winters is caretaker of a body that will one day house the souls of my beloved.

When will it happen? This, too, has concerned me greatly. As Nectanebo, my resurrection did not occur at the moment of my birth to Harriet Webb but, rather, thirty years thereafter when my souls rejoined the reborn body and consciousness arose anew.

I looked to the records of the second cloning, seeking the exact date when her new body emerged from the womb. The rebirth occurred just three moon phases and four days later than my own. Thus, her consciousness must reawaken soon. Then shall Lipta be resurrected and renewed. Then shall she step forth in all her wisdom and her knowledge to seek her destiny at Nectanebo's side.

With Lipta I shall regain my former glory. But not in Egypt. My ancient kingdom is no more and shall never be resurrected. My future now lies in the land of my rebirth. With the resources of the Regis Foundation and Lipta's cunning at my disposal, it must be child's play to win the popularity contest that will grant me control of America's vast armies.

Then, step after step, shall I conquer the world.

The Chronicles of Nectanebo: Twenty-Three

In the days of my glory, there were none save the gods who did what I do now. I am encased in the belly of a great metallic bird, and I fly!

It was made known to me that I now have in my possession several ships like this which ply the air as Pharaoh's navy plied the Nile and sometimes the open sea, but curiosity impelled me to use that which other men routinely use. The failing spirit of Luke Webb supplies me with the term "commercial flight." Thus I went to Egypt; thus have I returned. I am in the company of the powerful of this age (who know me not) and with my beloved Lipta (who knows herself not). I sail across the billows of a white sea made from clouds. As is my birthright, I have become one with the gods.

When I regain my glory, I shall issue an edict restricting this marvellous mode of transport to Pharaoh and His Great Royal Wife.

The End